SUCH SWEET SORROW

SUCH SWEET SORROW

A Novel

Carolyn P. Ellis

To order additional copies of this book, contact:
Xlibris Corporation
1-888-795-4274
www.Xlibris.com
Orders@Xlibris.com
80387

DEDICATION

FOR THE TWO LOVES OF MY LIFE, JIM AND JEFF!

PROLOGUE

Teacher's Journal—3 Springs School

Sometimes I feel burrowed into these mountains like a field mouse or one of those nasty white possums I've met on the school house porch. Life here is so very slow and monotonous. There's no energy or rhythm to life. Nothing for any of us to look forward to.

This, I have learned, is the way mountain people have cycled their lives. Complacency suits them just fine. They don't go looking for "changin' thangs." They don't care to know that life can be made better for them, or for their children. They feel they have lived perfectly all right and their children can live this way, too. This is how they were raised by past generations, and they see "no need" for "thangs" to be different for their "young'uns."

When I first came here, I thought this was an interesting way of thinking. I also felt I had a great deal to offer them as the new teacher in their two-room school. Now it seems as if they have worn me down, or cycled me down, to accepting this culture and stifling my educated enthusiasm.

I drove my brand-spankin' new Jeep Grand Cherokee back into this valley four years ago, imagining my life would become a piece of juvenile fiction: "Randa Stratton . . . Rural Teacher." I was excited to meet these children, ready to bring the outside world in here to them. I wanted to bear the message that life itself was over that big mountain, down the "super road" to Knoxville.

Coming here was like entering a foreign country: I struggled to learn their language, eat their food, to second-guess what they were thinking. Their stares at me were of wonder, disbelief, and a stubbornness to accept what I was all about. I soon learned the stares meant their attention had left me and gone on to something else. When both the children and adults don't want to understand, they simply turn a deaf ear and acquire a blind eye.

These children are similar to inner-city ghetto kids, scraping out the same kind of life. These hills and hollows are their mean streets. In the city, they acquire street smarts; out here it would be called survival of the fittest, even within their own family.

During that first year, I was fascinated with them, and I think I became their student. I was quickly told by the parents what I could not do. They implied I had boundaries with my "teachin's," and that I'd best just stick to "the readin' and the writin'." The children didn't need much else.

At our school Christmas party that year, I gave each of the little girls Barbie dolls and Walk-Man radios to the older children. My church in Knoxville had provided my shopping money.

One little girl's daddy apparently thought Barbie to be just a little too anatomically correct. He brought the unwrapped and undressed doll to me saying, "She won't be needin' such as this," and took his daughter out the door to go home.

It seems they all love to eat: the mothers and dads, the grandmas who wear their sun bonnets year 'round, the grandpas who gather on the grocery store steps to whittle and spit. Our best interactions have been at dish-to-pass suppers. They always come bearing what they're most proud of: country ham biscuits, homemade sausage, chow-chow from an age-old recipe.

They are saying to me, in some language, that they appreciate my work. But when I try to get close to them, they draw back, away from an outsider's questions that might expose something.

Their mountain vocabulary has taken me back in time. Antique words like toddy, salve, and dipper are still widely used here, as are silly words like "dagnabbit," "dadgummit," and "shoot fire." Phrases like "he shore is beside hisself," "she's rich as all git out," or my particular favorite "it's a snowin' to beat the band," have touched my heart.

I've learned that something might "get your goat" or be "clean as a pin," or someone would "not want to raise a stink." One might have "Sunday-go-to-meetin' clothes," a "holier than thou look," or be "caught between the devil and the deep blue sea."

It's very hard for these children to stay in school beyond the eighth grade. There is no encouragement for them to finish high school thirty miles away in Brandensburg. The boys are destined to work grubbing out a living on their family farm, or to work in the zinc mine. The girls will link up with the boys, get married early and quickly get pregnant, or vice versa. Our most successful alumnus owns a bowling alley in Trentville.

I have decided the blankness in their eyes has come down through the years within their mountain genealogy. It's an inherited blankness of heart, mind, and spirit. These families have been defeated by poverty and ignorance. Not one single person hereabouts has any kind of dream or motivation. Even the youngest of them seems wound up by key to perform the basic functions of living, and nothing more.

Obviously, my efforts to charge these children up with something that might spark an interest have failed. They give me no feedback. They come here, sit here looking at me, they eat the butterbiscuits in their sack lunches, look at me some more through the afternoon, and they go home. Nothing more, nothing less. We are all fulfilling someone's idea of the educational process!

CHAPTER ONE

The Gray Days of Winter—January 2000

The girls seemed quiet today. Forlorn and melancholy. Randa wanted to ask them what was wrong, but she knew they would only duck their heads in response. Yesterday, they had giggled quite a bit. She liked them when they were silly; it was as close to a spark of life as she could get.

Something was wrong with one of them. Randa had learned these children could feel each other's pain; they could bear each other's burdens. They were too young to have burdens. They seemed to be little old women in knot-kneed, little girl bodies.

At seven years old, Donna-Dean Silcox was the ringleader of her group. If she was sad, the other four girls were sad. If Donna-Dean giggled, they giggled. Randa couldn't understand how this shy, introverted little cutie had such an influence over the others.

Today, Donna-Dean had said nothing, not even when Randa called her up to her desk to give her some M&M's hidden in the drawer.

"Donna-Dean, are you sick?" Randa asked.

"No'm," she said softly.

Later, when the others were eating their lunches, Donna-Dean came over to Randa and said she didn't want to go home from school today. She said her mother did not want her to come home, and had told her this morning that they "wouldn't be there," if she did come home.

Donna-Dean was almost in tears. "My momma said I should jist go on off somewheres."

Randa believed what she was saying. Several weeks back, the mother had threatened to set Donna-Dean's hair on fire if she lied about doing some insignificant something. Randa felt this child's fear in the pit of her stomach. Her head flooded with all of the do's and don'ts she had been taught for situations like this.

Miss Mattie Lou Carnes, Randa's teaching partner and about thirty years her senior, would know what to do. They had divided their twenty three regular students into two groups. The young ones, grades first through fourth, were in Randa's classroom. Miss Mattie had wanted the older ones, grades fifth through eighth. Mattie was a teacher from the old school. She knew the people of this valley and met them head on. She demanded everyone's respect. And she got it.

Randa took Donna-Dean to Miss Mattie and asked her to tell her story about going home.

"Well, Donna-Dean," Miss Mattie said rather sharply, "where do you want to go?"

"I'll jist stay right here," Donna-Dean said. Randa thought perhaps Miss Mattie had met her match.

"Where is David-Jack today?" Miss Mattie asked about Donna-Dean's fourteen-year-old brother, who was absent from school. "I don't know," she replied. Randa led Donna-Dean back to her room and gave her pieces of colored chalk to draw pictures on the blackboard.

Moments later, Randa almost ran back to have a private talk with Miss Mattie. They reviewed many stories the children had been telling about Donna-Dean and David-Jack. Supposedly, the mother had stuck a straight pin through David-Jack's tongue when he dared to sass her at the supper table one evening. David-Jack had never said much more than 'huh' at school anyway, so no one could have possibly been able to detect a pin-sticking.

"We'll just have to call Sheriff Hawkins in on this. I'll go call and have him come on over here when school is out," Mattie said.

At three o'clock the school bus came. They all knew Donna-Dean wasn't going to get on it. Randa watched her go to the back corner of the classroom to sit on the floor while the others gathered their things to rush out the door.

CHAPTER TWO

Outside, Sheriff Royce Hawkins leaned against the front of his car. Randa went out to introduce herself. A handsome man under the Smokey-the-Bear hat he was tipping at her. He seemed rather young for this powerful job. A nice blend of Andy and Barney, she thought.

Randa invited him inside. As the two of them looked across the classroom toward Donna-Dean, Randa whispered that Mrs. Silcox had warned Donna-Dean not to come home from school.

"Her brother, David-Jack, was not here at school today."

"Is that right?" the sheriff said, as he raised a skeptical brow.

His first suggestion was they wait at the school to see if anyone would come to get her. He concluded they might send the brother for her once she didn't get off the school bus. Donna-Dean remained in the corner of the classroom, crouched on the floor. As the winter sky began to darken at four-thirty, the sheriff began to think of another plan.

"Thing of it is, these people can be really spooky about what they consider to be their business," he said. "They just wouldn't want us messing in their family matters."

"Oh well, that's fine, but am I supposed to let this little seven-year-old girl stay here in the school house overnight, or am I supposed to drive her out there and leave her to walk up her lane in the dark, not knowing if anyone is there?" Randa asked.

"The house is about a quarter of a mile back up that hollow, off the main road. She can't be left to walk to the house by herself," he said. "And I'm afraid if they see me coming up in the sheriff's car, there's no telling what they'll do to her after I leave. We have to try to approach this in a peaceable fashion until we need to do otherwise," he explained. "I do need to ask if you might ride with us?"

"Yes, I will," Randa said. "Let's convince her to go."

Donna-Dean had moved from the corner to the front of the room where she was playing with the erasers on the blackboard tray. She had been crying. The tear trails had etched their way down her dirty little face.

"Donna-Dean, this is Sheriff Hawkins. He's going to go with us to take you home. We'll get to ride in his car and you can show us the way," Randa said, trying to make this sound like a most exciting adventure.

Donna-Dean said nothing as Royce Hawkins offered her his hand to lead her out to his car. She grasped his hand quickly, eyeing him cautiously, and looked over her shoulder to make sure Randa was following.

The drive out past the stand, the mountain term for grocery store, and the three other buildings in the valley settlement of 3 Springs, was silent. Each of them was lost in their individual thoughts on this tense situation that had an uncertain outcome.

It was pitch dark on the two-lane highway, once they had passed under the street lights on either side of the post office. The dark gathered close into the sides of the car, with only the headlights streaking out toward the double yellow line. They made two or three turns onto smaller roads. Sheriff Hawkins seemed to know where he was going. Had he been out to this house before?

Donna-Dean sat between them on the seat. Royce stopped the car near a leaning mail box on the left side of the road.

"Is that your daddy's mail box?" he asked.

"Yessir."

"I'll turn in here." he said. "Hang on. This is probably a bumpy old wagon road."

Once off the paved highway, the trees and bushes folded over the car in a frightening thicket of darkness. The wintry arms of trees on one side grew up and across to gather in the arms of trees growing up from the other side of the lane, forming a canopy above them. Randa saw no sign of a house, just woods to the right and to the left as far as she could see. The road was passable, but branches switched heavily into the sides of the car. If they lived back in here, they were certainly camouflaged against the outside world.

Finally, up ahead, the car lights focused on the shape of a house. It was a two-story brick, antebellum country home, run down from the lack of funds to maintain it. There were no lights in any of its tall windows.

"Donna-Dean, do you see your daddy's truck?" Royce asked.

"Does he keep it around back?"

"No," Donna-Dean answered both questions, reserving any further comment. She kept her head ducked below the car dashboard, occasionally peering over to take quick glimpses of the scene before them.

The car lights, on full beam since they turned off the main highway, blared directly through the rickety yard fence, past a gate hanging by one rusty hinge. Randa noticed the wooden porch was bare. No porch swing to invite a visitor to sit, no flower pots with frostbitten winter plants, no outward indication a family lived here.

Royce blew the car horn, quite unexpectedly, jump starting Randa's heart and scaring Donna-Dean. He blew a second and third time. No lights came on, no one appeared at the door. The three of them sat in silence, waiting.

"Well, I'm going to go up there," Royce said. "Maybe walk around back. I need to show you how to use this, in case you need to."

Randa felt her head turn toward him, almost in slow motion, not sure what he might be talking about . . . God, don't let it be his gun. No, he was holding the microphone to his dispatch radio. She was to call for help.

"Oh no. If I think you're not coming back, I'll drive this car out of here, into town. You'll just be out here to fend for yourself until I can get help," she found herself getting a loud panic to her voice. "I would need to get Donna-Dean out of here," she said, using the child as a mental hostage against whatever his arguments might be.

"Well, give me time to investigate the situation. I've got to at least walk around the house to see if they're out back. Maybe they are out at the barn," he explained.

"Look, if they couldn't hear this blaring car horn, why don't you try giving the siren a little whirl. That should bring the relatives up out of the cemetery," Randa said. She immediately regretted that Donna-Dean had heard the dead relatives remark.

"Okay, that's an idea," he agreed. "Donna-Dean, do you want to push that button right there?" She seemed to have the hint of a smile. She pushed and the blue light on top swept across the front of the house and yard, scanning the place like a Hollywood beacon light. The siren shrieked two or three times, then Royce turned it off. No use, no one was roused, from the dead or otherwise.

"All right. Now. I'm going in. Give me ten minutes by our watches." They checked their wrists as if they were espionage agents in a movie.

"If I'm not back in ten minutes . . ." he began a scripted dialogue as Randa interrupted.

"I'll tell you, Royce," she disregarded the formal reference to "Sheriff" in an effort to make her point. "I'm not going to sit back in this thicket, in the black dark, with this little girl, while someone over the mountain somewhere tries to decide if they're going to come help us or not. If I drive up to the county courthouse in your car, they would definitely know you needed help . . . wouldn't they?"

"Well, what if I . . ." He stopped in mid-sentence, realizing he couldn't lay out a scenario in front of Donna-Dean. "Okay," he conceded. "Do what you have to do, I'm going in."

He grabbed a flashlight from under the car seat and was out the door. As the door slammed shut behind his boots, Randa slapped down the car door lock, feeling only a tiny bit of security. Donna-Dean scrambled over and pulled herself up to "drive" the steering wheel.

CHAPTER THREE

Royce unsnapped the holster which had clasped around his gun. He made his way to the gate and punched it open with the end of the flashlight. The rusty hinge made a loud creak that broke through the silent darkness. A cold wind swept across his feet, racing a cluster of dried leaves into the far shadows of the yard.

He stepped quickly to the left side of the house. The flashlight traced along the fence where Mrs. Silcox had cleverly topped each picket with a glass fruit jar. The light caught the word "Mason" on the inverted glass. Odd place for jars, he thought.

There was no light anywhere from within the house. Royce pointed the flashlight up to the second floor . . . nothing of interest there. When he approached the back corner of the house, he switched the flashlight off and stepped in close to the brick wall.

There was no moon on this cold winter night. Royce turned up the collar on his leather jacket. He strained into the wind as he leaned out trying to see, or hear, something, anything, across this great backyard. Nothing. No truck. He hated to admit it, but nobody was here. God, what would he do with this child? His mind raced through the possibilities.

He turned on the flashlight, and walked toward the screened-in back porch. The yard was covered with trash and clutter. The light found its way to a mattress that had been tossed out the back door. It smelled as if it had been recently burned. He put his hand across the charred end to see if it was smoldering. It wasn't. Don't jump to conclusions here, he warned himself.

The torn screen door to the porch was slightly ajar, no light from within. Suddenly, there was a sound. What was that, he thought? He stood quiet. Maybe he would hear that again.

Nothing.

Scanning with the flashlight once again, through the screen door, Royce decided to announce himself.

"Mrs. Silcox? It's Sheriff Hawkins."

Nothing.

"Anybody here?" he shouted.

Nothing.

There . . . that was the sound again. It sounded like a gurgle. It seemed to be coming from the far right corner of the porch.

Royce jerked the light beam across the emptiness to what appeared to be a pile of clothes on the floor. He pulled open the screen door and jumped quickly up the steps onto the creaking floor boards. The light fell across the boy's head and face.

"David-Jack?"

Propping the flashlight under his chin, Royce quickly gathered him into his arms.

The boy was bleeding from a massive head wound, as well as from a deep-seated gash across his stomach. Blood was everywhere.

He was obviously close to bleeding to death. There was no struggle, no response to Royce's supporting his head, no groan of pain. His eyes were almost fixed. There was only a glimmer of life.

"DAVID-JACK! Who did this to you? Can you tell me?" The boy slowly rolled his eyes toward Royce.

"Who, David-Jack, who would do this? Tell me, NOW!" Royce leaned close to the bloody mouth eager to hear a whisper.

"My ma . . . ," he said.

Royce didn't know what to say to him, what hope to offer. "Where is she . . . David-Jack, where did she go?"

Royce felt the body go limp. He watched as the boy's eyes told him life had gone. The Lord had mercifully called him home.

"Thank you, Jesus. Take him to the best part of Heaven you have." He rested David-Jack back down onto the floor.

God, what kind of mother could have done this to her child? What could he possibly have done to make her do this? Royce rubbed his coat sleeves across each other to paw away the streaks of David-Jack's blood, and fumbled for the shirttail inside his jacket to wipe his hands clean. Donna-Dean can't see this, he thought.

He ran, now, off the porch at a full gallop around the corner of the house to get to the car. Oh God, please let her still be there. He wanted to scream to get his temper under control before he had to act cool and calm for them, but there was no time. He bounded across the front yard into the beams of the headlights. He was glad he had left the car running to keep the heater on for them.

Royce was so cold. Chilled not only by the weather, but chilled all the way to his heart by what he now knew.

Randa had pulled Donna-Dean up onto her lap and was trying to entertain her with items from her purse. She saw Royce and reached over to unlock the patrol car door.

He slid in under the steering wheel and turned his eyes to meet hers.

She read his panic and anger.

"I'll need to get some folks out here," he began.

Above Donna-Dean's head, he tried to roll his eyes and shake his head from side to side in a sort of sign language that might indicate things were bad.

"I'm going to have to call Judge Ferrell to have him decide some things. Who should come in on this? I don't know who I can get to come out tonight."

He realized he sounded lost in the situation.

"We'll need to get Donna-Dean to town. I have to make those calls as soon as possible. Could you stay with me for a little while to help out with her?"

He could tell Randa was trying to mentally follow all he was saying to her. There were questions in her eyes. Oh Lord, he couldn't remember her name . . . and this wasn't the time to ask.

Randa put her hand softly onto his arm and asked, "What's going on?"

CHAPTER FOUR

It was 7 o'clock now, and the sheriff's department was perking more than strong coffee. Randa had watched each of the three hours inch around the clock, although time seemed to be at a standstill and tomorrow seemed light-years away.

Their ride in the sheriff's car, some thirty minutes across Hurricane Ridge to the county seat of Brandensburg, was memorable. Royce buckled Randa and Donna-Dean in and told them to "hold on" as if he were a carnival ride operator. He sped away from the Silcox place like a bat out of hell, steering wildly with one hand and shouting alphabet codes into the radio handset.

Donna-Dean seemed thrilled by the siren screaming above their heads and Royce's careening the car around the mountain curves. Randa noticed her burrow herself back into the car seat to snuggle closer and closer to Royce Hawkins' hip.

Royce had not wasted a moment of time since bringing them there. Randa sensed that Donna-Dean posed quite a dilemma for him, and had offered to stay with her until further arrangements could be made. When they first arrived at the office, Royce sat Donna-Dean on the high counter in front of the radio dispatcher and introduced her to the wide-eyed staff. They seemed eager to entertain her. He led Randa to a nearby conference room to explain what he had found on the Silcox back porch.

Randa admired his emotional involvement. He was near tears as he told her that David-Jack had died in his arms. It made her remember the sad-faced young man who never spoke.

"Can you tell me what you know about this family?" Royce asked in obvious interrogation.

Randa told him the rumors she had heard from the students about threats and supposed tortures that had been done to the Silcox children. She added that there had been no outward signs of abuse, and that neither David-Jack nor Donna-Dean had come to her for help.

"All of our students are under what I call a 'don't-you-go-tellin' syndrome. They're not to tell things at school, like their mother is going to have another baby or that they don't have enough money for food. I can guess they have been threatened with a 'whoopin'."

"I met the Silcox parents only one time . . . at the grocery store," Randa said. "They were just like all of the other mountain families, distant and withdrawn . . . a domineering father, and a submissive mother."

"They're all cut from the same cloth," Royce offered. "They didn't seem at all interested in their children's schoolwork. They would never come for parent conferences. They would never sign report cards, but that isn't out of the ordinary, most of the parents can't write. These people never came to the school for any reason."

"Did these children ever talk about trouble at home?"

"No. In fact, David-Jack didn't speak at all. He would only say 'huh' in response to me and to the other children. There was a time when we suspected he might be deaf, but the Health Department comes every other year to do hearing tests and he always passed those."

"God . . . ," Randa fought back her own tears. "I should have been more concerned with what was behind the 'huhs'. Maybe I could have helped him out of some maddening situation."

"What about Donna-Dean?" Royce asked.

"She can be incredibly shy, but every now and then she likes to be an entertainer. Isn't it odd that she hasn't asked about her parents coming to get her, or worried about where they are?"

"I've told her that both of you are going to be staying here for a while. She seems quite content with that," he said.

"Oh," Randa said, wondering just what "a while" might mean to the county sheriff.

Later, Royce hurriedly explained that he had placed a call to Judge Ferrell, who was away from home and was not expected to return until late. Legally, they were on hold. Royce truly did not know where to go from here as far as Donna-Dean was concerned.

"I surely want to thank you for your time. I couldn't have managed anything here without your help," he smiled at Randa.

"Right now," he added, pulling on a long, black coat, "I need to find this mother, or father; if for no other reason than to notify them of their son's bleeding to death on their back porch."

He seemed to get his second wind as he left with several others to go back to the Silcox farm to wait for the Medical Examiner. Randa had been left with the mental picture of David-Jack lying stone cold dead in a puddle of blood, alone in the dark.

CHAPTER FIVE

One of the deputies brought them steak dinners from the truck stop restaurant over on the Interstate. Randa thought the food tasted wonderful.

Donna-Dean had eaten like a wild animal. Now, this bedraggled, confused little girl was sound asleep on a cot brought from a jail cell and placed in front of Royce's desk.

A bustle of activity in the outer office brought Randa's attention up from an issue of *Field and Stream* magazine. Royce had returned and everyone out there had a question that only he could answer.

He came to the door and whispered across Donna-Dean, "Do you want a cup of coffee?" Randa nodded and asked for two sugars. He reappeared with a giant mug in each hand. He carefully stepped around the cot and walked over to sit on a window seat by the double windows that rose almost to the ceiling.

"Watch this stuff," he warned as Randa took a seat beside him. "Danny makes that old Luzianne coffee really strong. It sure will keep us awake."

"Oh, I'm pretty much a night owl anyway," Randa said.

"You know . . . I must admit to you . . . that with all of this excitement . . ." he said shyly, peering through the steamy fog rising from his coffee mug, "I have forgotten your name."

"Randa. Randa Stratton."

"Well, Randa Stratton . . ." he seemed to look at her for perhaps the first time.

Blue eyes, she thought. Extremely blue eyes.

He must have felt his look to be too personal, for he quickly diverted those blue eyes down to check the ball-point pen he had taken from his pocket.

"I really appreciate your coming over here to help me with this," he said softly. "I'm a single man and I just didn't know what I should do with this little girl. I hate that this is the best I can do for her right now."

"Royce, I've been thinking about all of this and I've decided I would like for you to ask the judge if I can have her stay with me until a good arrangement can be worked out for her. She could go back to school."

"That would be wonderful for her," he said, "but are you sure you want to do that?"

"I'm sure."

"She seems to be crazy about you. I can tell Judge Ferrell that she would probably be real happy being with you. Of course, he may want to turn her over to the Social Services people."

He laughed as he shook his head from side to side. "There are so many cans of worms we will be opening here."

CHAPTER SIX

Two or three knocks and the door swung away from a voice that said, "Chief? It's Judge Ferrell on the phone."

"Thanks, Danny," Royce said. "Are you sure you want to make your offer?" he asked Randa as he put his coffee mug on the desk.

"I'm sure." Randa watched him side step Donna-Dean's cot as he left to take the phone call in the outer office.

Randa smiled as she overheard him begin the conversation, "Judge Ferrell? Sorry to bother you, but I've got quite a situation over here tonight."

As the office door slowly closed, Randa recycled the "Would this be the right thing to do?" question. Had she answered the Lord's call, or had she merely misunderstood His beckon?

Royce returned, "Judge Ferrell would like to speak with you."

Walking toward the phone, Randa tried to recall all she had been witness to. Would he need to know that Donna-Dean had been told not to come home from school today? Would he need to know about the pin-sticking with David-Jack? Would she have to admit she had overlooked a child in deep distress?

"Hello?" she said, cautiously.

"Miss Stratton?" the judge said in a booming Santa Claus voice. "I've heard all about how you've helped out tonight, and I thank you for that. Royce said you have offered to take this child home with you?"

"Yes sir. I would like to do that."

"The way I see it is, we need to have shelter for her at least until I can get someone to come over there tomorrow. I'll leave it up to the social workers to decide if she can stay with you and return to school," he boomed. "They may not have a place to put her right now. And, I think she'd be better off with you than for them to take her all the way down to Knoxville."

"Yes, she would," Randa agreed.

"Of course, you know that once you get started with something like this, it could go on forever. Do you think you want to get that involved and attached?" he said.

"I am already involved . . . and because I am her teacher, I am attached."

"Certainly you are."

"She doesn't need any more trauma right now, and going out of her familiar surroundings might cause some pretty bad mental damage." Randa tried to recall trivial bits from her child development classes in college.

"Well . . . tell you what . . . I'm going to let my boy Royce use his good judgement. He'll do things by the book for me, and he'll take good care of you and the little girl. If you need anything, he'll know how to get it. I'm going to draw up some of the legal paperwork that will record all of this, and open the case we will develop for Donna-Dean. I'll be checking back with Royce to see how y'all are gettin' along. Thank you, again, for all you have done tonight, and for all you will be doing."

Randa handed the telephone receiver to Royce, wondering if she should have said a "thank you" in return.

CHAPTER SEVEN

"Now . . ." Royce pulled up a chair for Randa, alongside Danny's desk. "We have to think of what to do next?"

Danny moved over to guard the open door to Royce's office, to keep a close watch over Donna-Dean.

"Okay." Randa seated herself.

Royce pushed papers, and the phone, away from the edge of the desk and sat himself there hovering over her so his words wouldn't travel toward Donna-Dean.

"I'll need to keep you two under guard. That means you'll have a deputy with you twenty-four hours a day. Technically, she's a ward of the state, and she's my responsibility. My main thought, or fear, is that the murderer or murderers are still out there and they may be slinking around to get ahold of this one," he pointed toward his office door.

"We need to plan where you want to go from here," he said. "Do you want to take her to your house, or take her to my house, or do you want us to put you up at a motel . . . we can do that, if you had rather?"

"I think I would like to take her to my house. She would probably like that. What do I do about taking her back to school tomorrow?" Randa asked.

"Well, I think we might get you both off from school for tomorrow and let you go back on Monday. That way the kids might not be so talkative about this."

"Or, they might be really wound up about it after going to church on Sunday," Randa offered.

"Guess you're right. Where do you live? Over by the school?"

"About two miles to the east, off Trawber Creek Road. I have a trailer," she explained. "You know, I'm regretting that I left my car at school. Do you think it will be okay?"

He read the worry in her eyes. "I'll have Danny go over there to get it and take it to your place. Just to be on the safe side, y'all will be traveling with me for the next few days."

"Do you think you can find her parents?" Randa asked.

"Well, what's happening right now is, we're searching about a ten mile radius of the house. We've gone to all of the neighbors and, of course, they claim they don't know nuthin' about nobody. We've got an all points bulletin out on the dad's truck. The Highway Patrol is on that. We know that Silcox did go to work at the zinc mine this morning, but he got a call to come home about ten o'clock."

Randa arched a brow.

"Yeah," Royce arched a brow back at her. "She was probably on her rampage then."

"They may be gone from this whole area, maybe even out of state by now," Randa said.

"Or, they may be hiding close by, even watching us do this investigation. Someone could be hiding them. They could even be forcing someone to hide them. Remember, these are mountain people who know the backwoods. They know where they can lay low like Brer Rabbit. You know him from your schoolwork, don't you?" Royce said, trying to get a smile from her.

"Yes. But, if you remember, he was very smart."

"The Tennessee Bureau of Investigation will be here in the morning. Their dog unit is on the way from Knoxville now."

"I'll bet they can pick up a scent," Randa said.

"One of the things that stays on my mind, is when David-Jack answered my 'Who did this to you' question, his answer was 'My Ma.' But . . . was that an answer to my question, or was it the beginning of something he wanted to tell me about his Ma? Like maybe, 'My Ma is lying out in the woods dead,' or 'My Ma was set afire on the burned mattress out there,' or 'My Ma's gonna try to get to Donna-Dean.' And . . . it's that last one that worries me."

"Oh goodness," Randa said.

"Everything will all come together, sooner or later," Royce added. "You should understand that any involvement you have from here on out brings you buck up into the middle of this case. In fact, right now, you know almost as much as I do and that makes you a witness."

"I know," Randa said softly.

"Also you'll probably be the one Donna-Dean tells her story to. She may open up to you about what brought all of this on. That's what Judge Ferrell meant by the term 'involved'."

"He also used the term 'attached'," Randa said.

"You have to realize that her dad may show up wanting to get her. Of course he can't have her, since he apparently abandoned her and now we have found his other child murdered on his back porch. He'd play hell with Judge Ferrell to be able to take Donna-Dean without a court proceeding.

"Now an aunt, or a grandma, or someone from out of state with proof they're a relative, might have some right to take her. So . . . what I want you, and me too, I'll have to include myself in this," he put his hand gently on Randa's arm and focused those deep blue eyes directly at her, "is to try hard not to fall in love with her."

"Oh, I agree," Randa said. "Completely."

"And of course, you know, if at any time you want to bail out of this, you can do that. Just let me know, because I really want to spare your feelings, and you've got a job to go back to," he said.

"I'll bet you never dreamed you would be spending half the night in jail with one of your students, did you?"

Again that sweet humor. Randa thought it seemed like a flirt.

*   *   *

Randa was glad to be making plans to go home. A quick inventory of herself revealed she was beginning to smell bad, her teeth needed brushing, and her hair felt matted to her head.

Royce had excused himself to, among other things, locate an unmarked car, alleging it would not "do" for them to arrive at Randa's trailer in the sheriff's car. He asked Danny and Jake to bring Randa's car from the school to her trailer, and it had taken at least twenty minutes for them to discuss and question the map she had drawn for them. Randa began to doubt their crime-solving abilities.

Finally, she could tell by the uproar in the outer office that Royce had returned. He appeared at the door. God. He had transformed himself from a backwoods county sheriff, into a movie star. There must have been a film crew outside on the courthouse steps, and this was their hero.

He had shed the sheriff outfit and was wearing jeans and a white, long-sleeved shirt under an L.L. Bean P-Jacket. He had over-doused himself with cologne.

"Wow," she managed to say. "And here I am looking like I've spent the night in jail."

"I guess we should go on over to your place now. Get you two out of here," Royce suggested. "Looks like I'm going to be your night-watchman for tonight. I have a sleeping bag in my truck. I can just camp out on your living room floor."

"I've got a feeling that when we wake her up, she will be awake all night," Randa warned.

"That's okay, I'm going on adrenalin now, so I can entertain her while you get some good rest."

CHAPTER EIGHT

"Mornin'."

A strange voice greeted Randa as she walked into the living room. Danny spoke cheerily over a can of R.C. Cola he had marauded from the refrigerator.

"Royce has gone to work already. Said to tell you he'd be back as soon as he can get away from things over at the office today. Said to call if you need food for lunch and he would send something in with the deputy who comes in to replace me."

"Okay," Randa managed to say. Suddenly she felt as if she had been off the planet for three days.

"Hi Miss Randa." Donna-Dean popped up from in front of the t.v. set. She looked like a leprechaun in the green sweatshirt Randa had given her to sleep in. They had made a nice bed for her on the couch. Royce had slept in his sleeping bag on the floor below.

Randa remembered she had been too sleepy to have any further conversation when they arrived at the trailer. She hoped, now, that she had at least said good night to him.

Randa's goal for the morning was to get Donna-Dean into a bubble bath, and to get her clothes washed and dried.

"Hey, Donna-Dean, do you want me to make some pancakes for you and Danny?"

"You got any Beanee Weenees?" Donna-Dean asked.

"No. They're not very good to eat for breakfast. Let's have pancakes instead." Randa began to search for the teflon griddle.

"This little friend is an eatin' machine," Danny said. "She's already had a baloney sandwich and a bag of chips."

Randa cast a backward glance into the pantry and noticed it had been tumbled through.

"You got any Oreos?" Danny quizzed.

"No. Sorry," she said.

"Donna-Dean, after you eat your pancakes, you can take a bubble bath in my big bath tub."

"Can I still wear your shirt?"

"Yes. You can wear it while I'm washing your clothes."

Donna-Dean hopped onto the couch beside Danny to continue watching "The Beverly Hillbillies."

"When's my momma gonna come?" she asked out of the clear blue.

Danny gave a startled look in Randa's direction.

"We're waiting to hear from her, Donna-Dean. You and I are taking the day off from school today. Maybe we can find something around here for you to play with after you've had your bath."

Randa hoped to divert the child's attention with idle chatter.

Wonder what had triggered the thought about her mother?

After eating over half of a very large pancake, Donna-Dean begged for the promised bubble bath. Randa laughed when she realized she had bloated the child's little baloney-filled stomach with pancake and syrup, and now would be heating all of that up in warm bath water.

Minutes later, Donna-Dean was at the bathroom door, beginning to shed the sweatshirt. Randa told her that after the bath they would need to wash her hair at the sink.

Donna-Dean was almost naked, as she danced around trying to step out of her panties. She quickly flung them skyward and they landed kerplop in the water. Randa picked them out, and handed Donna-Dean the bubble bath to pour under the running water.

As the child leaned out over the tub to reach the faucet, Randa caught sight of the spots on her legs. Oh my God, what's that, Randa thought, almost afraid to look any closer.

"Donna-Dean? What's this on your legs?" Randa asked.

Circling each leg, around the area where the elastic of her panties had been, were raw, crimson-red circles. Were these sores that she had scratched? Donna-Dean quickly turned herself away.

"My momma says to tell that these is chigger bites. She don't want no body knowin' that they's been done by a cigarette."

"Oh, baby. Who did this to you?" Donna-Dean jumped at the suddenness of Randa's question.

"I dunno," she lied.

"Does it hurt? Maybe you ought not get in the water with these places so irritated."

Donna-Dean looked disappointed.

"Maybe you should just take a shower instead, that way you can wash your hair at the same time," Randa explained as she let the bubbled water out of the tub.

Donna-Dean said she had taken showers before, and knew how to keep the shower curtain pulled close around the tub. Randa preset the water and helped her in, then ran to the door to call for Danny.

"Stay here by the door and listen in case she needs anything. I've got to get in touch with Royce."

She hurried to the phone as Danny shouted the telephone number behind her.

She stubbed her toe on the corner of the bed, as she pulled the phone by its cord across the bedspread. It took only moments to hear his voice on the line.

"Royce. This is Randa Stratton."

"Hi. How's it going? Did you get some rest?" he asked politely with no thought that she was in a panic.

"Royce, you need to get right over here. Donna-Dean has some nasty signs of child abuse. This is something you need to see. I think we will need to get her to a doctor. These places need to be treated." Randa could sense the smile fading from his face.

"I'll be right there," he said somberly.

Crossing back in front of Danny, Randa shouted to Donna-Dean. "Do you need some help washing your hair?"

"I can do it with the shampoo you have in here," Donna-Dean said.

"Finish on up now. We'll use the blow dryer to dry it, okay?"

"Okay," she echoed.

To Danny, who was holding both the bathroom door and his mouth ajar, Randa explained that Donna-Dean had what looked like cigarette burns all around her legs.

"It looks infected."

"Damn," he whispered.

"Royce is on his way. He may get here while I'm drying her hair. You can just let him in. He may want to take her to a doctor."

Royce appeared at the door all too quickly. Obviously, he had driven the thirty miles at some daredevil speed.

Randa had finished Donna-Dean's hair and was rummaging through her closet to find a long tee-shirt that would be a makeshift dress to wear with the dirty panties and dirty socks.

Donna-Dean was sitting in the middle of Randa's bed, still wrapped in a big terry-cloth bath towel. Her face lit up like a Christmas tree the minute Royce entered the room.

He glanced a panicked look at Randa, but to Donna-Dean he said, "Good morning, Miss Ma'am."

"Donna-Dean, I need for you to stand up here and let Sheriff Hawkins see these places on your legs, maybe he can tell us what kind of medicine to put on them. We want to heal them up so you can get that bubble bath sometime soon," Randa said.

Donna-Dean stood up, mainly to be held up by Royce. She readily hugged his neck. He returned her hug, then pushed her back so he could see what Randa had discovered.

"Yeah. We need to get her over to the hospital. Y'all put on something warm, we're going to go . . . now." he said. Donna-Dean's face fell as she absorbed his aggravation.

"We'll be right out," Randa said to his back as he left the room to make further arrangements with Danny. She could hear several "damns" being passed between the two of them.

CHAPTER NINE

Dr. Brodie Caldwell had been a good friend to Royce; all the way back to high school when they were drag racing their old rattle-trap cars. Seemed ironic that these hometown pals, who had done quite a bit of gully-jumping in those old cars, would today be discussing this little girl's butt! The Lord truly works in mysterious ways, Royce thought as he paced the floor of the emergency room.

Royce and Randa had been asked to "wait" while Brodie and his staff did a thorough examination on Donna-Dean. Randa had not wanted to be a part of that, neither had Royce. Donna-Dean had cried frantically when they left the room.

"Damn," Royce repeated the swear to Randa as if she had not fully understood the last two or three times he had used it. He stopped pacing to sit down by her.

"You know . . . I've seen a lot of stuff over the years. Stuff that was bloody and gory from a shotgun blast. All kinds of stuff from car wrecks and suicides. I've even seen a human head that was brought up into someone's yard by hunting dogs who were prowling in the woods. But when it comes to kids . . . it just makes me so mad I feel sick! Brodie knows I can't take this."

Randa patted his arm. "You seem to be a very caring and compassionate man, and those are really wonderful traits."

"Yeah, for any other line of work I suppose," he said. "You need to be tough and un-caring to get into sheriff'n. It's taken me a while to learn that. I can be tough on the drunk drivers, or people on dope. And the wife beaters . . . I can really come down on them. But when it comes to child abuse, that gets me. Or, maybe I'm just trying really hard to impress you," he flashed that smile.

"Oh you are, are you?" Randa nudged him with her shoulder. "Well, I think I am beginning to be impressed . . . and hungry. I am very hungry. Do you think they have a candy machine, or something, around here?"

They walked a lengthy maze of hallway toward the front of the hospital. Someone said the vending machines were located near the main entrance.

Randa smiled at passersby who greeted Royce. They stepped aside to let him pass, all but saluting his badge and Smokey-the-Bear hat. Vestments of the political office, she thought.

Royce smiled at everyone, offered his hand, and even slapped a few backs. He was working his crowd.

They found the machines and Royce quickly collected change from his pocket. "What's your choice?" he invited.

Suddenly the overhead speaker blared "Sheriff Royce Hawkins . . . Sheriff Royce Hawkins? Please return to the emergency room admit desk."

"Damn," he muttered as he chunked coins into the candy machine. Randa said she would take a Hershey. He retrieved her bar from the drop box and quickly chunked in more money to get himself a Mounds.

They hurried back to the emergency room and as they approached the desk, two ladies in dark business suits and high heels turned toward them. Randa found a seat among the sick people in the waiting area.

"Sheriff Hawkins?" the younger of the two ladies stepped toward him.

"I'm Cheryl Crenshaw with Family and Children's Services," she extended her hand to his with masculine gusto, and kept hold of it with feminine allure.

"This is my associate, Christine Moss," she reluctantly passed his hand away.

"We are here regarding the Silcox girl. They tell me the doctor has finished with her and wants to see you. We will need to review her situation after you have met with him."

"Sure," Royce said, suddenly missing his back-up, Randa.

CHAPTER TEN

The hospital cafeteria was an odd place to be deciding Donna-Dean's fate. Randa thought it should be a more formal, court-room, judge's chambers-type place.

Royce, Brodie Caldwell, and the two social workers huddled in a far corner away from the lunch crowd. From her booth across the room, Randa kept a careful watch. They had taken turns in laying out their points of view. Now all eyes were focused on Dr. Caldwell as he gave his medical conclusions.

Randa read Royce's body language. He was squirming.

*   *   *

"Donna-Dean has gone through several very painful episodes," Brodie read from his notes on the chart before him. "She has six burns encircling the upper right leg. These burns are in a pattern, almost as if they were trying to tatoo her. They probably put them in this area because they would not be visible to the public. There has been an interval of time between each burn; we can tell that because of the healing and scaring sequence of each burn.

"She has told me that she was burned each time her mother thought she had told a lie. She said her mother burned her with a cigarette while her father held her down."

Royce slammed his "Smokey" hat down hard on the table.

"Fortunately," Brodie continued with an eye toward Royce, "she has not been sexually abused. In fact, they have carefully avoided her vaginal area in placing these burns.

"There is no sign of infection . . . yet. One place is quite irritated and we need to watch it closely. Her blood work shows no signs of drugs. I had originally thought they may have drugged her, or sedated her some way, in order to do this so . . . artistically.

"I think the physical damage will heal completely with time. She may even outgrow the scarring. Obviously, the real damage here is mental.

"She seems convinced, or brainwashed into believing that she has been bad, and this was a perfectly normal punishment. She may even believe that all children are disciplined this way.

"She has asked me about her mother. Royce, have you explained anything to her about her mother?"

"No. I just keep stalling. I haven't told her about David-Jack either."

"Well, maybe these ladies can advise you on how do that. It's one of those sooner or later things. Is there a minister, or grandmother, or somebody who could tell her?"

"No. I want to be the one to tell her. I just haven't found the right moment to do that. I guess I wanted her to get a little settled. I'll tell her when I feel the time is right," Royce promised.

"I've got to get back to my patients now. Do you have any more questions for me?" Brodie looked at the two women.

"We will need to get a statement from you regarding your findings, and we have some forms to leave with you to fill out. Will you be giving us instructions on how to take care of these wounds?" Ms. Crenshaw asked.

"Those instructions will be given to Sheriff Hawkins when we dismiss Donna-Dean.

"Royce, I'll get with you later. Get a grip, buddy. She'll get over this, in time. It's awful to have to accept these things, but you need to put this out of your mind and go ahead and do your job here, okay?" Brodie patted his friend on the shoulder.

"If you need me, you know I'll come running." Brodie backed his chair away from the table and walked toward Randa sitting across the room.

Chapter Eleven

"Miss Stratton? I'm Dr. Caldwell." They shook hands.

"I have examined Donna-Dean and I've just discussed her injuries with Royce," he said.

"Is she all right?" Randa asked.

"She's made it through lots of pain. My main concern now is to keep down infection. I would like to see her again in a couple of days."

"Has she been sexually . . ."

"No."

"Thank God," Randa sighed.

"The nurses will be releasing her to Royce shortly. To tell you the truth, I'm a bit worried about him. This stuff just throws him over the edge. He has my home phone number, so if y'all need me in any way just make him call. Call even if you just get to worrying about her."

"That's nice. Thank you," Randa said.

"I've got to get gone now. The nurses will have some written instructions and medications to give you."

"Thank you, again."

"You're welcome," he said over his shoulder as he walked away. "She's a sweet kid."

Moments later, Royce wound his way through the lunch crowd to eagerly announce, "She's going to get to stay here with us until the last of next week."

He could not hide his excitement. "Let's go find her, and get her out of here."

*   *   *

Donna-Dean was in the last exam room on the left-hand side of the hallway. They approached the door cautiously, Randa stepped back to let Royce be the first one in.

Donna-Dean was sitting on the exam table. The nurses had made a blow-up balloon out of a rubber glove and had let Donna-Dean draw a face on it. When Royce appeared at the door, she was eager to see him.

"Hi," he said. "Let's go."

A nurse stepped over with several papers for him to sign, at the same time explaining that Donna-Dean was heavily bandaged around her leg.

They helped her down onto the floor where she practiced walking with a strange waddle.

"Let's see if Miss Randa would like to go to McDonald's," Royce said, expecting to see a smile.

"What's that?" she asked.

"You just wait and see, girlfriend."

CHAPTER TWELVE

"Royce, she needs something to wear," Randa said as they drove away from the golden arches. "Maybe we should stop at Walmart."

"Okay. Danny can cover for me at the office until the T.B.I. investigators get antsy."

Moments later Royce chose to use the V.I.P. status of his patrol car to park in the fire lane at Walmart. He also decided to carry Donna-Dean in his arms as they entered the store. Shoppers turned their heads to look at them. Wondering why? Imagining what?

"You got any girls at your house?" Donna-Dean asked the question into his face.

"Nope. Not a single one."

"You got any boys?"

"Nope." Royce smiled at Randa, as he added, "All I've got is a dog at my house."

"No fool'n," Donna-Dean said skeptically.

Royce gave a hearty laugh as he put her down from his arms. Little did he know he had just answered one of Randa's lingering questions.

He brought out his wallet from his hip pocket and grabbed bills. "Here, buy her what you think she needs. If this won't cover it, I'll use a credit card."

Randa jerked on the front of his jacket and whispered the word "attached." He snapped off a quick wink at her over Donna-Dean's head.

They had fun picking out a new wardrobe, hoping the trauma of Brodie's physical exam had been erased. There was no mention of the hospital, or any further reference to the burn marks.

Donna-Dean was thrilled with all of their choices. They piled the shopping cart with several tops and jeans, a corduroy jumper with two special blouses to wear under it, and a Barbie nightgown with matching house shoes. She had chosen socks and mittens. Royce wanted her to have a long toboggan hat, which he said he could "keep up with her" by holding on to its tasseled end.

When they approached the girl's underwear section, Royce excused himself, alleging that they could handle those choices without his help. He said he would meet them in the toy department.

Randa noticed Donna-Dean's eyes light up. Obviously the word "toy" ranked right up there with the word "food" in her vocabulary. When they rejoined Royce in the "toys", Donna-Dean thanked him for all he was "gittin'" for her. She had been taught to be respectful and mannerly by someone, Randa thought.

Royce fanned away her thank you with his hand and diverted her eyes to the rows of pink Barbie doll boxes across the aisle.

"I'll treat you to a Barbie," Randa said, remembering the Christmas she brought Barbie to the valley schoolgirls. Barbie could be quite a pick-me-up for a second grade girl.

Donna-Dean ran straight to the Bridal Barbie. Randa gasped at the price, then decided "what the hell," if the sheriff can be extravagant, so could she. They decided that Barbie's sister, Skipper, could not be left behind and she, also, was tossed onto the stack of items in the cart.

"Does Barbie have a momma?" Donna-Dean asked.

"Probably."

Royce had been strolling further down the aisle, saying to them over his shoulder that he would meet them up front at the check out counter. Randa noticed him walk out to the center of the store toward a group of constituents who were eager to shake his hand, slap him on the back, and toss out their questions. Randa smiled at the thought of shopping at Walmart with an abused child and the county sheriff.

Randa and Donna-Dean circled around the toy department and headed for the coloring book rack.

"I got some colors at home, if I can go git em'," Donna-Dean said as Randa grabbed up two coloring books and the largest box of Crayola's.

"We'll get these," Randa said, "They have a sharpener on the back of the box."

Randa decided to take a quick pass through the cosmetics section. Donna-Dean seemed fascinated with the careful decision-making necessary to choose the right makeup. Randa let Donna-Dean choose some fingernail polish, promising she could "paint" her fingernails later that evening.

Suddenly, Randa was all too aware that Royce was away from them. He was totally out of sight. They hurried toward the front of the store. The momentary panic was eased when he stepped alongside them. He was carrying a package that had been paid for, bagged, and stapled closed.

"What you got there?" Donna-Dean quizzed.

"That's for me to know, and you to find out, Miss Priss." She giggled.

When they loaded Donna-Dean into the back seat of the patrol car, they piled all of the bags around each side of her. She begged to open her Barbie, but Randa told her she needed to wait until they got back to the trailer. Randa found herself using her own mother's warning, "you might lose something."

Royce opened the passenger door for Randa. "I think we've just thrilled her to pieces with all of this stuff. Maybe it will take her mind off of things," he said.

"Let's see," Randa teased. "What were those words 'attached' and 'involved'?"

"Yeah. Guess you could say I'm gettin' attached to the two of you," he said. "Which reminds me . . . I thought of this in the middle of the night when I was sleeping on your living room floor . . . do you have a boyfriend, or somebody who might be offended by the sheriff hanging out at your place?"

"No, I don't," Randa smiled. "You got any girls at your house?"

"I got no girls . . . no where." Royce gave a big smile and said "Let's ride, lady."

Once in the car, they were again caught up within the sheriff's whirlwind world of crime. Royce grabbed the dispatch radio handset to report his whereabouts and to tell them he was headed toward the courthouse. He asked that Danny be ready in an un-marked car to take Randa and Donna-Dean home.

"The Medical Examiner will probably have something for me, and the T.B.I. people are probably going to want me to be with them throughout the afternoon. It would be great if they have made some progress this morning. I sure hope the whole crew of them have not just sat around waiting for me to get them going," he worried.

"Sorry we had to make this extra stop," Randa said.

"Oh no, we have to make her our number one priority. This had to be done. It was fun, wasn't it," he grinned.

"Yes, it was."

"I probably won't be with you tonight. It will have to be Danny or Jake," he said.

"I'll miss you," Randa said. "And your girlfriend back there . . . she's going to miss you, too."

"I'll be giving you a call." he said. "Oh, you might want to avoid the evening news on television, if you know what I mean. I can't promise you that news of this has not traveled over the mountain onto the airwaves."

"Gotcha," Randa said.

CHAPTER THIRTEEN

Royce bundled himself against the wind as he raced across the courthouse lawn up the ten stone steps to the ornate double doorway. The skies were grey and somber. Snow, he thought. How nice that would be if he were not caught up in the middle of a murder case.

Now get your mind off of them and back to this investigation, he reminded himself. Gotta find out what the hell happened out there.

As he opened the door to the sheriff's department his eyes raced across at least a dozen people who sprang to attention. Each of them shouted an admonishment that seemed to end with "and where have you been all morning, anyway?"

"Look," Royce called the room to order, "let me tell all of you . . . and file this away in your brains so that you don't have to keep inquiring where I may have been . . . I have an abandoned child that I am responsible for until other arrangements can be made. This child is the sister of the murdered boy. She is now under protective custody. This morning she has needed medical attention. And, because her home is now a crime scene and I can't get to her clothes, I had to buy some for her. I am back now and my attention is here on the work at hand. So, what's been going on?"

The three T.B.I. detectives clamored forward and requested to be Royce's first appointment of the day. "Gentlemen . . . my office," he swept his hand toward the door behind them.

During the next hour or so, Royce was inundated with information these guys were so very proud to be able to spout out for him. They seemed greatly impressed with being T.B.I. agents in the first place, Royce thought; and to be called in, to more or less take over and make a backwoods sheriff take a back seat so they could use all of their crime-solving stuff, well it just about made them feisty.

Royce had to admire their ability to re-create a crime. Other than using common sense, Royce felt his skills at piecing together crime puzzles were a bit lacking. He didn't particularly want to end up hearing that he "could have," or "should have," done this or that, or to hear the most dreaded words, "why didn't you do" so and so.

Many times a situation could be clearly surmised, but the gathering of evidence was crucial. These T.B.I. guys were at least very skilled at gathering evidence. Royce had coaxed himself into believing he could learn from them. He may not always have known what to do in various circumstances, but through the years he had very well learned from them what not to do at a crime scene.

"Sheriff, we were able to extract several good latent prints from the bloody ax handle," one of the agents said. "There was quite a struggle to get something heavy down the stair steps. Something other than that bloody mattress out back."

"There was blood on that mattress?" Royce asked.

"Yeah . . . a good deal of blood," the agent said.

"But it seemed to me he had axed the boy there on the back porch."

"Well now, that we don't know . . . yet," a second agent stepped forward. "As we pointed out to you last night, there was quite a bit of activity that went on outside of the house. Remember you had entered and exited the area from the left side of the front yard. Well, around to the other side of the house something had been drug out across the yard to a parked vehicle perhaps."

"You know . . ." the third agent peered over his bifocals, "If we could take that little girl out there she might tell us quite a bit."

"Hell no," Royce said sternly. "She won't be going out there . . . ever again . . . for any reason."

"Oh . . . kay. Well. From the scrapings and splinterings we have found on the hardwood floor, this thing they were dragging was a heavy, wooden item. Something like a trunk. Maybe they had hastily packed all their clothes in it. The only clothing we have found was two piles of dirty work clothes, underwear, and a few towels."

"Uh, huh," Royce muttered.

"Could you at least ask the child if her mother had a big, ole trunk?" one detective begged.

"No. Not now . . . maybe in a day or two. Right now I'm trying to come up with a way to tell her about David-Jack and about her folks. We have no idea what all this child may have been in the middle of out there, and I don't want to excite her any more than is necessary."

"We'll be working with the dogs today. You know that we'll need you to be there with us," the detective looked over to get Royce's agreement.

"Sounds like a fine plan to me, sir," Royce gave his cheesiest grin.

"Also," another voice piped in from over Royce's shoulder, "the Medical Examiner says he will have something for you after five this afternoon."

Royce sat listening to each of them. Usually this sort of fact-finding, and the thrill of the chase, was exciting. Not this time. He felt his attention drift away and his eyes go into a non-complacent stare.

Snap out of this . . . they'll think you're crazy, he warned himself. Take notes, tap a pencil, or something to show you are still functioning.

"We have checked each bank within a hundred mile radius. There are no bank accounts. Apparently Silcox cashed his pay checks at the grocery store," the lead detective said.

"Probably kept their money in a fruit jar, buried in the ground," the other agent said.

Royce's mind went back to the fruit jars inverted on the pickets of the fence. Usually people kept their canning jars in the cellar.

"Did anybody check the cellar under the house?" Royce seemed proud of his thought.

"Was there a cellar?" the question went from one to the other. Each of them returned a quizzical look to Royce.

"Well, most of these old farm houses have some sort of root cellar, or basement, or crawl space back under the foundation," he explained.

"I think most of our work has been throughout the house, concentrating on the blood evidence and the fingerprinting that was necessary on the back porch," the bifocaled detective said. "They've done a thorough check of the attic, the barn, and the sheds behind the barn. Nothing there, but of course we'll take the dogs back through . . ."

"We do need to look for an entry to a cellar," Royce interrupted. "Possibly down under that back porch. I can't believe that old house wouldn't have a cellar." Royce grabbed his jacket and scurried them all toward the door. Let's get back out there while we still have some daylight."

CHAPTER FOURTEEN

The drive out to the Silcox place had led Royce within a mile or so of Randa's trailer. He wondered what they were doing. The interest in Donna-Dean had diverted his attentions mightily. At least he was trying to convince himself that it was Donna-Dean. Perhaps she was just the "front" for his real interests here.

The ribbon of bright yellow crime scene tape seemed to glow against the darkening clouds of the cold, blustery day. It scalloped its way through the trees bordering the Silcox property, obviously announcing to the whole community that some god awful thing had happened here. Word of mouth had surely traveled some sort of story by now.

Royce flashed his lights at one of his own patrol cars parked near the ditch alongside the Silcox mail box. Jake Sullivan sprang up from the head rest to hop out of the car and raise the yellow tape. Royce and the two cars behind him drove into the dirt lane. Royce tipped his hat. Jake smiled and nodded in return.

As Royce drove up in front of the house a sick feeling roared its way through his heart. He sat for a moment trying to get a feeling, or a sixth sense, or to make a psychic connection with his place. What in the world had gone on here? What had eaten its way into this family?

He imagined Donna-Dean swinging on the front gate. For a moment he saw her in his mind's eye as she ran to jump into his arms. Suddenly he saw the mental image of them holding her down to do the cigarette burns. DAMN. He pounded the steering wheel.

Two T.B.I. men, who had been working the scene, walked across the yard to greet him. They were eager to get Royce's attention before the other guys got out of their cars.

"Sheriff Hawkins, we have something out here in the woods we want you to see."

"Okay," Royce replied. He locked the car door and went around to the trunk to grab his camera. On difficult cases, he took extensive notes and pictures, when need be. The lawyers would refer to these puzzle pieces he would mull over at his desk in the middle of a sleepless night, as the "totality of the circumstances."

He stuffed the camera into his jacket and zipped the zipper.

"Let's go before these other fellas divert my attention."

CHAPTER FIFTEEN

The hike back into the woods was down a worn pathway. Royce suspected the trail had led to an outhouse in years gone by.

The stiff branches switched back from the T.B.I. men leading the way. He put up his arm to keep the limbs from slapping across his face.

They had walked about a half mile when the detectives pointed to a dugout trench off to the side of the pathway. It appeared to be a shallow grave. Oh God, Royce thought. What now!

"It's not what you think, Sheriff," one of the voices said over his shoulder. "This is what was down in there."

Up ahead, in the middle of the path, the detectives had laid out a partially burned valise. An old leather carpetbag, Royce thought as he grabbed his camera to take a picture.

"They sure did like to burn things." He found a large stick to pry away some of the coiled, burned leather. The contents had been set afire within the open bag.

"I'll bet this wouldn't burn fast enough. So they closed it up and buried it," Royce said.

"What is this crap anyway?" Royce bent down to stir carefully through the ashes, gently turning over small charred cylinders.

As he dug beneath the mound of ashes, he noticed that one of the cylinders had not burned entirely. Royce recognized the bright yellow with black lettering and the ASA 200 on the side. "It's film."

He came down on his knees to see what else was there. Lengths of film had been pulled out of the film canisters and piled together for burning, only they had not burned easily. With the plastic spools inside, the film canisters had probably burned like miniature furnaces, Royce concluded.

"Film. Why the hell was this ole boy burning up the family pictures?"

The T.B.I. guys shrugged their shoulders in a dumbfounded choreography.

Royce took pictures of everything, as well as the area where the valise had been buried.

"I think the lab guys will want to take this whole thing in to the lab. They will be able to tell us what this is all about," one agent said.

"Anything else worth seein' back in here?" Royce stood up from the ground to look further down the trail.

"The path continues on back a little further. They've planned to take the dogs back in there," a second agent explained.

"Let's go back to the house," Royce said. "Whatever this stuff was, they took time out of all of their mayhem to bring it way out here to burn and bury. There had to be a real good reason for them to do that."

The remainder of the afternoon involved looking for the cellar. Royce was convinced there would be one, and like a jack-in-the-box, Mrs.Killer-woman would pop up out of it.

But, as the day wasted away, no entry could be found. The dogs tracked and re-tracked. They searched the barn over and over, nothing out of the ordinary there, except that Silcox wasn't much of a farmer.

Royce spent quite awhile in the house. Standing quiet, listening . . . hoping something would call out to him.

What kind of people were they?

Downstairs the rooms were fairly clean. Cluttered, but clean. They had not lived in filth. It looked as if they were a normal, low income family. She had been a suitable homemaker, Royce supposed. It seemed as if she had provided for these children, at least the basics of life. What had been the sickness that overcame her?

Royce found what may have been Donna-Dean's room. No pictures on the wall, no cute little bedspread, no bedclothes at all . . . but they may have taken those away for evidence. There were a few toys, a storybook, one dirty, pink mitten on the floor of the closet. And there were clothes hanging from a wooden rod. Sad little things.

The mattress out back had been taken from David-Jack's single bedstead. Why? Royce could let his imagination run wild. The attic, the bedrooms, the stairway and front hall had a creepy feel to them; a sad feeling that these children struggled here. There was an absence of love in this place. No coziness. Nothing to nurture a family. This seemed more like a drab, tenement hotel than a home with children. There was no celebration of life here. This was shelter; not much more.

CHAPTER SIXTEEN

Maybe some of this mystery does lie with Donna-Dean, Royce thought. And, I do need to talk with her about David-Jack. She's going to hear it from the wrong person, he found himself preparing an excuse to go by Randa's. And of course, he would need to see if they had anything to eat for dinner tonight. He told himself to ignore the fact that Randa probably had that handled. He would just make a quick stop. After all, he did have to be back in town for that autopsy stuff that would be in from the Medical Examiner.

Without further contemplation he grabbed the dispatch radio handset to have them relay a message to Randa. No, he re-thought. I won't involve them. I'll just go on over there.

Who's the guard there with them, he tried to remember. Danny. Okay, Danny needs to go home. I'll have Jake stay there tonight, if he wants the overtime. Royce backed the patrol car away from the Silcox house, leaving the crime scene behind in the rear view mirror. The T.B.I would be leaving soon.

He drove out the lane and pulled the car to a stop and stepped out to ask Jake if he wanted the night watch at Randa's.

Jake was eager for the extra money.

"Why don't you come over there by about six o'clock. I'll stay with them until then. I'll see if these T.B.I. fellows want to guard this place tonight. Thanks, Jake. Appreciate it." he shouted back over his shoulder.

Suddenly he remembered that he should not drive up to Randa's trailer in the sheriff's car. For safety's sake he would swap cars with one of the T.B.I. detectives. So far, he had managed to keep marked cars from Randa's driveway. The neighbors might think she was bootleggin' or into prostitution.

Twenty minutes later he pulled into Randa's driveway, and gently tapped the car horn to announce himself. At the door he was greeted eagerly by Danny who seemed quite ready to go home. Donna-Dean squealed in delight and ran to get Randa.

"I can't stay very long. I have to get back to town. Jake will be coming here at six o'clock. When he gets here, I'll have to go," he found himself over-explaining.

Since the visit would be short, he decided to postpone getting into David-Jack's death with Donna-Dean. Randa would have to pick up the pieces. He would have to do it later.

"How y'all gettin' along?" he asked. Donna-Dean ran to gather all of her Barbie stuff to pile on his lap the minute he sat down on Randa's couch.

"Hello Barbie," he greeted the doll Donna-Dean held up to his face.

"I wanted to see if you needed anything to eat for tonight," he asked Randa.

"No. As a matter of fact, I have supper ready now. How about you eat with us? Do you have time?"

"Well . . . I don't know . . . do I, Donna-Dean?" he said as he quickly separated his legs to let Barbie and Skipper fall through to the floor below. She giggled that little girl giggle that wrapped its way around his heart.

"We made a banana puddin'," Donna-Dean said. "I learned how to write the word 'banana'."

"Well, now, if you're talkin' banana puddin', then I'm stayin' for supper," he tickled her ribs and brought forth more giggles and squeals.

"We're having hot roast beef sandwiches and gravy, with mashed potatoes and cole slaw," Randa said.

"And B-A-N-A-N-A puddin'," Donna-Dean carefully spelled the word.

"Sounds great," Royce followed Randa to the kitchen table, flinging Donna-Dean into the air as if she were a toddler.

When Jake arrived, Royce and Danny headed out to Brandensburg. Royce said goodnight to Donna-Dean telling her to settle down and get a good night's sleep in her new Barbie nightgown.

He grabbed Randa's hand quickly turning the handshake into a subtle hand squeeze.

"Thank you for supper. It was wonderful. My stomach is not used to good home cookin'."

"Call me when you get back," she said. "You know . . . I just want to know you got there . . . okay."

"Okay," he smiled. "I was going to ask if I could call you later anyway. I will have that autopsy report on my desk when I get back. I'm dreading it. I think I would like to talk to you after that. God, what a topic of conversation . . . ."

"Call," she said.

He squeezed her hand he had continued to hold. Then stupidly tipped his hat at her.

CHAPTER SEVENTEEN

At eight p.m. Royce couldn't stifle the urge to call Randa.

"Well, the Medical Examiner's conclusions are just plain awful," he began.

"What does it say?" she asked.

"David-Jack died from a ventral wound to the abdomen, which avulsed the pulmonary artery causing a massive internal hemorrhage," he read.

"Oh my Lord," Randa sighed.

"You know, it normally takes a body about ten minutes to bleed to death," Royce pondered. "So that means they were doing all of this as we were driving over there with Donna-Dean. They may have still been lurking around the place when I got to David-Jack on the porch."

"Oh Lord," Randa said.

"The misery continues," Royce read further from the report. "He suffered a cerebral trauma to the head, possibly from the hammer-head side of the axe. But the forensic team said that blow may not have killed him. That's probably why they axed him in the stomach."

Royce noticed Randa's silence.

"Oh, damn. I shouldn't be reading all of this to you. It's too upsetting. I don't want you to worry . . ."

"No . . . I want to know. I really want to know, read," she said.

"He was sexually molested, with extensive evidence of repeated sodomy. There was the presence of a piercing of the tongue."

"Lord bless him," Randa said.

"This is the most dastardly thing." Royce found his temper creeping back in. "Why in this world would they have killed this boy?"

"I feel so bad that Miss Mattie and I didn't question David-Jack when we heard the other children talking about the abuses. He must have told somebody. Or Donna-Dean may have told somebody. Mattie and I saw him every day. We should have been more concerned. We should have . . . ," Randa paused.

"I should have gone out there to the house, by myself, to see why they didn't want their child to come home from school. Me. Let's get the blame over onto me. You and Miss Mattie had turned the situation over to me, remember," Royce said.

"Well . . ." Randa struggled to continue.

"Well . . ." Royce laughed. "See where this kind of talk goes . . . around in a big circle."

"I'm feeling guilty because we over-looked all the classic warning signs," Randa whined.

"He wasn't about to tell you anything. He chose to turn his misery into his personality," Royce concluded.

"Donna-Dean was shy and a bit withdrawn, but she would communicate. And she has really come to life since she has met you. It was really good that you stopped by today, she wanted the banana pudding to be for you," Randa said.

As they continued to talk, Royce began to feel that he could close the autopsy report on his desk. Randa quoted Scarlett O'Hara in reminding him that "tomorrow is another day."

They said their goodnights. He thanked her for being with him at the hospital, and for helping him provide that little girl with new clothes, and especially for teaching her how to spell banana and make a banana pudding. He hoped Donna-Dean would remember that happy memory for the rest of her life.

CHAPTER EIGHTEEN

Friday morning they again gathered around Royce for their morning power session. The T.B.I. guys came with their breakfast bags in hand. Amid their Egg McMuffins and slurps of coffee, they perked up their ears to hear him out.

"Let's go to the Silcox house and really plow through the place today. We need to look for that wooden trunk, or chest . . . ," he paused. At the mention of his own word "chest," Royce thought about his mother and grandmother.

"Cedar chest," he almost shouted to their sleepy faces.

"Most women have cedar chests for their valuables, don't they. You know hope chests . . . that sort of thing . . . ," he smiled at their raised eyebrows.

"Let's go," he urged. "Danny I need you to ride shotgun with me. Oh, do you know if the dogs are working today?"

"Can't seem to find out, chief," Danny shouted, across various heads, from the back of the room.

"Well, hell," Royce sighed. "If we're up and rollin', let's make sure the damn dogs aren't getting to sleep late."

By 10 a.m. everyone, including two K-9 officers with four dogs, gathered around the steps leading up to the back porch of the Silcox house. Royce laid forth his plan for the day, beginning with a head count of how many people were there, and who would be working on what. He frantically took notes and names, although names were meaningless.

Agents and lab people, who preferred to be called forensic scientists, appeared from all corners of the yard. There were three of them, plus three lead detectives.

Too many people here, Royce thought. All of this expertise, and we're going no where on this case.

The vision of David-Jack being sodomized had stayed on his mind all night. The emphasis seemed to have shifted from the mother to the father. Royce was secretly hoping they might flush the son-of-a-bitch out of the woods today.

"I should remind you that this is a doosey of a crime scene. I suggest we keep the number of investigators inside this house to a minimum. Only two or three of us in there at a time. Go in with your hands behind your backs . . . gloves on. Don't so much as fart in there, unless you do it in a bag!"

Danny tried to stifle his giggle with a gasp.

"Danny?" Royce bellowed.

"Yessir," Danny stepped out of the crowd.

"I will need for you to note down what is coming out of here; what has been bagged and who bagged it."

"Gotcha on that, chief."

Royce asked each man to give a report as to what they had found previously that might be relevant to the case. He brought out a small tape recorder to tape their comments, again for his late-night reviews.

He learned what evidence had been gathered and paper-bagged from the back porch. Fiber samples from the bloody, burned mattress had been collected. Baskets of dirty laundry had been taken away intact, and would be sampled, labeled, and bagged in the lab. They had taken bedclothes from the parent's bed, as well as shoes from the closet, hairbrushes and combs from the bathroom.

Another agent reported on the extensive lifting of prints throughout the house, beginning with the back porch murder scene. Another agent thoroughly described sampling the blood pool beneath David-Jack.

Royce thought things had been done by the book. They had used all of their sophisticated tricks to collect what was there. They had photographed, video taped, and sketched. Puzzle pieces to form the "totality of the circumstances."

One of the lead detectives had busied himself for hours trying to find a footprint to cast, joking to the group that "if a suspect's print is anywhere around, it had no doubt been trampled over by size 13 Highway Patrol boots belonging to Sheriff Hawkins."

"I believe we should concentrate on the thing that was dragged through the house," Royce said. "This may be an important piece of the puzzle. And I still say, most of these farmhouses have some sort of underground cellar. A root cellar. A storm cellar. We need to look for any entry into an area like that. Who knows, these folks may be hiding in there when we find it," he joked to the deadpan faces before him.

"You dog people need to earn your money today. We have to know if there is anything in these woods. Get with me if you find something," Royce said.

They all scattered quickly. Each seemed to be challenging the other. Royce felt like offering a lollipop to the first one who yelled out, "Over here!"

Royce turned to go through the screen door. For what seemed to be the hundredth time, he passed the blood soaked area where David-Jack had died. His mind traveled back to that feeling against his arm, when he felt the boy's body go limp.

"Damn," he swore.

CHAPTER NINETEEN

Looking back and forth across the worn kitchen floor, Royce followed the scratch marks of the "dragged" item. He pictured one person, possibly two persons, tugging with the bulky thing, perhaps arguing that it would not fit through the doorway and out onto the steps. The marks seemed to twist around here, over there.

On closer look, one particular curved etching in the linoleum streaked out away from the others, toward the refrigerator.

Royce knelt down on one knee and rubbed his hand across the marks. He let his eyes wander slowly up the front of the fridge, as if it were a beautiful woman.

He stepped up to pull the door open. The smell of rotten food jumped out to fill his nose and fog his eyes. White hair, or cob-web like growth filled the entire space inside. Butter oozed in its saucer. Sandwich meat had grown mold that appeared to be an inch thick. Bread had reached a moldy iridescent green.

He slammed the door and wiped away the smell on the arm of his jacket. The freezer compartment had four packages of rotten meat. The stench again jumped right out into Royce's face.

Why had the refrigerator been off? The electricity in the the house was on. He began to pull at the big appliance to get it out away from the wall. The plug was lying on the floor.

Royce then saw that the linoleum flooring had been pulled up and away from the baseboard behind the refrigerator. Let me get the boys in here, he thought.

Within minutes, they had the fridge moved out into the middle of the kitchen floor.

The finger-printers were there to dust for prints on the edge of the linoleum where it had been re-nailed. The nail heads were shiny and new, and not nailed all the way down to the floor. As they finished with the printing, someone produced a crow bar and began to pry up the wide plank flooring beneath the new nails. When they jerked up the boards the smell from below rose up into the kitchen.

Everyone there had met that kind of smell before. There was nothing on this earth to compare with that order of death. Everyone of them, in this line of work, had been knocked off his feet by it.

Beneath the floor boards of the kitchen was a small door with a ring pull for raising it.

"Ah, hah," Royce couldn't help but gloat. "Here's my cellar!"

The finger printers leaned down through the planks that had been torn away, to dust the ring pull. Everyone waited quietly while that very careful work was being done. Two of them quickly tied handkerchiefs across their faces.

"Okay, we're going to pull it open now," a voice warned. Suddenly it was up. Everyone jerked their heads to the side as the smell roared its way out from captivity heading up into the kitchen.

"Jesus!"

"Shit!"

"Lord-a-mighty!"

The group of them struggled for words.

"Sheriff, do you want the honor of going down first . . . if you do . . . ?" They stepped aside to make way for Royce.

He backed himself down five steep, plank steps onto the damp, earthen floor. Someone handed him a large flashlight. He scanned its beam around the area, noticing there was a string pull for the light bulb suspended from the socket fixture over his head.

Royce asked for the finger-printer to come ahead of him to check for a print. Several minutes passed as Royce held the flashlight focused on the string while the guy carefully decided what he would do.

"I think I'll cut it off about two inches away from the fixture. We'll take that to the lab. You can still use the light with the stub part that's left," he explained.

"Okay," Royce said. "Just hurry."

Another guy appeared with cutters for the job. Royce stepped away from this operation and crept along the dirt wall to the left. Up ahead he saw an area in the dirt floor that had been dug away.

"Here it is," Royce relayed back through the group. "It's a grave . . . I suppose."

They all tumbled down the steps to him now. Eager to see. Eager to advance this mystery. A shovel lay nearby and was the next target for the finger-print team. Someone was sent to the outside to bring in two T.B.I. shovels. They would soon begin to unearth this smell.

Minutes later, Royce had to come up into the kitchen for air. All of this was beginning to make him nervous. Thoughts of Donna-Dean and what he would have to tell her tracked across his mind. Last night he had only to tell her about David-Jack, and he had chickened out. Now what?

"Sheriff?" A head appeared at the floor level from the cellar opening.

"You know how you said you had found your cellar . . . we've just found your cedar chest."

Royce almost said his favorite "Damn," but damn didn't seem to be working for him lately. This was getting to be beyond any expletive he could think of.

Within the cedar chest was the chopped up body of what would later be formally identified as Donna-Dean's mother. Royce knew instantly; Donna-Dean was a carbon copy of her mom.

The body had been dismembered. Someone had chopped her apart as if she were a side of beef. Her naked torso was surrounded by the severed head, arms, and legs.

As the T.B.I. guys used tongs to lift the pieces away from the body, they could see the most grotesque thing of all. Her tongue, and the nipples from her breasts, had been carefully stuffed up inside of her vagina.

"What the hell . . ." had been someone's remark that broke through the complete silence within the cellar.

Royce left. Just let me get out of here, was his driving thought. He raced out of the kitchen across the back porch, sniffing the brisk winter air that blew through the tattered screening.

"God, David-Jack," he turned to speak to the bloody splotch on the porch. "What did you mean about your ma?"

Now the case had taken a big turn. No longer was "ma" a suspect. Other possibilities would have to be considered. Still the haunting question of who, and why, remained.

Royce thought they were no longer looking for a killer . . . they would now be looking for a blood-thirsty beast. How in this world had Donna-Dean escaped being its target?

CHAPTER TWENTY

Royce opened the trunk of the patrol car and slung his gear into the wheel well.

Suddenly, from the deep-rutted lane that lead back out to the main road, there came a shout.

"Hey?"

"Who is it?" he shouted, reaching for the shotgun lying to the back of the trunk.

"Hey?" the voice repeated, louder now.

The old man inched his way carefully along the yellow ribbon of tape telling him this was a "crime scene." He moved to the center of the lane, avoiding the worn tire tracks etched into the hard, frozen ground.

"I need to see somebody out here!" he yelled.

Royce came forward with the shotgun clearly visible at his side.

"I'm Sheriff Hawkins. You're walking into a crime scene, fellow. You'd better have a good reason."

"I need to tell somebody somethin," came the return shout.

As he came closer, Royce could see the man was elderly . . . perhaps 80. One of the neighbors, probably.

"What's your name, sir?" Royce asked.

"I'm Aubrey Claiborne," the man said, trying to catch his breath.

"What can I do for you, Mr. Claiborne?" Royce put himself into a respectful mode.

The old man stepped up to Royce, proudly gathering attention as he pushed back his worn, green John Deere Tractors cap.

"This ole boy who lives here gived my son some money yes-tiddy to come by up here 'n git his mail," he said dourly. "I tole Dwayne not to do it . . . tole him you-ens might jist shoot his sorry hide if'n he droved up to thet mailbox out yonder."

Royce moved toward the old man.

"Where is Dwayne? I need to talk to him."

"Wellsir, he's done gone back over to his place. Lives out on Tater Peeler Road 'tuther side of Tazewell."

"Where did he see Silcox?"

"Said he come up to him when he was a pumpin' gas down to the store, yonder. Offered him twenty dollar."

The old man dug into the watch pocket of his faded overalls.

"Here's the twenty dollar."

Royce took the money. "What did he want Dwayne to do with the mail?"

"Wanted him to put it up under that big ole Dempsey Dumpster that's across the road from the store." Claiborne grinned. "Guess he's done give up on Dwayne by now."

"Yeah," Royce said, "and he's probably mad about losing his twenty dollars."

"Wellsir, I jist want to git Dwayne out from the middle of it. Dwayne's been in and out of plenty of trouble hisself 'thout gittin' into a thang like this here. My wife sez the boy don't have sense enough to pour piss out of a boot."

"Do you live around here, Mr. Claiborne?"

"Yessir . . . 'bout half a mile down thet away," he pointed. "Them T.B.I. fellers wuz at my place the other day tellin' us 'bout this boy being killed over here. Askin' if'n we know'd these here folks. I tole them I used to know the old womern who lived here, 'fore this daughter moved in. But thet's been a while back. Mebe five year ago. I thank they moved the old womern up to Middlesboro. Put her in a home up thar . . . nursin' home," he said softly.

"What was her name?" Royce asked.

"Me and my wife been thanking on thet. We believe it wuz Stallings. This girl wuz a Stallings before she went off and murried this Silcox."

"Would you know where Silcox might be hidin' out? Did Dwayne say he was driving his truck?"

"Yessir, he wuz in his ole truck. You know I bet he's around here close . . . somebody's got him hid out. Ain't me though. I'd hope to have better sense."

"Mr. Claiborne, we need to get the word out that Silcox is very dangerous. He's done an absolutely savage thing here," Royce said. "And if anybody is sheltering him, they could be in big trouble."

"I sure will tell 'em down to the Nazareen Church this Sunday, believe you me," the old man said as he turned to leave.

Ah ha . . . Royce thought. Why hadn't he thought of something so simple.

"How many churches are up through this valley?" Royce stepped alongside Claiborne.

"They's three others besides us, thet I know uv. The ones we all call Holy Rollers are 'bout three mile down thetaway," he pointed. "Then the Methodists . . . you know they don't believe in water baptisin' . . . are down thetaway, off of Paint Pony Road.

"And them Fire Baptized Apostolic somethin-nuther, about five mile onto the mountain yonder. They let on like they's all goin' to Heaven and we's all goin' to hell."

"Is that right?" Royce said.

"Yessir. You jist ask airy a one of them . . . they'll tell ye."

"Well I would like for you to tell everybody you know that if they have seen this man, or have any information that might help us find him, they need to come right here. There's always someone from my office here, who can locate me at a moment's notice. We need to get to Silcox, before he gets to his little girl."

"I know thet to be true," Mr. Claiborne said.

"I'm going to have to go now," Royce explained. "I can drive you back to your place if you want me to."

"Nossir, I'll jist walk on back. I don't get into cars much any more. Got arthur-itis in my hip. Can't even git up onto the runnin' board of my truck 'thout it hurtin' me."

"I thank you for stopping by," Royce said. "Tell Dwayne he's wise for not trying to do this for Silcox. Good decisions like that will keep him on the straight and narrow. Tell him I appreciate it," Royce offered to shake the old man's tremoring hand, but Claiborne didn't notice; he had turned to leave, carefully placing his feet to walk back down the lane.

"Houston!" Royce summoned one of his loitering deputies. "I've got to go. Would you walk on down there with him. See if he'll tell you anything else. He's just told me that Silcox is among us. I'll have to step up security out here."

CHAPTER TWENTY-ONE

The phone rang at five o'clock. Randa answered, secretly hoping it would be who she had been thinking about all afternoon. Like a giddy teen-ager, her heart gave an anxious leap at the sound of his voice.

"Hey," Royce sounded a bit out of breath. "Guess who has the evening off and is looking for a hot date? How about joining me over here for a steak dinner, or a Chinese dinner, or a Red Lobster dinner, or a . . ."

"Hold on Sheriff," Randa teased. "This is kind of short notice, considering we have a child to think about."

"I've got that handled."

"You do."

"Yep. If you'll agree to go with me, I'll bring the baby-sitter," he pleaded.

"It sounds great," Randa hoped she sounded cool, calm and collected. "Are you thirty minutes away, or are you just down the road?"

"Actually, I could be there by about six thirty. Is that okay?" He was beginning to sound somewhat pitiful.

"What do you want me to tell Donna-Dean?"

"Tell her I'm bringing her a special sitter, and a big bucket of Kentucky Fried Chicken."

"But she's begging for Beanee Weenees," Randa laughed.

"We can stop by a store and get some for her. I was going to ask you to plan a grocery shopping trip. Judge Ferrell will reimburse me, or you, for whatever we spend on her upkeep. Just save the receipts. In fact, I should give you some cash money to use with her until I can get with the judge on Monday. He'll probably do whatever he does for foster parents.

"But now, tonight is your night. I think you need a little diversion from all of this. I know I do," he seemed to be struggling to disguise his obvious intent.

"Thank you, that's very nice. I appreciate your thoughtfulness." Randa squinched her eyebrows at the thought of her words sounding like a Hallmark card.

"I'm sorry for the short notice. I didn't know I could get things worked out this quickly. I guess I do things on the spur of the moment. I don't always know that I can get away from here. But, right now, I've had my fill with this investigation. I haven't had a thing to eat all day. I'll probably make a pig of myself, wherever we go," he said.

"Then you get to choose the restaurant. Any place is fine with me. I'm looking forward to getting away from here, too. You must remember that I'm used to getting away from children at three in the afternoon."

"Well, then, I'll hurry on home to get ready and I'll be on the road in a little while. Bye."

"Bye." She wanted to warn him not to "split the road wide open," but decided that might sound a bit reprimanding. She would worry about him, though.

"Donna-Dean!" Randa yelled across the kitchen counter into the living room. Donna-Dean was stretched out on the floor, coloring in her coloring book. Barbie and Skipper were posed on the nearby couch keeping a close watch.

"Guess what?" Randa sounded as if she were talking to her teen-age girlfriend. "Sheriff Royce has asked me to go out to dinner with him."

"You mean on a date?" Donna-Dean giggled.

"Now what do you know about dates?" Randa quizzed.

"Well, Ellie Mae Clampett has dates with fellers, and on the Andy Griffin Show, Barney wuz always datin' Thelma Lou. And even Andy dates Helen Crump."

"Oh, you know whut!" Donna-Dean seemed awestruck with her own idea.

"What?" Randa asked.

"Andy Griffin is a sheriff, and Helen Crump is a teacher just like you." Donna-Dean rolled across the floor in a big flurry of laughter. She bumped herself into the crossed legs of Deputy Jake who was asleep in Randa's recliner.

"Oopsey-daisy. Sorry." she whispered. Jake didn't seem to be disturbed.

"Well you can call us Andy and Helen. I've got to get ready. He says he's bringing someone special to stay with you tonight." Randa walked over to spin Donna-Dean around and up from the floor.

"He says he's bringing you Kentucky Fried Chicken for supper. Have you ever had that before?"

"No'm," Donna-Dean made an imitation whine. "But I seen it on t.v."

"Let's get me ready. I'll need you to help me pick out something to wear." They sped off to the bedroom.

Deputy Jake, snoring lightly, was totally unaware that they were no longer in the room.

Chapter Twenty-Two

Six thirty sharp Randa was ready. She had chosen her navy blue wool pantsuit, complete with brass buttons on the double-breasted jacket and epaulets across the shoulders.

Randa looked at herself in the mirror. She hoped Royce wouldn't think she looked like a midshipman from Annapolis.

Donna-Dean wanted her to wear her gold earrings to match the brass buttons on the coat.

When the door bell rang, Donna-Dean made a quick jump to answer it. Jake was right behind her, in case this was some unexpected caller. He pulled Donna-Dean back and opened the door to greet his boss.

Royce made his entrance carrying a large chicken bag, and a wrapped gift in one hand. His other hand was offered to help Miss Mattie Lou Carnes up the trailer steps into the doorway.

For a moment the trailer was filled with squeals of delight from each of them. Miss Mattie grabbed for Donna-Dean, who was always eager to be drawn close to anyone.

Royce headed for Randa's kitchen table. He was delighted with the reaction to his surprise. Jake edged himself around the backside of Miss Mattie Lou who was now beginning to take off her coat. Randa gathered in the great cloak and peered over to look at Royce. She caught his eye. He gave her a quick wink.

"You are a sly one, Royce Hawkins," she teased.

To Miss Mattie, Randa said, "Are you sure you're up to this?"

"Honey, if this is what I can do to help, I'll be up to it. We'll have fun eating our dinner that Royce has brought for us."

"Donna-Dean, this is for you," Royce said as she ran to him. She jerked the box quickly out of his hand and tore away at the wrapping paper.

"Donna-Dean, what do you say?" Miss Mattie Lou coaxed.

"Thank you." Donna-Dean pulled and tugged frantically until she broke through the scotch tape. "It's Ken," she yelled. "It's a Ken doll. Now Barbie can have a date tonight, too."

Oh Lord, please don't let me blush, Randa thought. Royce would surely know she had talked the dating situation over with Donna-Dean. However, he was preoccupied by Jake's eagerness to go home for the evening. They walked toward the door talking about a replacement deputy who would be arriving shortly.

Miss Mattie Lou stepped closer to Randa. "You go on now and have a good time. Royce has things all worked out and has given me full instructions. We'll be fine."

"How are things at school?" Randa asked. "I feel like I'm off of this planet into outer space somewhere."

"Everything's fine. You're doing the Lord's work here, Randa. Just think of this as your calling for the moment. We'll all get by there at school. Everything will get back to normal soon. I just want you to enjoy this evening. He's quite something, you know," Miss Mattie said, giving a nod toward Royce.

"I'm beginning to find that out," Randa admitted.

Chapter Twenty Three

A light rain speckled across his black, Ford F-150 pick up truck, making tiny wet rhinestones glimmer in the muted glow of the porch light.

"I'm sorry I don't have a car," Royce said as he opened the door for her. "But, this is a brand-new truck."

"Why would you need a car?" Randa asked.

"Oh, I don't know. Seems like it would be more appropriate . . . more special."

He offered his hand to help her step up into the "new" smell of the leather interior. She noticed her hand in his. Their eyes met in a heart-stopping stare.

"Nice," she said to his eyes. "I mean . . . ," she stammered, "the truck . . . it's very nice."

Trying hard to overcome the awkward moment, Royce said, "I gave it to myself for Christmas. You're the first one to sit here on the passenger side."

"Now see, that's very special." Randa sat up onto the seat and let him close the door.

Settling in under the steering wheel, he turned to say, "I have to tell you something, now. But I don't want this to ruin our evening."

Randa's mind raced ahead of him. Here's where he reveals his romantic past: an alimonied ex-wife, a fling with the mayor's wife, a romp in the hay with some nurse Brodie had fixed him up with.

"Promise me you'll just file this away and not let it linger too long on your mind." He took her hands as she turned to face him.

"What?" she said.

"We found the body of Donna-Dean's mother this afternoon."

"Oh . . . my God," Randa pulled one hand away from his to cover her mouth.

"Her body was in the dirt cellar, beneath the kitchen floor. She had been axed, like David-Jack, only they chopped her up and put her inside a cedar chest. Whoever did this wanted to make some sort of statement, I suppose. They had cut her tongue out."

They let his words fall away into silence.

"That's what they hated about her . . . her words, how she used them. Her hatefulness," Randa said.

"There was some sexual stuff, too . . . but I don't want you to know all of that. It's hard enough for me to deal with it," he added.

"Royce, whoever did this is a maniac!"

"You're right."

"An absolute maniac," she muttered.

"But we'll get him. It may take us a while, but we'll outsmart him. Now . . . let's put this out of our minds."

"Is this why you asked me out?" she asked.

"No." He reached up to touch her cheek. "I don't want you to think that. There was no ulterior motive here."

"Are you sure?" she smiled.

"I asked you out because I wanted to be with you . . . alone."

"That's what I had hoped, but . . ."

"I wanted to tell you this now so we could deal with it before you had to go back to Donna-Dean. And, I guess, somehow, you're the only one who can really help me get past this."

"What are you going to tell Donna-Dean?" she asked.

"I don't know."

CHAPTER TWENTY-FOUR

An hour later, they were at the Flaming Steer Steakhouse in Brandensburg waiting to be seated.

"You know, I have to tell you," Randa began. "Donna-Dean has noticed that Sheriff Andy Taylor on t.v. is dating teacher Helen Crump."

Royce laughed. "She's sharp."

"Yes . . . yes, she is. In school, she's always seemed a bit shy, but now I have seen a different side . . ."

"Shhh!" Royce put a finger gently to her lips. "No more talk of Donna-Dean," he whispered.

The waiter led them to a corner booth, lit only by a sea glass hurricane lamp in the center of the table. Royce asked if she would like some wine.

Randa answered "yes" all too quickly. She hoped he would not think she was an alcoholic ready to lay back a few.

Royce ordered the house Cabernet, and they began to review the over-sized menus. Suddenly a man approached their table from across the room. He was carrying a giant bouquet of red roses in a crystal vase.

"Miss Stratton?"

"Yes," she answered as he sat the roses in front of her.

"These are for you," he said, almost bowing his exit away from the table.

"Thank you," Randa said, not quite able to hide her excitement.

God. She had never had roses! She grabbed for the small florist card tied with silver ribbon to one of the long stems.

The hand-written card, with a scrawled loop-over-loop signature, was an "F" piece of penmanship. It seemed to read "Thank you so much for your help."

"Royce? Is this you?" She clutched her chest trying to pump breath into herself.

He was smiling, almost laughing now. "Yeah . . . it's me. Can't you read that writin', Teach?"

Randa shook her head. "Oh sure. There is no "R" here, no "Y", not even a decent "H" for Hawkins. I've got to teach you how to write your name."

She cupped the roses in her hands. "I've never had anyone give me roses. They're beautiful. What a thrill! Now I can understand why women carry on so over roses."

She grabbed for his hand across the table.

"You didn't have to do this . . . but, I'm so glad you did. Thank you."

Dinner was perfect. They laughed and joked playfully as if they had known each other for years. Both avoided thinking about the little girl back at Randa's trailer, and how circumstances had led her there. This seemed to be their time and these hours were being well-spent.

Randa found out quite a bit more about Royce. She had observed his beautiful smile many times before, but now noticed that it actually began with the tiny lines at the corners of his eyes.

He was, again, quite dapper in his dark charcoal suit with a banded collar to his white shirt. Danny had told him he looked like a mafia kingpin, especially the spit-shined church shoes.

Royce explained that he lived in what had been his parents' lodge "out at the lake." Randa didn't know which lake, or where, since there were many in the area.

He had spent the previous summer refurbishing the place. He had put in french doors leading out of the living room onto the patio, and had the 100-year-old fieldstone chimney cleaned.

He said he liked the house and had kept it really nice through the years he had lived there, in case he "wanted to sell it sometime." He thought it was beautiful there, but sort of lonely. He found himself spending more and more time on the job back over the last few months.

Suddenly, as a thunderbolt idea, or to possibly change the subject, he asked: "Oh, hey, do you by any chance like roller coasters? I know it's an odd question, but have you ever been on one?" He was quite anxious to hear her answer.

"Yeah. It's been a long time ago," Randa said. "Why?"

"Okay . . . after we stop to get the Beanee Weenees for you-know-who . . . I'm gonna take you on a roller coaster ride! You won't believe how much fun it is!" he promised.

Randa couldn't keep up with his exuberance. She had difficulty adjusting to his spontaneity, but felt herself blocking out any questions or doubts she may have had. Is this "throwing caution to the wind?" She told herself it simply didn't matter; somehow it was okay that the county sheriff had wined and dined her, and was now offering a great adventure into the night.

Chapter Twenty-Five

Later, as they exited the all night market with a sackful of Beanee Weenees, Randa began to feel a great sense of anticipation. Royce had continually promised her that this was "just gonna be the thrill of her life." She began to wonder not only what this was, but where it was. There were no amusement parks around here.

They drove in the general direction of Randa's Trawber Creek Road, but forked off at the main highway that spiraled its hair-pin turns and switch-backs high up into the mountains.

They were the only ones traveling the dark, two-lane highway. The truck cab was warm and cozy. Randa found herself clutching the vase of red roses tightly with both hands.

As they headed downhill, Royce began to prepare her for what he remembered the teen-agers calling "7 Dips." Soon he was warning her to "hang on."

The road leveled out before them. They had to be in the next county by now, Randa thought.

Royce raced the engine to the top of what appeared to be a small hill coming up ahead of them. This was the first of a series of small hills, spaced close together, in a row of rises and falls. Randa couldn't quite see the glowing green speedometer, but the truck had to be doing at least 70, possibly 80 mph. She clutched the vase tighter.

Suddenly, they crested the top of the first hill and the roadway fell completely away from beneath the truck to drop them off into the "dip" below.

They both gasped and laughingly screamed a simultaneous "shhhh . . . it!!" They laughed wildly at the coincidence, and that the roses seemed to rise up out of the vase to almost touch the roof of the truck. Sprinkles of water flecked onto Randa's face.

Royce gunned the engine to climb up the next hill. They were each shrieking with laughter.

"See. I told you. It's great, isn't it?" Royce yelled as they plunged down into the second "dip." This one was a stronger drop and the thrill even greater.

Ever cautious, Randa hoped they would not meet another car or truck topping the hill on the other side of the road. She was lauging so hard now, she almost lost the grip she had on the vase of flowers.

This marvelously dangerous fun lasted several more minutes until the last hill had fallen away behind them. Randa thought no one would ever believe she had gone over "7 Dips" on her first date with this hot-roddin' county sheriff!

They continued to laugh all the way back to Randa's trailer.

"What in the world would you say if someone had caught you doing that?" Randa asked.

"Well, you know," he said, as he began to dance around her question, "what you really try to do is get airborne enough . . ."

"Airborne?" Randa laughed.

"To sort of fly from hilltop to hilltop, and not drop down into the dips. Of course you don't really lift off the ground. Now if I could bring us out here in that patrol car, I could kick that thing up to about 120," he bragged as he turned on the Dolby-stereoed radio to his favorite oldies station.

Randa joined him in singing along to "There's a Kind of Hush All Over the World Tonight." They both enjoyed over-emphasizing the "hus . . . sh" part.

Randa thought it had been fun to laugh and enjoy the same things. The date was, sadly, coming to an end as Royce pulled into Randa's driveway.

"Royce, this has been wonderful. I appreciate your asking me out, and I really appreciate the roses," she said.

He brought the truck to a stop, cut off the engine and headlights, and snapped off the radio as Elvis was walking in the "Cold Kentucky Rain."

"It was great fun, wasn't it. I hope we can do it again, soon. I'll try not to give you such short notice the next time. You know . . . I'm kind of a loner. I don't really do this . . . I mean, I don't really go out enough to know what's proper," he explained.

"You did just great," she said putting a hand on his arm. "Everything you planned was wonderful, even '7 Dips'."

"I'm glad you didn't think I was going to kill you," he clasped his hand over her hand. He leaned in close to say, "Do you get the feelin' that about three sets of eyes are peeping through the blinds, looking out to see if I give you a good-night kiss?"

Randa's gaze moved slowly around to look up at the trailer windows.

"Well, we shouldn't disappoint them," she teased. "Here, hold the roses."

She purposefully avoided his eyes as she shoved the vase into his hands. He moved back in total amazement. She used both of her hands to grab the lapels of his jacket.

Pulling him to her, she looked deep into those smiling blue eyes and warned him to "hang on."

CHAPTER TWENTY-SIX

Randa pulled back, letting her kiss settle across his lips that were mouthing the word "Wow."

"I guess you might say I've just assaulted an officer of the law," she joked.

Suddenly, a horrifying THWUNK! hit the rear window of the truck, shattering the glass into a million shards that crunched together like ice crystals. Only a handful of the chips fell down onto Randa's shoulder. The window held itself suspended around the hand-sized hole that now let in a blast of cold, night air.

Royce placed the vase of roses on the seat and immediately threw Randa to the floor of the truck.

He bolted out of the truck door, crouching low, and fumbling into his suit jacket. He drew out the gun he had snuggled in the shoulder holster under his arm.

He flung himself back into the truck cab and pounded a fist on the horn.

Randa thought the deputy on duty inside must be awake, for the horn's blast was followed by the porch light coming on.

Royce could see some movement at the trailer door and quickly recognized Danny's stocky form edging cautiously out and down the front steps. He wondered if all of this commotion would wake Donna-Dean.

Royce told Randa to stay down for a few more minutes, until they could get her out of the truck. "Whoever threw this is probably still out here somewhere," he whispered.

Danny was creeping around the front end of the truck.

"Hey, chief. You havin' some trouble out here in the romance department?"

"Yeah. Seems that somebody wanted to knock Randa's head off. It's taken out the rear window. They're probably still out here in the bushes, or across the road. I don't think I heard a car drive off."

"Now, how would you have known if a car went by or not, Mister Date-man?" Danny couldn't resist another poke.

"Danny!" Royce snapped.

"Okay . . . I'm sorry. I'm back to work . . . my mind's out of the gutter! So, are we gonna see what this thing is, or are we just gonna sit out here under the truck?"

"You cover me. I'll take a look. I think it bounced down into the truck bed."

Royce moved around to the side of the truck. "Stay down, Randa," he reminded her in case she had thoughts of moving.

He stood in a crouched position, weapon drawn and visible, in case anyone might be watching his every move. He quickly peered around and down into the truck bed. It was pitch dark and the porch light did not cast its light out this far into the yard. He could see the round object, but was afraid to touch it.

"Sheriff Hawkins?" Miss Mattie called from the trailer door. "Are y'all alright out there?"

"Yes ma'am. You go back inside. We've got trouble going on out here. We'll get in there to you in a minute. Go back in and close that door. NOW!" he spat out the words and hoped she wouldn't take offense.

"Randa?" he said

"Uh-huh."

"Are you okay?"

"Yeah. Just scared . . . for you," she said.

CHAPTER TWENTY-SEVEN

Later, the four of them huddled at the kitchen table, staring at the "round" object that had been retrieved from the bed of the truck. It appeared to be an old wooden croquet ball. A paper was tied around it with twine.

"I need to get this in to the office," Royce said. "We'll open it up there."

"Danny, I need you to take Miss Mattie home. I'll have to locate a deputy who can come over here for a while tonight because I need you to come on back to the office with me."

Randa walked to the front bedroom to get Miss Mattie's coat. She checked on Donna-Dean, who had remained fast asleep in Randa's bed.

"I don't think she heard a thing, she's sleeping pretty soundly."

Miss Mattie gathered her purse as Danny began to help her on with her coat.

"Now Randa, I could stay here with you tonight, if you need me to," Mattie offered.

"Well," Royce interjected. "I think I'm going to come back to do the late shift."

"I bet you will," Danny muttered, getting in yet another joke.

"Danny . . . I think I need to find some really hard, disgusting job for you to do . . . you know, something to occupy your mind! You must just be bored to death with your little life 'cause you've jumped over here into mine!"

Royce spun his sidekick around and pointed him out the trailer door, guiding Miss Mattie along behind.

"Remember now, find your way back over to the office when you leave Miss Mattie's."

"Aye-aye, Sir," Danny saluted.

Now, the trailer had an eerie stillness; no little girl giggles, no quips from Danny, even the t.v. was off. A few hours earlier everyone seemed to be alive in anticipation of the evening ahead.

Royce was at the kitchen wall phone concluding a series of good-natured commands by adding, "Well, wake him up and send him on over here, now. Please. Thank you."

Randa glared at the paper-wrapped ball that had brought her thrilling date to a dramatic end.

Royce moved over to her, reaching out to grab both of her hands.

"Hey . . ." he smiled. "Don't worry about this. Probably some prankster."

Randa returned his smile. Her attention had drifted away from his words, he had made the move to hold her hands and inch himself closer and closer.

"I'm sorry this had to happen," he rambled. "It certainly wasn't part of my plan for the evening. I wouldn't have had it happen for the world."

"Your evening was perfect. Especially the roses."

"Well, I wanted to thank you for all you have done for Donna-Dean . . . and for me. I don't know what I would have done without you." He dropped her hands and drew her into his arms.

He's shy, Randa thought. This big, hunk of a bear is shy!

She reached her hands around his chest to hug him.

"Is this a gun?" she joked patting at his shoulder holster.

"Yeah," he whispered.

"Would you have used it?"

"Yeah."

He pushed her back to look down into her eyes.

"You know, I think I remember what we were doing when that thing hit the truck window."

"Oh you do, do you?" Randa said.

"We were saying good night." He leaned down.

"Goodnight Randa." He kissed her with three soft kisses. The third one seemed to last forever. He hugged her as if he were settling her soul with his.

"Wow," Randa whispered.

"I . . . uh," Royce stammered.

"Don't analyze this," she warned. "It's the perfect ending to this perfect night you have given me."

CHAPTER TWENTY-EIGHT

"Randa?"

His voice seemed long ago and far away. Where? Who?

"Randa?" His voice was a little firmer now.

She sensed she should peep one eye open to see . . . ah, there he is . . . sweet prince. He's going to wake me up with a kiss. Does this mean I am Snow White? No, I don't think so . . .

"Ran . . . da!" He was pushing on her shoulder now.

The voice seemed to bring her quickly to the present. She was sleeping on the couch. Why? Oh yeah . . . after Royce left she found Donna-Dean sprawled out all across her bed. Don't wake her up.

One eye began to focus on Royce who was now sitting on the edge of the couch pushing at her.

"Oh, you're back," Randa said sleepily, at the same time thinking she should be sharp and alert so she could sit up and talk. Maybe he wanted to continue their date.

"Randa, I need to tell you something. Are you in there?" he said, pecking his fingers on her forehead.

"I suppose I am. What's going on?" she said.

"Remember the croquet ball with the paper tied around it . . ." he hesitated in that shy, little boy way she was becoming familiar with. "Uh, that paper was Donna-Dean's birth certificate. Someone had written across it, 'We know where she is. We're going to get her.'"

"Oh . . ." Randa said, quickly getting up from the couch. Royce was up alongside her. She glanced at the clock on the t.v., it blinked the red numerals 2:45.

She gave a deep sigh. Somehow fear could make the body want to hold its breath. It could shroud the heart in a dark covering, and draw expression from the face. Fear suddenly made Randa's spirit lose its kilowatts.

"I'll have to move you and Donna-Dean now," Royce said. "There are three deputies here with me to do that. I need you to gather up clothes and things you will want to take for yourself. We'll need the stuff we bought for Donna-Dean."

"Oh . . ." she said. Her body had begun to shiver.

"Randa," he grabbed her shoulders. "Are you hearing me?"

There was a seriousness to his eyes.

We need to leave in the van outside. Danny will follow us in your car, so he'll need your keys."

She looked at him now. Tears formed in her eyes. He reached out to draw her close.

"Everything will be okay. I'll make it okay. Nobody is going to get to you, or to Donna-Dean. I'm taking you to stay with me at my house, and there will be a whole team of us guarding you."

"Randa," he pushed her back from his hug. "Talk to me . . . say something."

"I don't know what to say," she managed a smile as she walked out of his arms.

"Remember that word 'involved'?" he said. "Well, here we are knee-deep in involvement," Royce turned to gather the Barbie dolls and Barbie house shoes on the floor by Randa's couch. "We need to move out now. Let's wait until we get things together before we wake Donna-Dean."

"Yes . . . we should wait." Randa agreed.

"Jake is bringing in some boxes. Just toss in as much as you want," he said to her back as she hurried toward the bedroom.

Randa began to mentally "pack." She immediately grabbed for the security of her purse: keys, I.D., real money. Plastic money, her favorite headache medicine, her little spiral notebook with phone numbers.

Once again, there was the feeling that she was going with the sheriff on yet another adventure into the night.

Chapter Twenty-Nine

The three cars raced convoy-style across Hurricane Ridge toward Brandensburg.

In the side mirror of the van, Randa watched as Danny made a diversionary turn in her Jeep onto a back road that wound its way into town. She thought about her $239 car payment as she saw the Jeep's taillights fade away into darkness.

When they had backed out of her driveway, Randa had said a silent "goodbye" to her trailer, wondering when she would be back to the often dull and lonely life she had led there.

"I'm glad you two can come to my place," Royce struggled to make light of the situation. "I think you'll like it. If this were summer, I'd have y'all fishing and boating . . . even water skiing if you wanted to."

"That would be nice," she muttered.

"We'll build a big fire in the fireplace. Who knows, maybe it will snow!" he said, peering out of the side window up through the star-filled night.

"Are you all right?" he asked.

"I guess I'm just stunned," she said. "I wasn't sure how this might all turn out, but this is a little unexpected. Where do we go from here?"

"Let's just go from moment to moment," Royce said. "If we lay too many plans, things might come along to blow those plans out of the water. Unfortunately for you, this is probably going to seem like you're incarcerated . . . with me . . . and my posse!"

They were approaching the turn off to the house.

"This place is difficult to find, even when I give someone a map. This is Texas Hollow Road. Once we are back up in here, we'll be hidden by Mother Nature herself. I'll have to go in and out to continue this investigation, but you'll be well protected by the team of people we have put together."

Randa's sleepy-eyed first impression of Royce's home was that it was beautiful. The glow from the porch lights revealed a rustic stone and log structure that was much larger than she had imagined. This was a lovely mountain retreat, ideal for a bed and breakfast.

Why in the world was this man choosing to be a county sheriff, when he could be an Innkeeper?" she thought.

Royce hurriedly shuttled her across the wide fieldstone walkway that meandered its way up onto the front stoop. The deputies were unlocking what seemed to be a hand-carved front door. Royce was carrying the sleeping Donna-Dean close across the front of his body, shielding her from the cold, or from other things.

Two deputies, who had gone into the house, were turning on lights and passing quickly from room to room, searching like search dogs. Randa began to realize that she would now be living this investigation up close and personal.

"The guest room is down this way," Royce motioned with his head to the small hallway leading out of the living area. "It will be ideal for you two. I have other rooms upstairs, but I don't want y'all to be that far away."

He was moving ahead now, careening around a wall to turn on a light switch with his shoulder. Randa stepped into the room that held an antique sleigh bed, a double dresser, and a large pine cupboard that would serve as a closet.

"This is beautiful, Royce," she said, amazed that this bachelor had such a flair for decorating.

"I have to admit that I've spent over a year of spare time redecorating it. And I did have to have female help with the colors and things," he whispered as he put Donna-Dean down onto the bed.

Randa's weary mind jumped to visions of ex-girlfriends, or possibly an ex-wife.

"The sheets and the bedspread are all brand-new, right out of the packages," he explained. "I've had them stored away . . . for when I had company," he said never realizing the mention of another female had almost sparked Randa's second panic attack within the last hour.

The deputies were bringing in the boxes of things from the trailer. She moved out of their way wondering what to do next. She decided to get over to Donna-Dean to take her coat off and put her under the covers. It was amazing that she could sleep so soundly.

"Randa, let me talk with you for a minute or two, then I'll let you hit the sack. You look like you are about to drop," Royce said, leading her out to the living room.

She chose the putty-colored leather couch that sat before the giant fireplace. Royce stepped around to start a fire. He soon had a strong crackling flame rising high up into the stone chimney.

He sat down next to her and quickly put his boots up onto the coffee table before them. He took Randa's hand.

"It's been a long night, hasn't it? I just wanted you to know that tomorrow I'm going to talk with Donna-Dean about David-Jack, and about her mother. I don't think I want to get real specific about how they died, even if she asks a lot of questions. I think those social workers wouldn't want me getting into detail, or saying things that might damage her, you know, psychologically."

"Maybe she can tell you what was going on out there," Randa said. "I think it's odd that she hasn't worried about going home, or back to school, or anything. She seems very content to be with us. Remember, Judge Ferrell has left everything up to our good judgement. He seems to think we can do this. Even if we make a few mistakes while we have her, I think the good we are doing will come shining through."

"You're right," he added.

"This fire is going to put me to sleep," Randa let her head fall over onto his shoulder.

"You need to get to bed," Royce said. "Unfortunately, this will all still be here when you get up in the morning. The guys are here to guard us, so don't worry about a thing . . . just get some good rest. My bedroom is upstairs, but I want to stay close so I'm going to sleep right out here tonight. Let's go," he said pulling her up.

"I'll try to get my wits about me by the time I get up in the morning. Oh, I must warn you that Donna-Dean is an early riser. She'll be out here at the crack of dawn looking for the t.v.," Randa said.

"That's fine. Goodnight, sweet lady, why don't you go and dream about our racing over '7 Dips'?" He hugged her tightly, gave her a quick kiss on the top of the head, and pushed her gently toward the bedroom door.

CHAPTER THIRTY

Royce simply did not know how to tell Donna-Dean about the deaths. Thinking and re-thinking the words he would say had been useless. Anticipating her reaction was making him nervous.

Gotta tell her tonight, gotta tell her in the morning, gotta tell her after lunch . . . what a nightmare. Gotta tell her now. Today was the day, and this was the morning.

He stood at the kitchen counter trying to figure out where the hell Becca had stored the Mr. Coffee machine. The coffee she had used three months ago was in the back of the refrigerator.

He flung each of the cabinet doors open, and searched all of the logical places. Maybe she took the damn thing home with her.

He eyed the hallway that led away from the kitchen toward the guest bedroom. Donna-Dean could come bounding out any minute. She would be confused at having been moved to a new place during the night. Royce knew her face would light up with glee the instant she saw him.

That would be the hard part, bringing down that joy with this awful news. Gotta do it, he coached himself. Can't keep harboring this in my mind, or keep hiding this from her any longer.

He wondered if she had been close to David-Jack. Would she have had any love for the mother, considering the cigarette burns? He guessed that any sort of human animal could form a bond with its mother, no matter how it was treated.

Royce secretly hoped she would have no reaction at all to the deaths. After all, she had not yet longed to go home, nor had she asked about them coming to get her, and this was the fourth day. She was being cared for here, and she was soaking up love and attention the way children are supposed to.

He would have to convince her that her home, and life as she had known it, was gone. He allowed the lurking counter argument to creep in, that maybe he should let the social workers handle this.

No. Notifying the next of kin about deaths had been part of his job for years. Godlandish stuff, too. He could handle this. Just because he had gotten close to her and cared about what her reaction might be, was no reason to think he should pass this over to someone else.

He planned to do the best he could do, and deal with what might be on the other side later. Hell, he should just tell her he would like to have her for his little girl and that might make everything all right.

Whoa . . . he warned himself. Better slow down. Do this right. Don't add in anything that would further mess up her mind.

CHAPTER THIRTY-ONE

Randa decided this would be a good day for jeans and a sweatshirt. Apparently, by sheer coincidence, Royce had the same idea for he was in jeans and a white tee-shirt. Across his pocket were tiny words that said "Lead, Follow, Or Get Out Of The Way!."

"Good morning," he beamed across the counter/bar that separated the kitchen area from the living room.

"Thought the smell of breakfast might rouse you guys."

"You'll have to settle for me," Randa said. "My body is telling me it's time to get up for school."

"This is Saturday morning by the calendar; you could have slept late. This is also day four of this madness . . . how are you doing with all of it?" he asked.

"I'm fine. I can roll with it a little longer. But, I should call my brother in Florida. He calls me often, and he would be worried if I never answered the phone."

"Sure. You're welcome to call whenever you want."

"Thanks," Randa said, "What do you have in mind for us, today?"

Royce reached for her hand.

"I like that . . . us . . . ," he said.

Randa pretended to jerk her hand away from him. "I was referring to me and Donna-Dean."

"I know . . . , I was just being silly," he said. "I'm nervous. I want to talk with her about these deaths, and if I don't get on with that I'm going to go nuts. I'd like for you to sit in on the conversation. I'll just be winging the whole thing."

Randa saw the worry in his eyes. "You'll do fine," she encouraged. "Just let your heart be your guide."

"Do you think she even knows what death is?" he asked.

"Possibly," Randa said. "Some of the other children at school have had relatives die, and we've had many sad tales about dogs and cats dying, or a calf being born dead."

"If I get off onto something you think I shouldn't, feel free to stop me," he said hoisting a giant skillet onto the stove eye.

"You're putting too much thought into it," she said. "You'll do fine. Are you going to cook breakfast for . . . us."

"For you and Donna-Dean?" he said.

"And you, too. You can be apart of . . . us."

"Well okay . . . I can do breakfast pretty good. I just can't seem to find the coffee maker."

CHAPTER THIRTY TWO

"You said you needed to call your brother. Maybe you should do that. You can use the phone upstairs?"

"I suppose now is as good a time as any," Randa groaned.

"Come on . . . we can do this together," Royce said, heading her toward the stairs.

"How do I even begin to explain this? Would it be better if you placed the call and told him everything?" she asked.

"You might want to get him on the line, and then whenever you think you need me, you can tell him that I'm here to explain further," Royce suggested. "What's his name?"

"Derrick."

They walked up the stairs and down a hallway that passed several bedrooms, to a small room Royce used for an office. His roll-top desk was a mountain of papers and files.

"Excuse the mess. This is my homework."

Randa noticed him knock over a framed picture of a girl, or a woman, as he dug for the telephone.

"Oh gosh," she said picking up the receiver to dial, "This will be long distance to Florida. How do I get it billed to my phone?" she asked.

"Don't bother about that, just dial. Do you want me to step outside the door?"

Randa grabbed his arm. "Don't you dare," she laughed.

"Why don't you tell him we went flyin' over 7 Dips?" Royce said.

"Or, buying Barbie dolls at Walmart?" she said, as she tried to recall Derrick's area code and telephone number.

The connection was made almost instantly, the rings answered all too quickly.

"Derrick?" she greeted him in her happiest voice. "Hi. How are you? What are you doing?" Royce would think she had lost her mind, and that cabin fever had finally taken its toll.

He shuffled around his desk, moving things from here to there, trying his best to be inconspicuous. Randa noticed that he had repositioned the framed picture of the woman.

Royce wondered what this man in Randa's life might be like. The name "Derrick" sounded sophisticated . . . a computer genius with NASA, a marine biologist at Sea World, maybe even the little man in the Mickey Mouse suit!

Randa began her conversation by saying that a "situation" came up at school last Wednesday afternoon, involving one of her students who had been abandoned. She told him that she had volunteered to take care of the little girl, to keep her from being sent to a foster home.

Royce could tell that things were getting complicated, when Randa suddenly said, "Here's Sheriff Royce Hawkins, and he can further explain," and thrust the receiver into Royce's chest.

"Hello . . . Derrick," he began. "Maybe I can help explain things. Uh . . . your sister has been doing a wonderful job for this child. We have gone from a child being abandoned at school situation, to a double murder investigation. The little girl's brother had been murdered, and then just yesterday, we found the body of her mother. So, we have Randa and the child under protective custody. They are here in my home with a team of deputies guarding them at all times. They are never alone," Royce continued.

"The Tennessee Bureau of Investigation is helping on this case. Legally, I can't discuss what we know, or what direction this case may be taking, but I can assure you that Randa will be safe. They both have been out of school since Wednesday.

"Right now we are concentrating on finding the child's missing father. At this point, I would say, he's our prime suspect.

"Randa felt like you should know where she can be reached, and you can call her here at any time. The call may be screened by a deputy, but they will have your name on a call sheet and put you right through."

Derrick had said "is that right," several times. He had not seemed especially distraught by the news. Royce thought he sounded like a very nice, pleasant fellow.

"Do you have any questions," Royce continued. "I know this sounds bad, but actually Randa has helped us keep everything together."

Royce felt like he was beginning to shoot the bull now.

"Judge Ferrell and I have really quizzed her about getting involved in this, and she made her choice wisely. To tell you the truth, we have all fallen in love . . ."

Randa's ears perked up, and her heart gave a giant leap.

" . . . with this little girl." Royce paused.

Randa allowed herself to draw breath.

"I don't know how long this will last, we're just going day to day," Royce said.

"I'll bet my sister will want to adopt her," Derrick offered his first comment.

"Well, that would be God's blessing for both of them, if it turns out that way," Royce said with a smile toward Randa.

"Take care of her for me," Derrick said.

"Oh, I can promise you I'll be doing that," Royce replied. "I'll let you speak back to her now. Just remember to call if you need to, and we will keep in touch with you," he handed the phone to Randa and made a "whew" sound beneath his breath.

Royce stepped out into the hallway to let her continue their conversation. He leaned against the wall and tried to interpret Derrick's reaction. Why had Randa been so worried; the man had seemed amazingly calm. At least he didn't get all excited and want to jump in his car to drive up here.

After she said goodbye, Randa came out into the hallway alongside Royce.

"He wants to come up here," she said.

"Why?" Royce tried to sound nonchalant.

"To help," she said.

"To help . . . you?"

"I guess."

"Do you want him to do that?" Royce tossed it out there like a bait-less hook, hoping to reel in nothing.

"No. No, I don't. I told him that wouldn't be necessary. He did offer for me and Donna-Dean to come to Florida. If we had to . . . you know . . . to be safe," Randa said, not wanting to tell Royce that Derrick had become a bit un-glued when she told him about the croquet ball being thrown at the truck window.

Derrick's comment had been rudely forthright. "And just what were you doing in the sheriff's truck?" he had inquired.

"That's for me to know, and you to find out," she had pulled the line straight out of her classroom, feeling it to be most apropos.

"I don't think Judge Ferrell would go for that with Donna-Dean," Royce reached for her hands.

"It's just Derrick's way of showing concern," she said. "This was a big surprise for him. He'll need a little time to absorb all we've told him. He does have a tendency to over-react.

"One thing about me and my big brother . . . I always hold my own with him, and I always take him with a grain of salt," she said.

"I think I'll go get Donna-Dean up and get her into the shower. That will give you some more time to ponder on what you will be saying to her," Randa said.

"Sounds good," he said nervously. "Take your time."

CHAPTER THIRTY-THREE

Later, Royce was sitting on the couch staring into the fireplace. He wished to hell it would snow. This was a snow fire. He glanced out across the lake to see if there might be any gathering clouds. No. Becca had all the snow out there in Colorado.

Randa and Donna-Dean came into the room. Donna-Dean bounded up onto the couch beside him.

"Hi," Royce said. "I'll bet you're surprised to be here at my house," he smiled.

"Un-huh," she said, squirming toward him hoping he would lift her up onto his lap. He did.

Randa smiled at Donna-Dean's obvious ploy, and at Royce's predictable response. She's got him wrapped around her little finger, Randa thought.

A thud against the kitchen door broke their silence. "Oh, I know who this is," Royce said. He moved Donna-Dean to the floor. He walked to the door and returned with a loud jingling following his boot steps.

The black and white border collie jumped up onto Royce's knees as he sat down.

"Gabriel . . . this is Donna-Dean, and Miss Randa. If you hold out your hand to him, he'll shake hands."

Donna-Dean reached her tiny hand down toward the dog, hesitantly, like a gunslinger sizing up things before making the draw.

"I call him Gabriel because he's my guardian angel," Royce said to Randa as she knelt down on one knee to pet the dog.

"He takes good care of the place when I'm not here. He'll let us know if anyone comes up to the door, or up onto the patio from the lake. And . . . he'll probably give us a bark if his friend, John Wayne, comes calling."

Randa stood up. "John Wayne?"

"The neighbor down the road has this big ole, battle-scarred, yellow tomcat, named John Wayne. He's Gabe's best friend. Sometimes they go off together and are gone for days.

"I've tried to tell him that if he's gonna have a night life, it ought to be with another dog," Royce laughed.

"Maybe he thinks John Wayne is a dog," Donna-Dean said as she hugged the dog around the neck. Gabriel gave a panting smile.

Randa and Royce shared a look.

"Well, I've told the two of them they had better stay out of that road down there while they're galavantin' around on their adventures."

Gabriel woofed.

"Yeah . . . you remember that stay out of the road speech, don't you. I don't want to find you, or John Wayne laying down there in the ditch, all run over," he patted Gabe's back and wooled his head from side to side.

"Sheriff Royce, can Gabriel be my friend too?" Donna-Dean asked.

"Sure he can."

"And he'll take care of me too."

"Yep."

"Good. I need takin' care of sometimes," she said.

Royce leaned back against the couch and closed his eyes tightly for a moment.

Gotta tell her. Now.

CHAPTER THIRTY-FOUR

"Donna-Dean, I've got to talk to you about some things . . . some sad things, about David-Jack and about your mother," Royce began.

She startled him a bit by leaning into his shoulder, as if she were snuggling in for a bedtime story. Go on, tell her, he said to himself.

"Do you remember the other day, when Miss Randa and I took you home from school?"

"Un-huh." Donna-Dean began to trace the letters on the pocket of his tee-shirt.

"Well . . . when I went around to the back porch, I found David-Jack . . . and he had been hurt . . . real bad. Somebody had hurt him so bad he wasn't able to live, and he died from his wounds. And now, we have found that somebody has hurt your mother, and she has died too." He waited for his words to settle. Waited for something from her.

"Do you know what it means when somebody dies?" he asked, softly.

"Uh-huh."

"What does it mean?"

"Means they go to Heaven," she said.

"Do you know about Heaven?"

"Uh-huh. They told about Heaven at Vacation Bible School."

"Well, when people die they are gone away from us and they can't come back."

"You mean nobody is going to come to take me home?" she leaned out away from him to look into his eyes. "I need to go home."

The words came as a shock to both Royce and Randa, but Royce plowed on.

"No, baby, you don't need to go home. You're going to stay right here with me and Miss Randa, and we're going to take real good care of you."

Royce rocked her gently, clutching her to his chest.

"Do you know where we might find your daddy? We can't find him. We don't know if he has run off, or where he might be." Royce pushed.

"I don't want you to find my daddy! I don't want to go with him! Please don't find him! Please don't let him come after me!" she shouted

She began to cry now, as she put both of her arms around his neck. Her tears led to a deep snubbing as she began to worry about what would happen to her.

"You don't have to go with him," Royce said as he rocked her. "I won't let you go with him," his voice cracked.

Randa moved over to the couch to sit by them. She reached out to hold Donna-Dean's hand.

"The only reason we would be looking for him is to tell him about David-Jack and your mother. Do you know where he might be hiding? Would he be staying with anybody?" Royce persisted.

"He mighta gone to my granny's," Donna-Dean stammered.

"Where is your granny?" Royce dreaded to hear there was a relative who might want this child.

"She's 90 year old and lives in a hospital building up in Kentucky. I don't know how to drive there. It's a long ways. She's mean and hateful, just like my momma. Neither one of them liked me or David-Jack," she said.

"Well, me and Miss Randa sure do like you. A lot! And that's what we want you to think about now. You won't be going back out there to that house. We're going to help you start a whole new life . . . a better life than you had out there with them." Royce promised.

Donna-Dean brought her arms down from his neck and sank herself back onto the words "Lead, Follow, Or Get Out Of The Way!"

"Do you think David-Jack is in Heaven?" Donna-Dean wiped the tears away from her face.

"Yes, I sure do," Royce answered. "I think the Lord is holding David-Jack close to His heart, just like I'm holding you to mine."

"David-Jack was a good brother to you, wasn't he?" Randa said.

"Un-huh." Donna-Dean paused for a moment. "He was sad all the time 'til he found him a safe place to go . . . way back up in the woods. He called it 3 Horses."

"Were there horses there?" Randa asked.

"No. It's a rickety old scary house that nobody lives in. It's got broke up walls and its winders are gone, kind of like a ghost house. Do you think the Lord will turn David-Jack into a ghost?" Donna-Dean seemed to have surprised herself at the thought.

"Uh . . . I don't know about that," Royce said.

"Well, he sure did like to make up stories about ghostees. He made up good stories about that old 3 Horses house."

"Why did he call it 3 Horses?" Royce asked. "Cause there was three little biddy white horses painted on the back door," she stroked the air in front of Royce's face as if she were delicately painting the scene she had described.

Royce looked doubtful and Donna-Dean sensed that he didn't believe her.

"It's true . . . three little horses . . . you'll see if you go there."

"Maybe you should draw me a map," he said.

"I will."

"Can you think of where your daddy might be? Would he be out at this old scary house?" Royce said.

"I dunno," she closed herself off.

"Donna-Dean, we know that your daddy was mean to you and to David-Jack. And if he told you to keep things a secret from people, we need for you to tell us those secrets," he pleaded.

He bore his eyes straight at her hoping to jar loose something that might be relevant to this case.

"Can you remember back to the other morning when your momma told you not to come home from school? What was going on that she would tell you a thing like that?" Royce waited for a spark, a glimmer. He got only a squirm.

"Was she mad at somebody . . . you, or David-Jack?"

"He wuddn't there," she said quietly.

"Where was he?"

"He had run off 'cause my daddy had given him a big whoopin' the night before." She looked at Royce to catch his reaction.

"Why did he whip him?" Royce asked.

"Well . . ." she stretched herself up from his lap. "My daddy was sayin' that David-Jack had better not tell 'bout some things. And David-Jack didn't say nothin' . . . just kind of rolled his eyes around and that always makes my daddy so mad."

"Does it." Royce said.

"Daddy calls David-Jack a stupid, shit-ass all the time and I think that hurts David-Jack's feelin's. But he don't ever cry . . . no matter how bad he's hurt. He just runs off. And the 3 Horses house is where he'd run to. And you know whut?" she said.

"What?" Royce took the bait.

"My daddy don't know where it's at. Only me," she boasted.

"Well, I sure would like it if you could draw me a map."

"I will. And you know whut?"

"What?" Royce smiled at Randa who was enjoying the banter.

"David-Jack might be sittin' right there."

"No." Royce turned her face to his once again. "No, Donna-Dean, remember I told you that David-Jack has died. He's with the Lord now."

"Well . . . maybe if the Lord turns him into a ghost he could let him go back up to 3 Horses to live." She began to cry again.

"You know, I think the Lord might have some great plans for David-Jack up there in Heaven," Royce began to fear he was running into uncharted waters now.

"You said your daddy didn't want David-Jack to tell about some things. What were those things, Donna-Dean?" Randa stepped in to redirect Donna-Dean's train of thought.

"I guess it wuz 'bout the burnin's they'd done on me. They wuz afraid David-Jack wuz gonna tell." she said.

"Did he want to tell?" Royce asked.

"Well, one time he screamed out that he wuz gonna tell and my momma got a hold of him and hurt his mouth with a pin," she continued to cry.

"Why did they burn you, sweetie?" Her eyes twinkled through her tears at his word "sweetie."

"When I didn't want to do some things, they would burn me until I changed my mind." Royce began to rock her from side to side.

She looked between her legs to the new bandages Randa had put on after her shower.

"This makes my new pants feel stuffed," she said.

"It's going to protect those places from rubbing against your pants," Randa explained.

"What were these things you didn't want to do, Donna-Dean?" Royce could feel his temper beginning to stir.

"I didn't want to kiss somebody's butt," she grinned.

"Oh, really," he said.

"And I didn't want to peep my head out from under my daddy's legs. And I didn't want them to put slimy things on me."

"Un-huh," Royce replied, not having the slightest idea where he should go from here.

"What slimy things, Donna-Dean?" Randa asked.

"My daddy's stick," she said.

Randa knew instantly what Donna-Dean's reference to "my daddy's stick" meant. She quickly looked to see if Royce may have made the same connection. He met her eyes. Oh yes, he knew.

He stood Donna-Dean down onto the floor, then seated her little stuffed bottom on the coffee table before him, much to her dismay at his breaking their bond.

"Donna-Dean, I need for you to tell me exactly what your daddy was doing to you. This is real important, so be sure you don't make up anything. Sounds like your daddy was doing some really mean stuff," he took her hands.

"You can tell me the secret things. You need to tell me, and Miss Randa, so we can help you. What did he do to you?"

"He made me lick a gun." she said.

"You mean a real gun, like for shooting?" Royce asked.

"Un-huh," she had begun to play pat-a-cake with his hands.

"I mean, you're not talking about a part of his body are you?" Royce asked in all sincerity. Randa almost snickered out loud.

"A real gun . . . like the one you have in your holster," Donna-Dean said.

"You licked it, like an ice cream cone?"

"Uh-huh," she seemed sheepishly proud of her accomplishment. She grinned into Royce's face, searching for his approval.

"Why?"

"I dunno."

"You mean, he just walked up with this gun and said, 'Here, lick this'?"

"Uh-huh."

"Well Donna-Dean, that was a very strange thing for him to do. I just can't imagine why he would want you to do that."

"He said I needed to look like it was tastin' good."

"Why?" Royce was getting an edge to his voice.

"I dunno," she whined.

"That other thing about somebody's butt. What was that all about?"

"One time that black man who works with my daddy came to our house and they was actin' all wild and mean. They kept flippin' things at me, pennies and things. Stickin' things in my hair. My daddy let that old man pull my hair up through a snap off top," she said.

"You mean a tab top off a Coke can, or something?" Royce quizzed.

"Uh-huh. It pulled tight and hurt my head a lot."

"What about the butt thing?" Royce was beginning to lose patience.

"Well, the next thing I know is they are showin' me and David-Jack how to moon somebody, and my daddy said I just needed to kiss that man's butt right then and there."

Royce gave an exasperated sigh, "Did you?"

"I didn't want to and daddy went and got my momma and they screamed at me about how I wuz gonna do it, and I screamed back that I wuddn't, and they took me to the bathroom and burned me," she lowered her voice to a low whisper.

"Bless it," Royce moaned.

"So when I came out of the bathroom, they led me right over to his necked butt and I kissed it. They put this peanut right down into his crack and they made me try to get it out with my lips. I think that part sounds funny," she giggled through her tears. "Like something that would be on t.v . . . "

Royce moved his eyes to Randa, whose eyes seemed to be transfixed on Donna-Dean. Stunned, once again, he thought.

A strange, unsettling silence fell over the threesome. Only Gabriel looked from one to the other, to the other, panting his happiness at being a part of the group.

Royce got up from the couch and walked over to look out of the french doors. He wanted to move his mind out across the lake, way up into the pine trees on the far bank.

Donna-Dean looked to Randa, puzzled that he had stopped asking questions.

Suddenly, he spun around and grabbed Donna-Dean up from the coffee table, and swung her up into his arms.

"Ladies . . . it's time we had some breakfast. How about y'all helping me cook up something," he said.

Over his shoulder to Randa he added, "I wish to hell it it would snow."

"I do, too," Randa said. "It would sort of wash away all the filth that's around us, wouldn't it?"

CHAPTER THIRTY-FIVE

"How about I make some of my fancy Velveeta cheese eggs?" Royce said.

"Sounds great," Randa was getting a favorable nod from Donna-Dean. "How can we help?"

Randa had been wanting to grab his attention, as well as a moment alone, to get his reaction to the horrible abusive situations Donna-Dean had described. There had been no such moment to grab. Randa began to realize that they would probably not have an opportunity away from Donna-Dean for quite some time. Was this little waif becoming "the other woman" in Sheriff Royce Hawkins life?

Their breakfast took several minutes to prepare, and by this time of morning it could have counted as an early lunch. Randa and Donna-Dean cut up potatoes to make hash browns, while Royce made his cheese eggs and Hungry Jack biscuits.

They made generous helpings and plates were given to the two deputies outside on the porch. The missing coffee maker was never found, so everyone had to be content with large glasses of chocolate milk.

Royce and Randa were surprised to learn that Donna-Dean had never tasted chocolate milk. She loved it, and quickly gulped down her glassful. Odd, Randa thought. What a childhood treat to have been denied.

Royce served Donna-Dean at the coffee table before the fireplace, and opened a large cabinet in the corner to reveal a t.v. set. He showed her how to operate the remote control that would introduce her to a wealth of cable channels.

Royce and Randa ate at a small table in the kitchen, alongside a bay window with a lake front view.

"My mother designed this area as a breakfast nook," Royce said. "Funny word for it . . . nook."

"The house is beautiful," Randa said. "And look at that view of the lake. Truly a beautiful place you have here."

"Thank you, ma'am," he said topping off the chocolate milk in her half empty glass.

"My dad bought this property with only that old stone chimney standing here. He had the house built up and around it. As best we could figure, the chimney is over a 100 years old."

"Really," Randa said.

"He built this place for my mother. It was their dream house. But, she died before the work was finished."

"Oh," Randa said softly. They ate in silence.

Moments later, Royce put his hand on Randa's arm. Her heart gave a leap. Finally a touch. He hadn't forsaken her for Donna-Dean after all, she thought.

"Oh, while I have you alone . . . which, by the way, is a pleasure, sir, I want to tell you that you did a marvelous job explaining the deaths to Donna-Dean. It may take her some time to absorb it all. Don't be surprised if you have to keep re-telling things, or re-answering questions. She may continue to ask about David-Jack, but I don't think she'll give a second thought to her mother."

"That was powerful stuff she was telling, wasn't it? What was that `my daddy's stick' all about. Was it what I think it is?" he asked.

"I think she was talking about his penis," Randa used the word without a flinch.

"Oh, damn."

"My childhood education courses come in handy every now and then," Randa said. "Some warning signs of sexual abuse can be detected in a child's art work. They might draw daddy with a third leg, or with what they might tell the teacher is a "stick" between his legs. Neither Donna-Dean, nor David-Jack, ever drew that. I wish they had . . . it would have been the big flag Miss Mattie and I needed."

"Randa . . ." he said. Again her heart skipped a beat at the sound of her name coming from the lips that had kissed her so sweetly only a few hours earlier.

"Don't keep beating yourself up over this. Somebody there was deranged . . . manic depressive . . . ignorant . . . or some such thing; and it's my job to find the bastard," he squeezed her arm.

CHAPTER THIRTY-SIX

Royce startled Randa with a "you know . . ." coming from out of the blue. It was that little boy in him sparked by some wild hair idea, she thought.

"Do I know, what?"

"I want to go out to the Silcox house tomorrow," he whispered so that Donna-Dean would not hear. "Would you go with me?"

Randa furrowed her brow.

"I think you might be able to help me get a feel about what was going on out there. You might see something that I have overlooked," he pleaded. It would get you away from motherhood for a little while," he teased.

"Well . . . ," Randa volleyed the tease back at him, "that might cost you, my fees for analyzing a crime scene are considerable."

"You can add it to my tab. I already owe you my heart and soul."

"And I would gladly take both," she smiled.

"Speaking of my soul . . . ," Royce sprang ahead of her to his next tactic. "While we are out there in 3 Springs, we will need to go to church. Three of them, in fact. Just to run in, pass out some flyers, then run out."

"Oh," Randa thought this outing was getting complicated.

"I want to get some flyers printed up with Robert Silcox's photo on them to pass out to these churchgoers. I phoned the preachers and they were very nice. Each of them seemed to understand what I need to do."

"Sort of a wanted poster?"

"Right."

"Remember . . . I know most of these people," Randa said.

"Sure you do. And you may have to interpret for me," Royce joked. "I have been thinking about letting you and Donna-Dean go back to school on Monday."

"Are you sure?" Randa asked, her eagerness all too apparent.

"If you see some of your parents tomorrow, you should ask them to sort of prepare their children for Donna-Dean. I'll probably put a guard with you for a day or two, so maybe they should be forewarned about that." Royce explained.

"I think I should stop by school, to get some books. I need to get myself back up to speed."

"We can do that. My plan is to be at that Nazarene Church by eleven, then on to the Methodist Church by eleven-thirty, then that other one before they let out at twelve-thirty. The preachers have said they will stop their services for me to say my little spiel."

"That will be something," Randa smiled.

"Can you imagine," Royce grinned. "Three hell-fire-and-damnation, fire and brimstone, feet-washin' preachers stepping out of the pulpit for me!"

"Listen up Lord, Royce Hawkins will be shepherding your sheep, today!" Randa teased.

"Yeah, right."

"But, if I go with you, what will we do with baby girl over there?" she squeezed his hand. "Maybe I should stay here."

"Hmm," he pondered. "Danny will be here about nine-thirty tomorrow . . . and he has a little girl about Donna-Dean's age . . . I wonder if . . ."

"Do you think he could bring her with him? That would be great for Donna-Dean."

Royce jumped up from the couch to grab the telephone, thrilled with the new idea he was working.

"Getting away for the day would give us both a break," Randa said, hoping he would fill in the blanks in her train of thought.

Royce looked away from the phone to give her a smile. She could tell, by the way he arched one brow, that he knew exactly what she meant. This little venture just might lead them toward being alone.

The remainder of the evening Royce spent in his upstairs office, while Randa and Donna-Dean popped popcorn and watched

"The Miracle Worker" on television. Randa took the opportunity to do a little teaching using the classic piece of literature. She and Donna-Dean took notes, on Royce's yellow legal pad, regarding the characters of Helen Keller and Annie Sullivan.

Randa had torn the top pages of the pad away, carefully tucking them into her pocket, since there were several handwritten scribbles referring to Robert Silcox.

It had taken a great deal of Royce's time to get Ed Cagle, the night deputy at the courthouse, to locate Silcox's work badge from the marked bags of evidence in his office. Royce had remembered the badge had a small I.D. picture on it.

"I'll hold on while you go look," Royce said. He could hear Ed's shuffling footsteps walking away from the phone. The muted sounds of the Grand Ole Opry broadcast set the mood for Saturday night in the sheriff's office.

Soon, Ed was back delighted at having found the badge in a box of miscellaneous things not previously sealed by the T.B.I.

"Good," Royce said. He then began to explain to Ed that he needed him to use the Xerox machine to enlarge the picture and to make 100 copies of this makeshift wanted poster.

Ed had great difficulty programming the Xerox machine. Royce gave instructions as if he were talking a non-pilot through landing an aircraft.

After four calls back to Royce, and one call to the office secretary, Francine, Ed was finally able to announce that the copies were made and on Royce's desk.

CHAPTER THIRTY SEVEN

Sunday morning streaked in through the french doors and found Royce mapping out the day ahead on various note papers laid across the coffee table. At 9:30 Danny arrived at the door followed by his eight-year-old daughter, Hannah, who ran quickly to Royce, eagerly jumping into his arms.

Lord, Randa thought. The man attracts children like flies!

"Hey, girl," Royce greeted Hannah with a big hug. "I haven't seen you since Christmas. Your hair has gotten redder and curlier since then. Can you stay and help your daddy babysit?" Royce cocked an eye to Danny.

"Yes," Hannah smiled. "My momma's gone to Knoxville. I had to daddy-sit anyway. Momma's glad we've got something to do."

"Well, I've got somebody here who really needs a special friend to play with today," Royce said, putting her down.

"I know. Daddy told me. And I'm not supposed to say anything about her momma or her brother. I brought all my Barbies, 'cause daddy said she likes Barbies."

"She does," Royce said.

"I brought my Barbie house that I got for my birthday. And my daddy wanted to stop at Walmart and buy one for Donna-Dean to keep her Barbies in . . . so we did," she pointed to the large box Danny had parked by the front door.

"Ah, Danny," Royce crooned.

"Danny!" Randa echoed. "Donna-Dean will be so excited. I'll go get her."

Royce stepped around the group to follow Randa. Moments later, they led Donna-Dean into the living room to meet Hannah.

Danny walked over and reached out his hands to Donna-Dean.

"Hey, sweetheart. I've brought my daughter, Hannah, to stay with us this afternoon. And she's brought all sorts of things for y'all to play with. Hannah, this is Donna-Dean."

"Hi."

"Hi."

"We bought you a Barbie house," Hannah began. "My daddy's gonna put it together. It's yours to keep. You can take it home with you."

Randa stepped in quickly, before Donna-Dean could think about not having a home to take it to.

"Danny, can you put this together?" she quizzed as he moved the over-sized box in front of Donna-Dean.

"Sure. I put Hannah's together. Now it may take me all day to do it, but I guarantee you Barbie will be sleepin' in the place tonight!"

They all shared a laugh.

Donna-Dean got down on her knees to look at the picture of the Barbie house on the box. Royce looked to Randa, who passed the look on to Danny. Even Hannah felt the tender moment as Donna-Dean put her arms around the entire box to hug it tightly. She looked up and said a tearful "thank you" to Danny.

Royce broke the silence.

"Not a bad day's work, buildin' a Barbie house, is it, buddy?" He patted Danny on the back. Danny grinned from ear to ear, knowing he would be drawing good, county money for working on Sunday.

The girls were making good friends, after about a thirty-minute warm-up. Donna-Dean seemed fascinated with Hannah and all that came with her. As Royce and Randa prepared to leave the house, Danny popped a tape of "Beauty and the Beast" into the VCR, and caught the girl's undivided attention.

Royce darted quickly upstairs, then outside to the garage. Randa assumed he was gathering things together for the two of them to leave. She sat down on the couch beside Danny.

"Thank you again, for the Barbie house. That was a sweet thing for you to do. She will always remember that you and Hannah were so nice to her."

"I know all about these little girls and their Barbies. They get something out of all of this, I don't know what," he admitted.

"They learn to be feminine, Danny. They learn about clothes, and hair, how to be prissy . . . and how to get that Ken," she laughed.

"How do you like being a mom?" he asked.

"I always thought I would be somebody's wife first."

"Well, how do you like 'somebody's' house?" Danny teased. Randa gave him a big nudge.

"It's beautiful, isn't it? He told me this was his parents' dream house."

"If you are from around here, you might remember the Maple Ridge Motor Court over in town?" he asked.

"No, I'm not from here," she said.

"Well, it was one of those 50's style tourist courts. His mom and dad owned that place for years. They had a little house around back, and that's where Royce grew up," he explained.

"They were building this place when his mother died. After that, his dad had absolutely no interest in moving up here. Mr. Hawkins wanted to stay in that little motel house, and he decided to open this place as a fishing lodge, sort of a hunter's retreat. Rented it out by the week. Well, that clientele nearly brought the place back down around that old chimney," Danny laughed.

"When Royce came back to town, he stayed down at the motel house, because his dad was in bad health. But, on the sly, Royce started to renovate this place, hoping he could talk Mr. Hawkins into coming up here to live with him. But he was never able to convince him to do that. I think the old man was glad that Royce had the interest to get the place back to the 'dream house' it was meant to be. Mr. Hawkins died later on that same year.

"In his will, he left this place to Royce, and the motor court to his sister, Becca. She's married and lives out in Colorado. She sold off the motor court to the bank next door, and they have turned it into a parking lot.

"Royce doesn't like to drive by there . . . says it's like his childhood is buried in asphalt!" Danny laughed.

Royce entered the room carrying an armload of strange attire and piled it on the kitchen counter.

"We will need to put some of this stuff on after we've been to church," he said.

Randa pulled out a Elmer Fudd-ish ear flap, hunting cap and put it on her head. Royce pulled the straps of the cap under her chin, "Can we call this our second date?"

"You can call it anything you want," she laughed.

Royce was dressed like a movie sheriff. His badge gleamed on his crisply starched uniform shirt, encircled with a bullet-loaded gun belt with added features she had not seen before. A different gun, she thought. Danny helped him make a Windsor knot in the long, brown necktie.

"My goodness," Randa said. "You are quite dashing."

"I need to dress the part for these folks," Royce said.

Danny flung the Smokey-the-Bear hat like a frisbee, curving it directly into Royce's hand. He put it on and promptly tipped it at Randa.

"You must have a special catalog for sheriff gear," she said picking up yet another jacket with giant reflective letters spelling out SHERIFF across the back. "This might as well be a bull's eye," she teased.

"My sister gave this to me when I was elected. I save it for special occasions, when I really want to make a fashion statement." He grabbed it from her hands and twirled it across his shoulder as if he were modeling on a designer runway.

"How long have you been sheriff?" she asked.

"This is the second year of my elected term. I served three years of the previous sheriff's term. He died in office . . . from a heart attack," he answered quickly, noticing her raise a concerned brow at the thought of death in the line of duty.

"You are so handsome in that outfit. You will really charm those little old country ladies."

"I'm hoping to scare 'em."

"Those big yellow letters might do just that," she said, "except for one thing."

"What's that?"

"Most of them can't read. You'll have to rely on the intimidation factor, alone."

CHAPTER THIRTY-EIGHT

Leaving the house together had been difficult. Donna-Dean had begged to go, then she had begged them not to leave her. The only excuse that seemed acceptable to her was that they were, indeed, going on another date.

The word "date" had piqued Hannah's interest, and she began an endless string of questions to both Donna-Dean and Danny.

Royce told Danny there were pizzas in the freezer, and warned him not to "burn the house down" cooking them.

"Don't try to contact me on the C.B.," he cautioned Danny. "We don't want to broadcast our business to this fool. I'll take the cell phone."

Royce got down on his knees to give a big hug to Donna-Dean who seemed to cling extra tight to him.

"You know that we'll be coming back in a little while . . . you go enjoy your time with Hannah," he said.

"Hannah?" he called and, she too, came bounding over and stepped into his other arm. "Y'all have fun now, and don't cause too much trouble for Danny."

"We'll see you later," Randa said and was the first to exit the front door.

"Where they gonna go?" Hannah asked as soon as the door closed.

"Huntin'," Donna-Dean answered. "They wuz takin' their huntin' clothes."

Outside, Royce and Randa hurried to the un-marked van. She looked back over her shoulder to get a good look at the front of the house.

It was set deep within a woods of towering pine trees, with the lake stretching out behind like a movie backdrop.

"This was a dream house, wasn't it," Randa said.

"Still is," Royce answered.

CHAPTER THIRTY-NINE

The ride into town was hazardous. An early morning rain was turning into a slushy sleet, and the county salt trucks were few and far between. Royce was able to show off his driving skills, which included demonstrating how to do a "donut" across the empty parking lot at the courthouse.

Inside his office, Randa remembered the hours she and Donna-Dean had spent there on the first night the three of them had been together.

Royce thumbed through the flyers with Silcox's face peering out from his work badge. They agreed he was a mean-looking man, who wore David-Jack's expression-less eyes.

Randa looked around the office to take in things she had ignored four nights ago. Several plaques on the wall, proclaimed Royce a top-notch civil servant by the Jaycees, the Civitans, and the Tennessee Sheriffs' Association.

The Vanderbilt University diploma, hanging on the wall behind his desk, declared Royce O. Hawkins a Bachelor of Science in Poli Sci, and a smaller degree announced that he was a Doctor of Jurisprudence.

"You have a Vanderbilt law degree." Randa read aloud from the acrylic plague, "Royce O. Hawkins. What does the O. stand for?"

"Don't ask."

"Why?"

"It's a personal thing," he quipped. "I don't discuss that with anyone."

"Come on now, you can tell me. What's your middle name?"

"That's just a real touchy subject."

"Royce . . . ?" she whined.

"It's not important."

"Is it that bad?"

"Truly awful," he said.

"Well, now I'm curious. What is it?" she begged.

"What's your middle name?"

"Diane. What's yours?"

"Now see that's nice, Randa Diane."

"Don't change the subject. What's your middle name?"

"Well, it's ridiculous. I never would use it. In fact, I'm kind of sensitive about it," he explained.

"Give me a clue. I'll try to guess," Randa said, trying another ploy.

"It starts with an 'O'."

"I know that, silly. Is it . . . Oscar?"

"Nope."

"Is it Oswald? Are you named after the guy who shot President Kennedy?"

"No," he laughed. "But it's about as bad as that."

"Well, I can't guess."

"So, forget about it."

"I can't. It will drive me crazy. Give me another clue."

"Okay. My mother was absolutely in love with this particular movie star. A real handsome, matinee idol. A better clue might be that she named my sister 'Rebecca'," he taunted her.

"Rebecca?" she puzzled. "There was a movie, 'Rebecca'."

"Starring . . . ?" he rolled his hands in a forward motion.

"Oh, what's his name?" she thought.

Royce walked around the desk to her.

"Oh, it's Laurence Olivier! Oh Lord, your middle name is . . . ," she found herself embarrassed to say it.

"Olivier. Royce Olivier Hawkins. Awful isn't it. But you know, considering that she named my sister Rebecca, I can be very thankful she didn't name me Heathcliff!" he said.

"It's not a name that suits you," she said.

"I hated that name so bad that I offered the principal of my high school $50 not to read it out when I went up to get my diploma. He wouldn't take the money, and he made me live in fear right on up to the moment he called out my name."

"Did he say it?" she asked.

"No. He just said Royce Hawkins and gave me a slap on the back when I took the diploma from him."

Randa moved to the window seat to look out over the town square. She sat down in the spot where she had waited, and watched Donna-Dean asleep on the cot in front of Royce's desk.

"You know . . . I don't think . . ." Royce said as he came over to sit down beside her. "I can't remember . . . ever," he paused, "kissing anyone in this window seat." He kissed her.

She touched his face with her gloved hand. "Olivier . . . huh?" she teased.

"Damn," he laughed. "Let's get up and go, girl!"

CHAPTER FORTY

On their way to the valley churches, Randa noticed Royce looking to the left, to the right, and looking back over his shoulder to see behind houses and barns. He was in a search mode.

The mood behind his aviator sunglasses was a serious one. Randa could tell he was mentally preparing himself to meet these people. He was anticipating questions, and calculating his answers.

A quick stop at Randa's trailer gave an opportunity for her to put on her Sunday coat; a long, maroon wool coat with big black buttons. Somehow it gave her an added sense of purpose.

Thinking ahead to school tomorrow morning, she gathered more clothes into a large suitcase.

She grabbed her mother's pearl necklace from her dresser drawer, and asked Royce to fasten it around her neck. She declared the clasp to be so difficult, you almost needed to be married to wear it. His serious mood bypassed her joke.

She brooded over the drooping roses he had given to her on their date. Royce warned her not to worry, there would be other roses.

As she closed and locked the trailer door, she told him that things seemed strange.

"Somehow my life here seems long ago and far away."

"Hey now, it's just been a few days," he reminded.

"But the world has spun really fast in those few days," she laughed.

"Yes, it has," he said pulling out of the driveway where he last had a wooden croquet ball thrown at his brand-new truck.

When they drove into the school yard, Randa immediately thought of the first time she had laid eyes on Sheriff Royce Hawkins. She

123

smiled recalling her first impression was that he was a little bit Andy, and a little bit Barney. Had she fallen in love with him in that first moment, when she saw him leaning against the front of the patrol car?

When she unlocked the school door, the familiar smell wafted out to them; that odor of waxed floors and forty years of mountain children who had spent time here.

Royce followed her to the back of the school building to a small cloak room she used as an office. He looked around for some personal item to tease her about.

She had boxes filled with teaching aids, all carefully labeled under subject matter, with related reading materials. Many things, she called "manipulatives," were hand made to carefully utilize the school's meager budget.

On their way out, they passed Miss Mattie's office. Randa noticed that she had pulled a desk into the far corner and had it covered over with a white tablecloth.

"That's David-Jack's desk," she told Royce.

"Good, she's hidden it away from Donna-Dean," he said, "and from you, Randa."

As they pulled out of the school yard onto the highway, Randa broke their silence.

"I think the best thing for me to do is just stand in the background. I don't want to say anything wrong. I'll defer any questions over to you."

"That's fine," he said flashing his sweet smile and reaching over to pat her hand.

CHAPTER FORTY-ONE

Services were underway at the Hickory Glade Church of the Nazarene when they came to the front door. They stomped mud off their feet to the pounding sound of a badly out-of-tune piano.

Royce gave a nod and the famous tip of his hat to the minister, as he led Randa to the back pew. She thought he might be a tad nervous. He seemed to squirm nervously, as he shuffled the Silcox flyers from hand to hand.

"Brothers and Sisters, we have an important visitor to our service today. Sheriff Royce Hawkins." He motioned for Royce to come forward.

"Sheriff Hawkins needs to speak a word to us today. Sheriff Hawkins."

Royce walked quickly to the pulpit, feeling every eye carefully scoping him out. He gave the flyers to the minister and asked him to make sure everyone got one.

"Thank you, Reverend Morris, and thank you all for letting me interrupt your service this morning. I am visiting each church in the valley today, to get the word out that we have had two terrible murders at the home of Robert Silcox over on Paint Pony Road.

"Many of you may know the Silcox family. Some of you men may work with Robert Silcox at the zinc mine.

"Mr. Silcox's wife, Rowena, and his fourteen-year-old son, David-Jack, are dead after being brutally murdered at their home this past week. Mr. Silcox has been missing from his job since Wednesday. We have not been able to locate him to tell him about these deaths, or to question him about these murders.

"Donna-Dean Silcox is the couple's seven-year-old daughter. She is being held in protective custody, pending the outcome of this investigation.

"I need to let you all know we strongly suspect that Robert Silcox may have had something to do with these killings. He is possibly still here in the valley.

"He may be hiding out, or he may be staying with someone who does not know they are hiding a criminal suspect. He may be holding someone hostage within their own home, in order to have a place to hide. If you have any information about this man's whereabouts, I need to speak with you.

"The flyers the Reverend is handing out have a picture of Mr. Silcox. He drives a red, 1985 Dodge Ram truck with Hancock County plates. This truck may be pulled back up into the woods somewhere. If you have seen this truck in the area, I need to know.

"This man should be considered extremely dangerous. If you do see him, do not approach him, but contact my office immediately. I do want you to know that if you are giving him shelter, you are breaking the law.

"If you have any information, I need for you to meet with me now, before I go on to the other churches.

"Also, tomorrow the little girl, Donna-Dean Silcox, will be going back to school. Her teacher, Miss Randa Stratton, is here with me to help you parents with any questions you may have about her re-joining the classroom. There will be an armed guard at the school for her protection, for as many days as we need him to be. We would ask that you parents prepare your children for this, and ask that your children be respectful of Donna-Dean in her efforts to return her life to normal after dealing with these deaths.

"I will be at the back of the church for a few minutes, and I would appreciate talking with you, if you think you have any information. And I would ask for your thoughts and prayers as we continue this investigation.

"Thank you, Reverend Morris, and thank you all very much."

Royce came down the aisle to stand at the church door. Several people gathered near.

"Mista Royce?" a large, grey-haired lady was edging her way in front of others to be the first to get to him.

"You 'member me, I'm Estelle Gleaves. You helped my boys git down off of that water tank over at Dowell Town a few years back."

Royce extended his hand to her.

"Yes ma'am," he smiled at the thought of the incident. "They haven't been back up there anymore, have they?"

"Nossir," she laughed. "You wuz jist so nice. You loaded those boys into the police car and made 'em thank you wuz gonna haul 'em into jail. But you drove them over to the Dairy Dip for a good talkin' to."

Another lady and her husband were standing nearby to add their two cents worth. "And you wuz jist so nice to that fam-lee over at Council Tree when their little boy drowned in their pond."

Heads around the gathering group began to nod.

"Yessir . . . I'd vote fer you. Anythin' you wanted to run fer."

"Well thank you," Royce said, "but I'm not looking for votes. Not today. I'm out here looking for this Silcox fellow. Y'all know anything about him?" he asked of all those who were grabbing for his hand.

Randa stood up from the back pew to join those rallying around Royce. She recognized two of the mothers of her students.

"Miss Randa, how is Donna-Dean?" one of them asked.

"She's doing very well," Randa replied.

"Pitiful situation," the other one concluded, shaking her head. "Motherless child."

"What will become of her?" someone from behind called out.

Randa scrambled to get away from them, heading herself toward the church door.

Reverend Morris had positioned himself there to shake the hands of his departing congregation. He reached for Randa's hand.

"He got their attention, all right. They think he hung the moon. I just hope they will take heed to the message he gave. But then I always wish that of this flock, for my own message every Sunday."

Royce had weaned himself away from his praise group to huddle with the men. Randa could not hear their words, but she could read their body language; fingers pointing down the highway, shoulders shrugging their "I don't knows," hands slapping Royce's back in allegiance. A few eyes squinted as mouths spoke words of violent retaliation.

Soon Royce was looking at his watch and edging himself toward the door. They followed him, not wanting to let him go on to another congregation.

He joined Randa. With a smile, he opened the church door for their exit. As he held her arm to keep her from slipping on the wet steps, they each felt the stares following them all the way to the van.

Inside the van, Randa shivered against the cold. Royce backed out, passing people who waved to him as they stood by their own vehicles.

"They sure do love you," Randa said. "I think they thought you were running for office."

"Did you see those quiet ones standing around the wall looking at the floor, or out the window?" he asked. "Those were the ones who knew something."

At the Methodist Church, they arrived to the sounds of "Amazing Grace," a hymn that always brought a memory of her dad's funeral, and a tear to Randa's eye.

The thought that this was Miss Mattie's church redirected her attention. She looked over the heads of the congregation to find the familiar blue-tinted French Twist her friend, and mentor, wore. When she spied her sitting alone, Randa left Royce to quietly ease into the far corner of the third pew from the back. Mattie was overjoyed.

"Goodness gracious, girl!" Mattie whispered loudly as she grasped Randa's hand. Randa gave a "shhh . . ." and redirected Mattie's attention to Royce who was stepping before the altar.

Royce's script was the same for the Methodists. Randa noticed Mattie drop her head, in silent prayer, when he mentioned Donna-Dean. At Royce's words "she is being well cared for," Miss Mattie squeezed Randa's hand.

Later, as Royce positioned himself at the door to greet the exiting parishioners, Mattie lined up to shake his hand. Much to her surprise, he reached out to hug her.

"You sweet thing," she said, wanting to linger in his arms. "I'll make sure everything goes just right at school tomorrow."

"I know you will," he said.

"There was a time when I could jerk a knot into any one of them that dared to say the wrong thing," she laughed. "Randa can tell you I've still got my ways of makin' them mind."

"Well, we've been talking to Donna-Dean about all of this, trying to explain things to her, a little at the time. She's got a lot of stuff to deal with."

"I think she absolutely loves you," Mattie said. She gathered both his hands and squeezed them with glee, as she was being gently nudged away from him by others in the line.

Randa followed Mattie to the doorway. "Yes, she has become quite attached to Royce. I don't know what will happen if she's taken away to a foster home. Royce would just die. And, it would be yet another heartbreak for Donna-Dean."

"And how are you doing with all of this, sweetie," Mattie asked.

"I'm fine. As soon as I can get back to teaching, things will be better."

"I mean, how are things with him?" she squinted her eyes in mock concern.

"Just fine, Mattie," she laughed. "See you in the morning."

One of the men stepped up to Royce. "I seen that ole boy be awful mean to that little girl."

"Is that right," Royce said.

"They wuz in my store down here to the crossroads right before Christmas."

"And . . ." Royce led.

"She wuz a beggin' for somethin' . . . some play purty. He got real mad and drug her out of the store. We all went over to the winder to see ifn' he wuz gonna whoop her. Wellsir, he did thet all up and down the front of the store thar. But that ain't all . . ."

"What?" Royce felt his blood pressure push his patience.

"He took her by the hair of the head and slung her up into the back of thet ole truck. I think he hit her head on the door handle. They left out with her layin' in the truck bed. We felt right sorry for her."

"And y'all just stood there watchin'?"

"Wellsir, we went out onto the porch, jist so's he'd know we had seen him. We seen his missus settin' up in the truck and figured she'd make him stop. They pulled out with thet little girl jista screamin' bloody murder."

Royce looked to Randa. His eyes squinted in anger. They both sighed in disgust.

"Did you ever see him with the boy?" he asked.

"They always made him stay up in the back of the truck. Seemed he wudn't right bright. If'n they all come in the store, he'd stay out thar in the truck bed . . . even if'n it war rain'." The men who had gathered around gave a group nod.

"If you even think you see Silcox in his truck passing by out here, you get me on the phone immediately!" Royce said firmly. "Don't waste a minute!"

He heard their promises: "Sure will, Sheriff," "Alrighty," "You betcha."

Lies, Royce thought. They were standing in the house of the Lord, lying through their teeth.

The third church was the one Mr. Claiborne had referred to as the Holy Rollers. There was a change in atmosphere here. These people were serious about their worship service.

They were sitting in complete silence when Royce and Randa entered the door. Their eyes said "now whut's he up to."

They remained in silence after he spoke. No one approached him to shake hands as he left. There were no words of commendation here. No one had a comment or question; no idle chit-chat to cause him to tarry. They acted as if they had been caught at something.

"Hmm," Royce said. "They were afraid we would see what they do during their service."

"Would they have handled snakes, or something?" Randa asked.

"Probably . . . and, thank you Jesus, they kept them in a box while we were there," he said.

CHAPTER FORTY-TWO

Half an hour later, they were approaching the Silcox place. Royce clipped the gold, seven-pointed "Sheriff" badge onto the pocket of the hunting jacket.

Randa had watched him layer on the attire he had brought from the garage. Buried deep within the orange and brown hunting jacket was a bullet-proof vest that would save his life, if need be. As for the vest he had made her wear . . . it was hot and scratchy.

When they were within a half mile of the Silcox property, Royce used the C.B. to forewarn the deputy on guard duty that "County One was coming in for a landing."

Royce pulled the van off the road into the rutted lane that led down through the overhanging trees. The deputy inched his patrol car forward from the shadows and hopped out to raise the yellow ribbon of crime scene tape. Royce lowered the van's tinted window to greet the deputy.

"Logan, we're going to be back in here for a while. I'll take the Walkie Talkie. You should have one there in the trunk. We don't want to use the C.B."

"Can I tell dispatch that 'County One has landed'?"

"Sure, why not," Royce said.

"I've always wanted to say something like that," Logan laughed.

"If I need you, I'll give you a holler on the Walkie Talkie."

"Oh . . . Sheriff?" Logan said. "The mailman's been leaving stuff here with me. I've been meanin' to get this to your office, but they always call me at home to come on out here to relieve somebody. I haven't even been in to the office. Anyway, I just figure it's their mail."

"What is it?" Royce said quickly.

"The postman says this is stuff that he always takes on up to the house, cause it's too big to get into the mailbox."

Logan began to pass things through the van window. "It's an arm load," he said.

Royce took the manila envelopes and put them on the seat beside Randa.

"Okay . . . we're going in."

"Alrighty . . . County One," Logan joked.

"Obviously, the postman is totally unaware of this situation," Royce said. "I guess I should have handled that."

Once they were parked alongside the rusty-hinged gate at the Silcox picket fence, Royce grabbed up the four over-sized envelopes. They were addressed to "R. Silcox" with a post office box number in Atlanta, Georgia as the return address.

"Well, 'R. Silcox' let's see what you've got in the mail," Royce said ripping open the clasped end of one of the envelopes.

Silence.

"What?" Randa was curious.

Silence.

"Royce?"

"Oh, my God," he managed to gasp as he looked over to Randa. She grabbed his arm. "What is it?"

"This is it. This is the damn secret. This is what the son-of-a-bitch was into," he said as he shuffled the stiff papers around in his hands. "This is the key to it all."

He looked to Randa.

"These are photographers contact sheets. Proof sheets of what he had on his rolls of film. It shows him what he's got so he can tell what is useable. What to enlarge. What to sell," he explained.

"He was into pornography with his own children," he pounded the steering wheel with his hand. "Damn."

He passed a couple of the sheets over to Randa.

"Oh my God in Heaven," she said. "Here's the gun picture with Donna-Dean. This is why they were wanting her to do those silly things," she pointed to one tiny frame on the film strip.

"So he could take pictures," Royce said. "That's the big secret. That's what she's not telling us. He was photographing her."

"Remember, she said something about how she was supposed to act like it was tasting good?" Randa said brushing away a tear.

"Makes sense now, doesn't it."

Royce looked out of the van window, back down the lane to where the Silcox mailbox stood at its odd angle.

"Wonder how often this stuff comes in the mail?"

He continued opening the envelopes. The photographs became more grotesque. Several sheets featured the pre-pubescent David-Jack. His hands were bound with rope, his legs spread apart and tied to stakes that were driven into bare ground.

"Oh Jesus," Royce groaned. "This stuff is very incriminating. I can do a lot with this."

Royce would not let Randa see any more of the pictures

"This is not the memory of David-Jack I want you to have," he explained.

"This just keeps getting worse, and worse," Randa sighed.

"If he has been using the U.S. Mail for this kind of crap, he may be in Federal trouble. But, most importantly, this kind of crap will keep him from being able to get custody of his child."

"How do you know he took the pictures?" Randa said.

"I betcha I can tie this back to the burned film, and film canisters, we found buried down that trail over there," he nodded toward the west side of the house.

Royce opened the last of the envelopes. It was full of money orders in various amounts, made out to Robert Silcox.

The safest way to make payment, Royce thought.

This was a great deal of money. Obviously, this was quite a lucrative hobby this backwoods farmer had gotten into.

"Oh, I almost forgot," Randa said, fumbling deep within the hunting jacket and bullet proof vest to find her jeans pocket.

"Donna-Dean drew a map to that old house she was talking about." Randa hoped this surprise would draw his attentions away from the ugly photographs.

"Well, look at this," he seemed surprised.

"It's crude, but maybe we could find some of her landmarks. She may have imagined some of them, though. Sometimes I think she goes off to a little fairyland in her mind," Randa said.

"I wouldn't blame her . . . living such hell as this."

"My Nancy Drew instincts tell me we should try to follow this map. It might be fun," she said touching his hand that was still gripping the steering wheel.

"You know, Donna-Dean thinks we are on a date?" he smiled at her.

"Seems quite romantic to me."

"Going into the woods with me already, and you've just known me three, or four days," he teased. "You are a brave lady, Randa Stratton!"

CHAPTER FORTY-THREE

Donna-Dean's map began at the front porch. Her trail led past the front gate, and followed the picket fence across the left side of the front yard. The skinny line on her paper corresponded to a narrow dirt path that wound off through knee-high weeds.

Royce carried what Randa imagined was a sawed-off shotgun. Earlier he had slipped on his, now familiar, shoulder holster with its gun buried under his left arm.

He offered Randa his hand as the path angled down a steep embankment.

"Here's the creek . . . and there are the four stepping stones, just like she has drawn them," he said.

"She really did her best work because it was for you," Randa said as she tried to balance on the slippery rocks.

"I tried to make it a school lesson. You know, a geography project. But she wouldn't go for that. It was to be a present for Sheriff Royce."

Randa had been looking for his little boy smile; he had not had time for one since viewing the pornographic contact sheets. This was no second date . . . this was an intense mission.

"Sure hope we can find our way back," Randa worried.

"So far, we are just paralleling the highway," he replied, holding tightly to her hand as they stepped away from the icy stream.

The path led them up a steep hillside, then trailed itself out along a bluff that overlooked dark woods below. Fog had settled in stripes across meadows in the distance, a scene that no doubt reminded the Scots-Irish, who settled here, of their homeland, Randa thought.

Clouds hung like dirty wads of cotton, bleak and gray over the valley panorama. Through the stillness, a cow bawled a response to the farmer's yelling "soo-calfer, soo."

"I wish to hell it would snow," Royce said.

"Maybe you'll get your wish, looks like the sky's willin'," Randa said, thinking that if she were home she would be gathering in a week's worth of groceries, just in case.

"It's pretty up here . . . peaceful, away from all of that horrible stuff down there," she said.

Royce reached an arm around her waist, holding the sawed-off shotgun by his side.

"I'll get him . . ." he said, somberly.

"I know . . . he's as good as got!" Randa said.

"Such grammar."

"It made you smile, didn't it?" Randa squeezed his cheeks.

"Yeah, illiteracy always makes me laugh."

"Hush," Randa pulled him by the coat to plant a quick kiss across his smile.

Royce responded with a surprising kiss that seemed too intimate for this time and place; yet, it seemed to be what they both needed.

CHAPTER FORTY-FOUR

Royce helped Randa cross over a low, stone wall, the legacy from some long-ago farmer who cleared this pasture land and stacked the stones together to make a fence. Now it served only to meander its way into nothingness.

Royce noticed that Donna-Dean had drawn this stone wall as a bridge. "I'll bet she used to walk across the top of it, rather than staying on the path along here."

They had walked more than a mile since leaving the Silcox front yard.

"Wonder how often David-Jack had to run this trail . . . after dark?" Royce said.

"And I would bet that he taught Donna-Dean how to run it, too," Randa ventured.

Stepping carefully as the path led down another steep hillside, Royce spotted the rusty tin roof of the old house in the trees below.

"I think that's it," he said.

As they came up to the front of the house, the sun peeked through the dreary clouds to momentarily light the scene before them.

Towering hackberries grew high above the old shell of a house. Their bony-fingered branches tickled the fragile boards under the tin roof, creating an eerie clattering in the silence that drew in and around the place.

Randa let go of Royce's hand to walk alone across the bare ground, to the rubble of wood that had been steps leading up to a caved-in front porch.

"Look . . . at . . . this," she said peering into the door-less entryway. "What history does this place have?"

"You mean, what ghosts does it have, or moonshiners, or murderers," Royce said as he poked the broken steps with the tip of the shotgun.

"Remember . . . Donna-Dean thinks David-Jack may be in here," Randa whispered.

"Randa, I know exactly where David-Jack's body is. Now . . . as for his soul, well . . ." he said as she shook her finger in his face.

"Let's go around back. I've got a feeling that's how they got inside."

"This makes me feel even more sorry for David-Jack," Randa said.

"Why? This was his secret hideout."

"Because, for David-Jack, this was his sanctuary. Think about it, as awful as this place is, it was the best he had going for him," she said.

Royce seemed at a loss for words.

"They really shouldn't have been back in here at a place like this," she continued. "So many ways to get hurt."

"But country kids go all over," Royce explained. "Exploring. 'Gettin' into devilment,' as my grandma used to say. They fall into wells, and old cisterns, and they seem to be natural-born spelunkers!"

At the side of the house, Randa stretched up to look through the broken window panes. The faded wallpapered-walls inside seemed to shudder in the crisp, cold wind. It was a sad place by day; what must it have been like at night, she thought.

The house spoke the voices of husbands and wives, of mothers calling their children in to supper, of sons going off to war, of a grandma singing as she sweeps the bare ground around the front steps, and of the old maid who waits to give a peddler-man a dipper of water.

Royce pulled the collar of the hunting jacket up around his neck. It was getting colder, he thought. Or, was it this place. He stepped ahead, holding Randa back with his hand.

"Let me see what's up ahead . . . just in case," he said softly.

"In case . . . what?" she pulled at his sleeve. "In case David-Jack is . . ."

"No," he said in a firm whisper. "In case Silcox is here!"

Randa shrank back in wild-eyed silence.

CHAPTER FORTY-FIVE

Royce crept along the eroded wall of the old house, and peered around the corner to view an emptiness, a nothingness, only a cold winter solitude.

He swung the shotgun up into the crook of his arm and moved in toward the back door.

"Anybody here?" His shout echoed down through the hollow walls of the center hallway.

Randa could hear the beat of her heart thumping through her ears. Did he really expect someone to answer? Would he soon be saying, "Come out with your hands up?"

Royce walked back to her.

"Come on, nobody . . . including David-Jack, is here," he said.

"There's the three horses," he pointed to the back door, that was propped wide-open by a seat-less kitchen chair.

"Just like she said, Royce. Three little biddy white horses!"

Royce stepped up into the open doorway. Randa followed, stepping cautiously across the creaking floor. The hallway lead toward the parlor room near the gaping front entry.

She imagined newlyweds coming through that door. The bashful groom carrying his bride away from the shivaree-ing crowd outside. What babies had been born in the front bedroom, that was now without its eastern wall? Maybe a premature baby that would have been warmed on the oven door of the kitchen stove.

Randa could hear Royce's footsteps fading away into the kitchen, each plank of the floor squeaking under his weight.

"Randa?" he shouted. "You gotta see this."

She was there beside him, quickly.

"I would say that David-Jack has been here," he stepped aside to let her see into the kitchen pantry.

On the floor was a pallet he had made with two drab-green Army blankets, and a stained feather pillow. Beside the blankets sat a Big Ben alarm clock, a metal flashlight, and a rusty Coleman lantern.

He had slept here, scared . . . alone . . . and cold, Randa thought.

Royce walked over to the left side of the pantry, to a large hand-hewn wooden chest. A bin, or larder, of some sort, he supposed.

Dusty footprints were everywhere.

Royce slowly raised the heavy wooden lid, to the shrill screech of its hinges. Needs a little WD-40, he thought.

The bin was empty, except for three planks placed side by side and wedged down almost to the bottom. Something between the cracks of the planks caught Royce's eye.

Something was stuffed under there, he thought. Two of the planks had been nailed firmly into place. The third one, was loose. Royce jerked it away.

Yes, something was there . . . carefully pushed back under the other planks. He edged himself around in order to slip his hand down and back.

BANG! The loud snap carried the force of a firecracker, and rang out simultaneous to Royce's scream of "Y . . . OOW!"

Randa's heart jumped at the sound. Had someone shot through the kitchen window?

Suddenly Royce spun around to her. He was holding his left arm out to reveal a huge rat trap dangling from three fingers and part of the palm of his hand.

"Oh my God!" she screamed.

"Help me get it off!" he shouted. If I sling it off, it's gonna take my fingers."

"Okay," she managed to say, running for the back door. "Let me find something." Over her shoulder she saw him sink down onto the filthy floor.

CHAPTER FORTY-SIX

Find something . . . quick, she told herself. A stick . . . something to pry it off . . . around front . . . the hackberry trees . . . she ran, turning this way then that way for what seemed an incredibly long time.

Searching for just the right thing, she stumbled over an old mop handle. Maybe this would be strong enough, she thought, pulling it up from its time-worn groove on the ground.

Running with it, she bounded herself back into the house to get to Royce. His hand was bleeding, badly. His face ashen.

"That'll work," he noticed the mop handle. "Wedge it under that hammer. Maybe I need to stand up?"

"No," she warned. "We can do it here, just let me get it centered, then I'll push when you're ready."

"Okay . . . push!" he shouted. Randa gave a forceful pry with the mop handle and broke the hold the trap had on his fingers. She flung the thing across the room, into a far corner.

"Holy . . . shit!" Royce grimaced, his fingers gushing blood.

"I need to get to my shirt . . . to use it for your hand. And I'm going to have to take all of this stuff off," Randa said as she began to unsnap the clasps of the hunting jacket, to hurriedly tear off the bullet-proof vest, then to pull her sweatshirt over the silly Elmer Fudd hat.

"Hold your hand up so the blood won't pump so fast," she yelled to Royce.

"You know I must be going into shock, because it looks to me like you're strippin' naked," he said.

"Well I don't think you'll be making any inappropriate moves," she quipped. "I want to get that hand wrapped tightly. Maybe that will stop the bleeding."

She jerked the sweatshirt over her head, suddenly wishing she had some sort of spectacular WonderBra, or at least something from Victoria's Secret to be flashing at him. But no . . . this was just her plain, old well-worn Cross-Your-Heart.

"This will ruin your shirt," he worried.

Randa gently turned his hand over to see where the blood was coming from. The three fingers had been smashed hard with the hammer of the trap, spiking deep into the flesh beneath one knuckle. This will need a stitch, or two, she thought.

"Royce, we need help. Let's call Logan."

"Nah . . . I can walk out of here. It's just a scratch. You need to get that vest and jacket back on before you get frost bite. That would be difficult to explain, now wouldn't it?" he managed to smile.

"You're right. I didn't have any petticoats like Melanie in *Gone With the Wind*."

"I'm thinking about standing up." He began to shuffle his boots around on the floor.

"Wait . . . one more thing," she said. "Stay down for one more minute."

She ran back outside.

Royce winced as he rocked back and forth, trying to absorb the throbbing pain. He held the white blob with his hand nestled deep inside, high in the air supporting its weight with his good hand.

"Damn," he said out loud, glancing at the rat trap that lay on its side in the corner. That thing was designed to kill a ten-pound rodent, he thought.

He tried to flex a finger, or two. They were numb. Something was beginning to swell. Did he feel blood filling up the sweatshirt, or was that his imagination? Thank goodness this was his left hand, not his right-hand trigger finger. Shit anyway, he thought.

CHAPTER FORTY-SEVEN

Randa appeared in the doorway, panting, and adrenalin pumping.

"I'm going to improvise on an old folk remedy. These mountain people have taught me that putting metal scissors onto someone's back will stop a nosebleed . . . I don't know the medicinal workings of that . . . sends some sort of clotting message to the brain, I suppose," she said hurriedly trying to convince him.

"But, since we don't have scissors, I'll have to use a very cold rock. I want to put it down your back."

"So, now you want to strip me?" Royce said.

"Now you are delirious," she said tugging at the front of his blood-spattered jacket.

"I'll just loosen this so I can pull it away from your neck. I need to put the rock between your wing bones."

"My what?"

"Wing bones. Angel wings. Don't you know that your shoulder blades are called wing bones?"

"Well, since you put your vest back on, my primary point of anatomy has been my fingers."

Randa pulled at the coat, then wedged her hand and the cold rock down beneath the bullet-proof vest to his back. When she gently let the rock rest against his skin he yelled.

"RANDA, honey, that's COLD!"

"Shhh . . . settle down, be still and quiet, and let it do its work," she reprimanded.

They were quiet now, as Royce tried to endure the shock of the cold rock treatment, as well as the pulsating pain in his fingers.

Randa took the rock out and refastened his jacket.

"How do we know it's worked?" he asked.

"We don't, we'll just have to have faith," she smiled.

"So now you're a faith healer?"

Randa had been kneeling alongside him. She rested herself back on her heels, and looked deep into his eyes.

"Honey, I can be whatever you need me to be," she boasted.

"I'll hold onto that thought."

He began to squirm, once again trying to stand up.

"Let me help you," Randa said. "Now, you may get a little queasy. Just stand still and quiet once you get up there."

She held his good arm to give him support. He was up. Bringing his head upright, she could tell he was seeing stars cross his eyes.

"Whoa," Royce said trying to steady himself.

"We really need some help. I'm afraid you'll pass out on me if we try to go back down that trail," she pleaded.

"Okay . . . okay," he said jerking open his jacket to get the Walkie Talkie from the inside pocket.

"Logan?" he spoke into the static.

Seconds passed. Just as Royce was about to repeat the name, Logan came in loud and clear.

"Yeah, chief?"

"We're back in here at an old abandoned house, to the north and about a mile and a half from the Silcox place. I've hurt myself. I guess I need for you to start walking toward me as I guide you back in here. I have a map and I'll give you directions to follow. We'll start walking out of here to meet you now."

"Okay, chief. Do you want me to call dispatch and let them know I'm leaving the patrol car?" Logan asked.

"No, don't do that."

"Do you need an ambulance?"

"No," he said impatiently. "Just come up to the front of the Silcox house, go to your left, down to the end of that picket fence. You'll see a little foot path leading off down a hill."

"Okay, chief, I'm on my way. I'll get back to you when I get to that path."

"Let's go," he said to Randa.

"Oh wait . . . I want to try to get whatever is in that wood bin. Can you look in there for me and see if we can pull it out? Be very careful . . . there might be another trap in there. Maybe you can use that mop handle," he said.

Randa grabbed for the mop handle with its rotting strands dangling at one end, and ran quickly to the bin.

Royce followed, grabbing up the shotgun by its barrel, and trying damn hard to disguise his stagger.

CHAPTER FORTY-EIGHT

Randa approached the large, white bin as if it were a hibernating polar bear; grouchy and cold. When she raised the lid, its screeching hinges seemed to call out "Do Not Disturb."

Looking into the emptiness she, too, saw something between the cracks of the remaining boards.

She positioned the end of the old mop handle and began to move it under, then back and forth across the bottom of the wooden bin.

"Careful," Royce said softly.

"There's definitely something here," she said. "I've hit it three or four times. I don't think there are any more traps."

"Let me get my good hand back under there," Royce said.

"No. I can get it," she insisted, bending herself down into the bin to make the stretch with her arm.

She began to bring out the items. Two cigar boxes, two Big Chief tablets, and a Walk-Man radio.

"Oh, Lord," she said tearfully. "That's the radio I gave him for Christmas."

"Is there anything else?" Royce asked.

"No," she said swinging the mop handle freely along the bottom of the bin. "No, that's all."

"If you can carry that stuff, I'll carry the gun," he said.

"Remember to keep your hand up," Randa said, struggling with David-Jack's treasures.

Several minutes later, they met Logan on the path. Royce had re-traced Donna-Dean's map on the Walkie-Talkie, a process that had been exhaustive, and he was quite glad to be handing over the shotgun which had become quite a burden to carry under his good arm.

Randa related the rat-trap story to Logan, who offered a soulful, "Well, I'll be dog!"

Together they edged Royce on up the path toward the van. An argument arose as to who would drive. Royce yielded to Randa, once again.

She thought she had heard a "damn" or two, but it was disguised under other pain-related groanings.

As they approached the picket fence, Royce looked at the Silcox house in disappointment.

"I really wanted us to go through there today," he said.

"We can come back another time, right now you're more important," Randa said as she hurried on to the van to unload David-Jack's belongings onto the back seat.

Randa pulled herself up under the steering wheel as Royce got into the passenger seat.

"I need to get this hand fixed, so I can think straight," he said.

"Maybe we should have Danny bring Donna-Dean to us at the hospital?" she suggested. "I don't know why . . . just my maternal instincts. I think we need her with us now. We could have those burn marks checked."

"Sure," Royce grabbed the dispatch radio handset to ask that they patch him through to his house. Moments later he managed a feeble "Hi, how y'all doing," to begin his conversation with Danny.

Randa jerked away the handset.

"Danny . . . ? Royce has injured his hand . . . bad. I'm bringing him in to the hospital. Can you call them and ask that Dr. Caldwell meet us in the emergency room? Tell them we are about thirty minutes away."

Royce leaned his head back onto the headrest. He could hear her say "rat trap . . . bleeding . . . I'm driving . . . how are the girls . . . could you bring Donna-Dean to the hospital . . . okay, bye."

He heard Danny's promise to call Brodie, and that they would meet them at the hospital.

"What was that other, about the girls?," Royce asked as he scrunched down lower in the seat.

"They are having fun. They were painting Danny's toenails," she said.

"You're kidding," Royce managed to chuckle over the pain in his fingers.

"Well, they couldn't exactly paint his fingernails, now could they," she said.

"Guess not."

He had decided it might be a good idea to close his eyes, as a great urge to puke was rising up from his rib cage.

CHAPTER FORTY-NINE

Brodie Caldwell met them at the admit desk in the E.R. waiting room. Danny had not gone into great detail, only that Royce was hurt and bleeding. Brodie had assumed the worst . . . that Royce had been shot. He was greatly relieved to see him walk in, wearing hunting gear.

"Nice hat," Brodie commented.

"Shut up," Royce quipped.

In the exam room Brodie unwrapped Randa's sweatshirt from Royce's hand, and with her help was able to get the bulky hunting jacket, and bullet-proof vest, off over the bleeding fingers.

Randa related the rat trap story as they made Royce lie back on the paper-lined exam table. A nurse quickly placed a pillow under his head, and gathered his bloody jacket to take it out of the room.

"Can I take your jacket, too?" she offered to Randa.

"No, I'll keep mine, thanks," she said with a wink to Royce who was watching for her response.

"When did you have your last tetanus shot?" Brodie asked as he gripped Royce's wrist to find a pulse.

"I don't know."

"Was it in the last ten years?"

"I don't know."

"This was a rusty, rat trap that bit you, man," Brodie warned.

"I don't remember ever having one," Royce admitted.

"Well, old buddy, today's the day!"

Randa moved to the top side of the exam table to take the Elmer Fudd cap from Royce's head. Brodie noticed her gently brush his hair back to the side.

"Uh . . . Brodie said, his thoughts momentarily diverted away from his patient to Randa.

"We'll need to get an x-ray before I close that little puncture wound that's doing all the bleeding. Now, am I to assume that you guys were out hunting rats today?"

"We were out at an old abandoned place Donna-Dean told us about. This was a booby trap just waitin' for me, I guess," Royce explained. "Do you think anything is broken?"

"Probably. We'll get you on down to x-ray, but first I'll send the nurse in to give you that tetanus," he said as he left the room.

"This will take forever," Royce groaned.

"Will you be okay if I go out there to meet Danny?" Randa asked.

"Yeah, sure." He caught her hand.

"Thank you for taking such good care of me. I'm not used to anyone fussing over me."

"And I'm not used to having anyone to fuss over," she squeezed what would become known as his "good hand."

"Once again, our date has been spoiled," he said.

"Now how can you think that. After all, you got to see me in my bra!" She spun around to leave before he could see her blushing cheeks.

Randa inquired at the desk outside the exam room, about Royce's jacket. Brodie walked up behind her.

"I appreciate your bringing him in," he said. "He probably would have tried to patch himself up at home."

"He really thought it was just a scratch until it began to bleed so badly," Randa said.

"You know, I can't help but notice that you two seem to be making good friends."

"I guess. We're both really concerned for Donna-Dean," she said, not quite sure where this conversation might lead.

"That's great . . . I'm tickled to death . . . remember, I told you he's an old friend of mine, we go way back. I love him like a brother," Brodie said.

"He's quite unusual for a sheriff. I mean, he seems so nice and gentle, and caring," Randa felt herself going overboard on the compliments.

"It just drives me and his sister crazy, that he wants to be a county sheriff, especially here in this hillbilly county. We're scared he'll get shot someday."

"Danny mentioned a sister," Randa tried to subtly lead Brodie toward satisfying her curiosity.

"Yeah, an older sister, Becca. She lives in Colorado . . . Breckenridge, I think. She's married to a structural engineer or contractor, somebody who builds those fancy ski resorts and condos. They were just here at Christmas. Well, I've got to go read his x-rays. Thanks again, for taking care of him."

Walking backwards away from her, Brodie said, "He's a great guy . . . might just be the love of your life."

He gave her a thumb's up sign as he turned to go down an intersecting hallway.

CHAPTER FIFTY

"Oh great . . . this is just great," Royce barked. "I've got so much to do . . . right now . . . this minute . . . and this here certainly wasn't on my agenda."

Brodie carefully strapped the two broken fingers onto a splint.

"Well now, maybe I should give you an another injection that would keep you from being so agitated."

"How long do I have to wear this rig?"

"Till these fractures mend themselves, and I'll warn you, buddy, the body don't give a flyin' shit what you've got to do today," Brodie joked.

"Just fix it so I can use it, to drive at least," Royce begged.

"I'll take the splint away in a while, that is if you've been a good boy and left it alone. Of course, if you go home and un-strap all of this, well, let's just say you will be in deep trouble. Don't do that, my friend!"

"At least it doesn't hurt any more."

"That's the injection I gave you to put in the stitches. I'll give you some pain medication to take home, for later when the feeling starts to come back."

"So now I've been x-rayed, stitched, splinted and tetanus-proofed," Royce said.

"Sounds like you got your money's worth," Brodie patted Royce on the shoulder.

"Where's Randa?"

"In the waiting room. Danny's here with the little girl. Randa wants me to take a look at those burn marks. You can go now. I'll have the nurse bring in a wheel chair."

"Now wait a minute. I walked in here and I can walk out," Royce stood up.

Brodie drew himself up close to Royce's face.

"Do not take these wrappings off," he spoke in slow motion, emphasizing each word. "You're very lucky you don't have any tendon damage. That would have required surgery. I want to see you sometime next week."

"Okay. You and Randa sure are ganging up on me."

"Speaking of Randa . . . ," Brodie teased.

"Oh, you want to speak of Randa, do you?" Royce said.

"She seems real nice."

"Yes. She is real nice. She is real pretty. She is real smart. I've only known her for a few days, but I really like her a lot. So that's about it in a nut shell."

"Well . . . well . . . . do we dare think that this might be . . ."

"There's something that's come between us." Royce said as Brodie helped him into the bullet proof vest.

"What's that?"

"Donna-Dean," Royce said with a slight sigh.

"You can work that out. Just hang onto to each other. She just might be the love of your life!"

In the waiting room, Randa carefully explained to Donna-Dean, Hannah, and Danny that Royce had "mashed" his hand in a trap. She made no mention of where, or how, or why. She feared Donna-Dean would make the connection to David-Jack's treasures hidden in the wood bin.

Royce's blood-stained jacket made Donna-Dean cry. Moments later Royce came walking down the hallway toward them. Donna-Dean ran to him.

"Hi," he said reaching down to touch her head. "Now don't worry over this," he held out his splinted fingers for her to see. "Dr. Caldwell has fixed me up just fine."

Donna-Dean hugged him around the waist. They walked over to the near-by row of waiting room chairs. He sat down and gathered her onto his lap. They sat quiet for several minutes, then he began to talk to her, hoping to settle her fears.

Randa and Danny watched from across the room. Danny held a tight reign on Hannah who pulled and tugged to be let go, ignoring

Danny's litany of "Stop! Quit! Don't!" She was all too eager to join Royce and Donna-Dean.

"Did you get a shot?" Donna-Dean asked.

"Yeah."

"I got one too . . . in my bottom. It hurt just a little bit. They said it was for the `fection.' I just had to cry some over it," she added.

"That's okay. Sometimes cryin' helps things," Royce said.

Hannah finally broke free of Danny's vise-like grip on her arm and raced to Royce. She drew herself up short before him.

"Hey," Royce greeted her.

Hannah looked him square in the eye, and put her hand on his shoulder.

"Bless your sweet heart!" she blurted out for everyone within earshot to hear.

"Well, right back at you, Hannah," Royce smiled over her head to Randa and Danny.

CHAPTER FIFTY-ONE

At home, Royce stretched himself back into the big leather chair before his roll-top desk. The house seemed still and empty, its usual feeling at this time of night. It seemed like hours since he left them to come upstairs "to go to work."

He found himself distracted from the pain in his fingers, not only from Brodie's medicinal potions, but from the master plan that had been spinning wildly in his head.

Royce gathered David Jack's belongings from the table across the room. All evening, he had felt their presence, as if David-Jack himself was ready to tell his side of this story.

It was sad to think these were the most meaningful things the boy owned. This was a pitiful representation of a child's life; yet such valuable treasures that he had wanted to protect them with a giant rat trap.

Royce opened one of the cigar boxes to find two Band-Aid tins. Each was packed full of money. Bills, mostly twenties, had been folded into tiny one-inch squares and crammed into the tins.

Quite a bit of money here, Royce thought, as the money in the second tin splayed out across the desk when he touched its lid.

How did this kid come by this amount of cash?

Moments later, thumping sounds of footsteps on the stairs reminded him that he was the guard on duty tonight. He drew his holster and gun near. Hold on "Quick Draw," there's a child in the house.

A small tapping at the open door frame broke the silence. Randa was there carrying two mugs of piping, hot something.

"Need some company?" she asked.

"Sure do," he said closing the Band-Aid boxes.

"She's sound asleep," Randa said anticipating his question. "Exhausted from her big day with Hannah."

"I'll bet."

"How's your hand?" she asked, pushing a mug of hot chocolate toward him.

"Okay."

Randa noticed the stack of things from the wood bin.

"Find anything interesting?" she asked

"I'm just starting through it. I've spent quite some time studying over Silcox's photographic work. It's awful. He seemed to specialize in David-Jack's emerging private parts. In most of the shots, David-Jack was tied down on the ground, with his hands and feet bound with leather straps to iron stakes . . . like they use for playing horseshoes.

"That alone could be considered child abuse, couldn't it?" Randa asked.

"Well I think they were rewarding him . . ." Royce let one of the Band-Aid boxes spill forth its squares of greenbacks.

"Royce!" Randa laughed. "That's quite a stash."

"Yes ma'am, it is. I'll bet it's at least six hundred dollars, maybe more than that."

"How . . . ."

"I would suspect, that they were paying him twenty dollars to do what they asked him to do for these photo sessions," Royce said.

"And to keep his mouth shut," Randa added.

"Oh, they probably threatened to kill him if he told anybody. The pictures of David-Jack are all out child porn, but the ones of Donna-Dean are more silly, artistic, arousal crap. Sexually stimulating to perverts, I suppose."

Royce picked up the other cigar box and the two Big Chief Tablets that belonged to David-Jack. He pulled out the wooden arm from within the roll-top desk. Randa drew a chair close as Royce gently opened the worn box.

Inside were two photographs; both had been crumpled then straightened. Randa recognized the school pictures of David-Jack and Donna-Dean.

"Wonder why these were crumpled up?" Randa asked.

"Probably somebody's temper."

Royce picked through the other items in the box. Two pencil stubs and the Barlow pocketknife he had used to sharpen them, six cats-eye marbles, a Duncan Yo-Yo with no string, and two sticks of Teaberry gum.

Royce stood the money tins side by side, pondering them, mulling over the probabilities.

"That's what he was guarding with the rat trap, isn't it?" Randa asked.

"Yep. Maybe he thought his mom or dad would steal it away from him."

Randa reached for one of the Big Chief tablets and flipped through its pages. The handwriting was small; a miniature script, mixed with miniature print. She turned back a few pages and read aloud to Royce,

"Miss Mattie says I can't read
Miss Mattie says I can't spell
I don't see no need to read
I don't see no need to spell
So Miss Mattie can just go to hell"

"Oh Royce," she grinned. "Please don't tell Mattie. She would die."

Randa turned a few more pages of the tablet.

"Oh my goodness . . . this is a journal . . . of all they were doing to him."

"This one is too," Royce said as he turned page after page of the other Big Chief tablet. "He's left us a great deal of testimony. This one here gets rather intense," he closed the tablet cover and tossed it onto the pile of paperwork cluttering the top of his desk. "Damn," he muttered.

Randa turned to the middle of the tablet she was holding, and read "My Daddy puts Vaseline on my bottom before he . . ." Royce quickly jerked the tablet straight up from her hands.

"Randa, this is what he wanted, or rather needed, to say. This is how he chose to 'tell'. I don't want you to have these words as a final memory of him."

"Oh, I just feel so sorry for him. Why didn't we realize something was terribly wrong with this boy?"

"You know, I think Silcox may actually have convinced him that this is what men do."

Randa looked doubtful.

"I mean . . . well, . . . think about it. This was a 14-year-old boy, who's messed up in his mind over raging hormones, anyway. Sexually curious. So, it may have been easy for his daddy to convince him that this was an okay thing to do."

"Well, these tablets could have some deep psychological revelations?" she said.

"They will be of great interest to the prosecution. Almost worth getting my fingers broken."

"These crumpled pictures," Randa said, pressing her fingers across the images. "Sad little lives."

CHAPTER FIFTY-TWO

Royce gathered the Band-Aid tins and re-packed them within their cigar boxes. Randa handed him the school pictures.

"You know, she's a pretty little girl, isn't she?" he said.

"Yes, she is. Danny told me that he overheard Hannah and Donna-Dean talking, and Hannah was saying that she wanted to be an airline stewardess when she grew up."

Royce smiled at the thought.

"Donna-Dean had no idea what an airline stewardess was, so Hannah went into great detail to explain."

"I'm sure," he said.

"Then Hannah asked Donna-Dean what she wanted to be when she grew up, and do you know what Donna-Dean said?"

He looked at her with skeptical eyes, fearing the answer.

"She said 'nothing.' When she grows up she wants to be . . . 'nothing'." The word fell between them like a cannonball. Their eyes met in worried concern. Royce simply shook his head from side to side.

"Well, she has come from nothingness. She was able to exist in it, and now, hopefully, she has survived it."

"And you know whut?" Randa said, trying her best to imitate Donna-Dean as she clasped her hand over his. "You're falling in love with her."

He laughed out a loud "ha," as he gathered up David-Jack's things to return them to the table across the room.

Randa hesitated, remembering her excuse for coming upstairs in the first place.

"My main reason for interrupting you, was to tell you something."

159

"What's that?" he said taking a sip of the hot chocolate.

"This is probably going to cause a major diversion in your work here. Are you sure your want a diversion, right now?"

"What is it?" he smiled.

Randa drew close to him to whisper, "It's snowing!"

"Really!" he jumped back, almost spilling the hot chocolate. "Let's go see."

Randa took his mug and set it on the desk. Royce was hurriedly grabbing for her hand to lead her downstairs.

The living room was dark, only the light from the kitchen and the fireplace made delicate glowing circles across the floor. Royce headed them toward the french doors.

"Wow, this will be beautiful in the morning," he said.

The snow was pelting down. The wind blew giant frozen flakes in a zigzag pattern outlining the stones on the patio.

"Wait here," Royce said as he turned away.

Randa thought it quite an anomaly that this powerhouse of a man could pull his mind away from the investigation of two grotesque murders, to marvel at something so simple and beautiful as snow.

He was back from the coat closet dragging an over-sized black coat. Randa stepped over to help him pull it on over his splinted hand.

"This is a prairie coat . . . like cowboys wear," he explained. Randa smiled, sensing another little boy adventure.

"Go get your coat on, girl, it's cold out there." She noticed him adjust the ever-present holster across his shoulder, and gun under his arm.

CHAPTER FIFTY-THREE

Randa ran to the bedroom to find her coat and gloves. Donna-Dean was buried deep within the down comforter, not realizing fun was close at hand and she would be sleeping through it.

Outside, Royce was dragging a lounge chair from the far edge of the patio. What in the world, Randa muttered to herself as she walked out of the house into the snow-filled night.

Royce reclined himself on the padded, cushion of the chair. "You've gotta see this," he said, holding the ankle-length black coat wide open. "Get in."

"Oh really!" she wanted him to think she was shocked.

"Climb in!" he urged. "You won't believe how great this is."

She sat down, then scrunched herself down and back onto the chair, as he folded the billowing coat across her.

"Now we'll zip up . . . all the way to your chin." He tugged at the zipper with his good hand. "Just let your face peek out." Randa thought this, indeed, would be one of those memorable scenes she would store in the scrapbook of her mind, when she wanted to recall their time together.

Royce held her in his arms and bundled her close to his side. "Now look straight up," he directed.

Randa looked up into the blinding flurry of ice pellets pinging at her face, sticking to her eyelashes and prickling her cheeks.

"Isn't it great," he laughed as he looked up through the giant flakes. "I love this kind of blinding snow."

Randa did think it was great. The snow seemed to be coming down heavier now. She could no longer see the roof line of the house. She could barely see Royce's face.

When she began to get too cold, she snuggled her face down into the prairie coat. Just as she was settling herself, trying to overlook the fact that her body was alongside his, but nonetheless hoping he would soon make some sort of romantic move, he zipped down the coat and jumped up.

"That's enough," he declared, "don't want to get frost bite."

As he began to help her get out of the coat, he said, "Wait . . ." he held her shoulders and pointed his finger in her face "wait . . . wait, right here."

Royce ran into the house and quickly grabbed the portable radio from the kitchen counter. He snapped it on as he raced back outside. Using his splinted hand as a snow scraper, he brushed away a perfect dome of snow to nestle the radio onto the patio wall. He reached for Randa's hand.

"Would you dance with me in the snow, my lady?"

Did he just bow to me in that flowing black coat, Randa asked herself, or could this all be a dream?

He pulled her to him, and as the song "You Are My Special Angel" blared out through the flying snow, the sheriff showed her that, among his many talents, he was quite a dancer.

Close, slow, dancing had never been Randa's strong point. The main problem had been diagnosed by many a college letter-sweatered beau. She simply could not, or would not "follow."

This could be embarrassing, she thought. The teacher was at the blackboard, chalk poised over the long division she could not begin.

"I . . . ," she began the explanation.

Royce drew her close.

"I . . . , don't do this very well."

"What?"

"This."

"You do it very well."

"I mean, I don't slow dance," she felt herself sliding closer, her thighs touching his, "very well."

"You just need to follow me."

"That's what they all say," she laughed. "That's the part I can't do."

"Just let my body tell you the direction to go," Royce said into the top of her head. This was their first intimate moment; they were clearly awed by it.

"That sounds a little nasty," Randa said, easing the tension.

Royce threw his head back in laughter, while Randa realized she was "following" his every step.

They danced, laughing and spinning around through two songs. He had wrapped the big coat around her, drawing her close with his good hand across her back. As he huddled over her, she put her head down onto his chest, thinking she had never had a more romantic moment.

As The Lettermen crooned their way into "The Way You Look Tonight," Randa said "You know, I think this might possibly make up for my not going to my high school prom."

"You didn't go to your prom?" Royce asked.

"I was invited . . . by a boy I had quite a crush on. I had bought a lavender prom dress with a long satin sash. I had fought with my mother over the color, and over the cost of it. But . . . the day before the prom he told me he was going to go with someone else. A cheerleader."

"God," Royce swirled her around to see her eyes.

"My mother took that dress out to our trash barrel in the backyard and burned it. Cremated the whole nasty episode."

They laughed.

"That was the one and only time I let a man break my heart," Randa said.

"So, I should take warning, you've got your dukes up, right."

"You won't break my heart. You're too sweet and charming."

"Sweet and charming?" he quipped. "Don't let that get around, you'll ruin my reputation."

"I hate to tell you, big guy, but I think that is pretty much your reputation," she teased.

"Now how would that look for my next campaign . . . `Royce Hawkins For Your Sweet and Charming County Sheriff'!" he said as he "dipped" her way back on her heels.

He brought her up quickly.

"Thank you for always going along with my crazy ideas. Somehow I think you bring out the silly in me." He leaned down to give her a kiss.

"All of this has really been something," he continued.

"All of this?" she asked.

"Oh, this with Donna-Dean, and the search for Silcox. All of this disruption I've caused in your life. And, our having had the opportunity to meet each other."

"I believe things happen for a reason . . . a purpose," Randa said. "Life's little plan."

"You mean there was a reason that guy didn't take you to the prom," Royce pondered.

"Well, now, that's going pretty far back in time, but ultimately . . . yes, there was a reason."

He held her tight and gave her one final Fred Astaire twirl across their snow-covered dance floor.

CHAPTER FIFTY-FOUR

"If you're not sleepy, would you sit with me by the fire for awhile?" Royce asked as Randa came back into the living room from putting her coat away.

"Sure. Remember, I told you I am a night owl."

They sat in silence. Royce put a pillow on Randa's lap to rest his injured hand.

"I just keep thinking about that creep who stood you up for your prom," he said.

Randa laughed. "That was a thousand years ago." More silence, punctuated by the crackling fire.

"Why are you thinking about him?" she asked.

"Just can't believe that he wouldn't have been thrilled to death to go to the prom with you. Wish I had been there."

"You should have driven down to Pensacola to take me. Of course, you were a big college man and you wouldn't have given me a second glance."

"Pensacola, huh?"

"Pensacola born and raised."

"Are your folks still there?" he asked.

"Just my brother, My dad died my junior year in college. My mom died of cancer about five years ago. That's when I came up here to U.T. to supposedly start work on my Masters. I shelved that idea after two semesters."

"And . . ." he said.

"And . . . . decided to look for a teaching position here in the area. I didn't want to go back home."

"It's kind of ironic that you just have your brother, and I just have a sister. My folks are both gone, too."

"Brodie told me that your sister lives in Colorado."

"Yep . . . Becca's not much of a home town girl. She got married, and they headed out to bigger mountains and pockets of gold."

Randa clasped both of her hands around his good hand.

"Please tell me that's her picture on your desk upstairs."

"It is. Why?" he looked at her. "Were you worried about that picture?"

"A little. Like you're thinking about that prom guy," she teased.

"I should have introduced you to that picture the first time you were up there in the office. God . . . you were probably thinking that was my ex-wife, or something," he nudged her with his shoulder.

"Something?" she quipped.

"You know, a long lost love. I don't have any of those around. Brodie says I'm married to my job . . . yeah, like a doctor isn't married to his!"

"If you're happy with that kind of life, then that's all that matters," she said.

"I think I've spent a lot of years building my life, like an old bird out here in the woods. I've put a twig in here and a twig in there; added a string of this, and a strand of that to get my nest just the way I want it. And, I've burrowed down in to it hoping to be happy. But, somehow it's just not right.

"Brodie, and Becca, and even Danny are all in a panic thinking that I've rooted myself firmly into bachelorhood. I think it's kind of cute the way I'm always on their minds."

"When I moved up here," Randa began, "I wanted to be alone. I wanted to be away from Derrick. After mom died, he turned into a basket case. I was twenty-six, living on my own in Tampa. I was enjoying my first teaching position in a big inner-city elementary school, and he started demanding that I quit and come back to our old house in Pensacola."

"Why?" Royce asked.

"He was in the middle of a million personal problems; women, money, alcohol, losing a business it took my father thirty years to build. He wanted me there to absorb all of that for him," she explained.

"But that twig didn't fit in your nest, did it?" Royce joked.

"No . . . I realized that was a bent twig," she laughed.

"So you tossed that twig out . . . threw it far away."

"And Derrick has been a bit peeved at me ever since. He thinks I'm living in a wilderness now. He nags at me that my living alone is dangerous. When I was in Tampa, he thought I was living and teaching in a ghetto. And . . . I was!" she laughed.

"Really." Royce said getting caught up in her story.

"It was a really bad area. A gangland. Guns and drugs, lots of multi-racial violence. All of the teachers literally ran from their cars into the building every morning, and ran out every afternoon.

"But I really liked teaching there. I loved working with those children. That's what attracted me to this job here. These are special needs children, too. With all of the grades combined, and only two teachers, it's a challenge to make sure they really master their work. I think it's worth my living alone, in the wilderness, to get this experience.

"Oh, speaking of this experience, I should go get things together for school tomorrow. Remember school. You do still want us to go back tomorrow, don't you?"

"Yeah. But the weather may be a factor. If the snow keeps up, there won't be any getting over Hurricane Ridge in the morning."

Randa moved his hand gently off the pillow and stood up to leave. He jumped up rather quickly for a man on pain relievers, to escort her down the hallway. When they reached the bedroom door, he pulled her close.

"Goodnight, sweet lady, thanks for . . ."

"If you thank me one more time, for anything, Royce Hawkins, . . ." she preached. He kissed her over her whispered voice, as if their parting for the night was a sweet farewell.

CHAPTER FIFTY-FIVE

As Randa was getting dressed, Donna-Dean walked into the living room in her Barbie nightgown and house-shoes. Her hair was matted and knotted in strands across her head. She yawned.

"Good morning," Royce greeted her. She made no response.

He walked over to take her hand to lead her over to the french doors.

"Look at the snow. Isn't it pretty?" They looked out in silence.

"School has been called off for today. Maybe we can go out and play in this stuff this afternoon. Want to?" he said.

"I'm gonna have to go home," she said.

Royce picked her up.

"Now, what are you thinking about?"

"I think I better go home."

"You are home, darlin'," he said. "You are as home as I can get for you right now." He hoped she would take the conversation no further.

"Hopefully, you and Miss Randa can go back to school tomorrow morning."

He looked for a reaction from her, but there was none. She's still half asleep, he told himself.

"Danny's coming in the back door. He's going to stay with you and Miss Randa while I go to work."

She put her head down on his shoulder.

He pulled up a nearby rocking chair and sat down with her to look out at the snow.

"You know, right down there . . . below the patio . . ." he pointed with his splinted hand, "there's this big ole, flat rock that points way out over the water."

"Uh-huh," she grunted.

"That's my favorite place to sit and look out across the water."

"Uh-huh."

"And when it snows like this, that's the perfect place to make a big snowman . . . because it looks like he's looking out across the water."

"Kin I make one," she sprang to life.

"When I get back, we'll get you all bundled up in some warm clothes and go down there. You be thinking about that."

"Gabriel, too?" she asked.

"Yep, Gabriel too." he said. "But you'll have to help me make him behave and stay away from the water."

"We'll just say, 'Gabriel, you be good'."

"That would work," Royce rocked her and soon she fell back to sleep.

When Danny came upon them, Royce looked up with a thousand questions behind his eyes . . . totally befuddled, as if he were asking what to do next.

Danny motioned for him to put her on the couch.

Later, Royce poured Danny the last of the chocolate milk, and glanced up into the carton to make sure there was no more before tossing it into the trash can.

"I'm going to be gone for a few hours today. I have a hunch to follow up on. Something Donna-Dean said last night reminded me of a bill, or a receipt, I found out there at the Silcox house. It was from a nursing home just over the border up here in Kentucky. The name of the person there is Dimple Stallings. I've got a feeling that's Donna-Dean's grandmother."

"You're going to go up there today?" Randa entered the kitchen, overheard his plans, and whined at the thought of him leaving.

"I'll make the trip as fast as I can. Maybe this lady can give me something to jump-start this case."

"I keep forgetting that you have a job to do," she said.

"I'll be back before you can even miss me."

Danny stepped around them, exiting himself out of the way, claiming a great need to clear cereal bowls from the breakfast table.

"I miss you already," Randa pouted.

"You do?" Royce reached out to pull her close.

The quick kiss he gave her would have to last the two of them all day.

CHAPTER FIFTY-SIX

Royce sped the patrol car along state highway 143 toward the Kentucky border. Several times he had thought about turning around ... here ... there ... the next good place. This trip to find Donna-Dean's grandmother was probably a wild goose chase; nothing more than a day away from this case that was quickly becoming a ream of paperwork spread across his desk.

He diverted his thoughts back to his date night with Randa. She's really a pretty lady. Cute. Just downright cute. Probably shouldn't have apologized for not having a car. Dumb thing to say ... must have sounded like I hadn't been out with a woman since God knows when.

Then there was that line "but this is a new truck," he chuckled at the thought. Damn. Not good. But who knows, maybe that would be the one line they could look back on and laugh over someday. One of those dog poop on your shoe memories. He chuckled to himself, remembering when Brodie went into a girl's house to pick her up for the prom, and tracked dog shit from his shoe all across her parent's new, white carpet!

He drew his mind back to the road as he whizzed by the Welcome to Kentucky sign. He began to watch for the turn off onto the county highway that would take him into Middlesboro.

Minutes later he pulled into a crossroads market for gas and to call ahead to the local sheriff's office. As he entered the store, everyone looked him over, up one side and down the other. He tipped his hat.

At the counter he asked a buxom, grey-haired lady with overlapping teeth if they had a pay phone.

"Nossir . . . but I reckon you could use this-un." She brought out a black rotary dial from beneath the counter.

"Do you have the number for the sheriff's office?"

"Yessir . . . keep it writ down by the register. You know, jist in case trouble walks in."

"Good idea." Royce took the grease-stained spiral notebook she thrust his way.

Minutes later, Sheriff Wilbur Crowder picked up the phone after keeping Royce on hold for what seemed like an eternity, and gave exact directions to the Cedar Crest Nursing Home. Royce used a pen, tied with a string to the counter, to scrawl the street names on his hand.

"You up here on b-ness, Sheriff?" Crowder's curiosity got the best of him.

"Just making a next of kin notification. Thanks for the directions."

"Well, if'n you need any help, lemme know."

"Sure will," Royce lied.

The nursing home was a v-shaped, motel-looking building, stretching across the hillside above the town. Royce noticed a group of elderly ladies sitting on a couch in the lobby. They looked like mannequins. Pill box hats, white gloves, pocketbooks nestled on their laps. He took a second glance to see if they were alive. He removed his hat . . . cautiously aware they would think that the proper thing for him to do.

"Morning," he greeted the nurse at the reception desk. She smiled, delighted to see a youthful face.

"Are they okay?" Royce nodded his head toward the ladies.

"Oh, yes. They're waiting," she whispered.

"For what?"

"The Senior Citizen van is coming to get them. They have doctor appointments downtown. Can I help you?"

"Do you have a patient here by the name of Dimple Stallings?"

"Yes."

"I'm Sheriff Hawkins from down in Brandensburg. I probably need to speak with your Director regarding the matter I have for Mrs. Stallings," Royce said.

"I'll go get Mr. Cox. You can take a seat over there by the ladies, if you want to," she flashed a flirty grin as she got up from her desk.

"Oh, no thanks. I'll wait here."

Mr. Cox came down the left corridor, with an outstretched hand. "Sheriff," he smiled. "Come on back here to my office."

They walked to a small maple-paneled room. The over-sized desk seemed to take up too much space. Too big, Royce thought, for the frail fellow who sank down into a worn leather chair behind it.

"How can I help you, Sheriff?"

Royce chose his words carefully, giving a condensed version of the murders and down-playing his investigative intent.

"I need to make the notification of the deaths. She is the only relative we can find. A neighbor knew she has been here at your home for a few years. How competent is she? Will she understand what I will be telling her?"

"Well, I'll tell you, Sheriff, the one you should talk with is our house doctor. He will be here just any time now for his morning rounds. To protect my own interests here, I need to have his approval on what you should do here. This is a critically ill patient. She is 96 years old. Not entirely lucid. There are times when she needs to be in restraints.

"Tell you what, let me call Dr. Fields and tell him you need to speak with him. Shouldn't be but a few minutes. You can wait back out in the lobby. I'll have the girls bring you some coffee and doughnuts," he ushered Royce toward the door.

The nurse at the desk seemed too eager to have him back in her care. She led him to a leather winged-back chair near a window, across the lobby from the ladies-in-waiting who were no more receptive to his presence.

Two volunteer pink ladies appeared bearing a carafe of coffee and two doughnuts. The coffee was weak and tasteless. The doughnuts looked stale. He wondered if they had been grabbed from a patient's tray. Think I'll pass, he thought. Especially on that pink one . . . doughnuts should not be pink!

"Sheriff?" Royce jumped his attention back to the white lab coat before him.

"I'm Dr. Fields."

"Yes, how are you?" Royce grasped yet another outstretched hand. "I need to talk to you about Mrs. Dimple Stallings. I have two murder victims in my county. One is Mrs. Stallings daughter, and the other one is her grandson. I need to know if I can discuss this with her?"

"Her mental condition is quite deteriorated. She has a hardening of the arteries, dementia situation. She sees things, hears voices. Seems to be living in her own little world. Most of the time she is rational, but I'm not sure what reaction she would have to your news. She might not comprehend it at all; in that case, she would probably be very unresponsive."

"I'll keep it simple. I do want to see if she can answer a few questions. She may have some questions for me," Royce said.

"I'll go with you," Dr. Fields offered.

Chapter Fifty-Seven

"Miss Dimple?" The doctor turned her wheel chair toward Royce who stood silhouetted against the open doorway.

"This is Sheriff Hawkins from down in Brandensburg."

"What?" she screeched through rotten teeth.

"He needs to talk to you."

Royce moved cautiously toward the frail body sunk within the arms of the wheelchair. Her eyes seemed to squint her disgust.

"He the law?"

"Yes, ma'am." The doctor shifted her catheter bag filled with its black 10-W-30 fluid to the left side of the chair.

"Well, what in the worl?" she sputtered.

"Mornin', Miss Dimple. How are you?" Royce took his hat from his head and held it at his side.

"Aw right," she mumbled.

"Ma'am, I've got some news to tell you about your daughter, Rowena."

"Rennie?"

"Yes ma'am. And about your grandson, David-Jack.

"What's wrong?"

"Well, ma'am, they are both dead." The doctor moved his hand over to her shoulder. Silence.

"Well, hell," she said.

"They were murdered there at your home place, a few days ago."

"Hell," she repeated.

"Yes, ma'am, something was going on there, and it's my job to find out what the trouble might have been," Royce said.

"I sure thought I would go before my chile," she played the sympathy card.

"I need to ask you where you might want us to bury them?"

"Hell, I don't know. The Lord will take care of thet."

"Yes, ma'am. Do you have a family cemetery somewhere?"

"I sed, the Lord will take care of thet, it's none of our doin'. When you go to the Lord . . ."

"Miss Dimple?" Royce interrupted, "I need to see if you know who might have done this?"

"Sorry folk. The whole lot of 'um. Just plain sorry folk. And this is how the Lord has taken care of it."

"Can you tell me anything about Robert Silcox?"

"No good. No account. Sorry ass. He's the ring-leader, you know. Sorry day when she took up with him. Thet other one she was with was better . . . ceptin' he led her into fornication!"

"Would you know . . ." Royce began.

"Fornication. Plain and simple. I tried to tell her thet would only lead to ruin and the next thing she's up and married the wrong one. Should have married thet boy's daddy."

"What?" Royce gasped.

"Never mind. That's our beeswax. No need to dredge it up. She made up her own mind, wouldn't listen to me. She sent me here so's I don't have no vote on nuthin'."

"Was Robert hurting these children?"

"Well, he never would in front of me. He'd always take them off up to the barn. But when they come back, you could tell. David-Jack was just senseless. Both them chil-ren would always let on like they'd had whoopin's or somethin'. But, they wuz powerful bad liars."

"So, you didn't do anything about this?"

"Nope, I didn't. It wudden't my place!" she glared up at Royce. "I betcha you think it wuz my place."

"Yes, I do."

"Well now, you warn't a 90 year old womern, a-livin' thar. wuz yew?"

Royce laughed. "No, ma'am."

"Did the best I knew how. Then got out. Didn't look back over my shoulder none when I left, neether. Sed I didn't give a hoot 'bout any of 'um . . . still don't."

Royce glanced up at the doctor, who was nervously checking his watch.

"Rennie wuz the one, though. Sorry to say that 'bout my own girl, but she wuz the one."

"The one who did what?" Royce said.

"Everythin' you could imagine. I got to thinking she was a witch. That's why I didn't raise too much of a stink when they wanted to move me out."

"Did she make Robert do things?"

"Hard to tell if'n he would make her or she would make him. They kind of drew the bad fire out of each other. A real match made in hell. She oughta stayed with that other fella she fornicated with."

"And who might that have been?"

"It was Robert's brother."

"Really." Royce remained calm, giving her time.

"It just wudden't my place to interfere thar. You think I'll go to hell for thet?"

"The Lord will take care of you, Miss Dimple," Royce turned to leave.

"However He see fit," Miss Dimple smiled Donna-Dean's impish little smile.

CHAPTER FIFTY-EIGHT

Royce had been rather tight-lipped about his visit with Donna-Dean's grandmother. He was angry . . . just out and out mad, Randa thought. The beautiful blue eyes were buried deep within squinted lids. His brow was lined with furrows that had lain dormant. His jaw was tightly set around clenched teeth. He was trying hard not to twitch his head from side to side, in response to a pissed-off pulse.

He explained a few things to satisfy Randa's curiosity, but hedged around the alleged "fornicatin'." These were still very scattered pieces of the puzzle.

He had convinced Donna-Dean that there was an urgent need for the two of them to build that promised snowman before they lost the afternoon sun.

Randa watched them from the bedroom window, wishing she had a video camera. Royce was helping Donna-Dean roll snow into big, round, dirty globs that would be stacked together to make their snowman. Gabriel was dancing a jig around them, as if the cold snow was burning his paws.

Royce carefully lifted the snowman's head up onto the ball that would be the belly. Moments later, he lifted Donna-Dean up to place two rocks into the facial snow. These would be the eyes to look out across the lake.

Royce pulled a carrot out of his hip pocket to use for a nose. Gabriel bowed himself down on his front paws and wagged his rear end, begging for what he thought was an orange bone.

They used Royce's L.L. Bean muffler to bundle around the snowman's neck. As the two of them stood admiring their creation,

Randa opened the french doors to shout across the patio asking Royce if he had a camera. He shouted back that there was a Polaroid in the bottom desk drawer in his office.

Randa ran up the stairs to locate the camera before the sun grew weaker. The Polaroid was among binoculars, a small microscope, an over-sized magnifying glass, and a tape recorder.

She glanced at the framed photograph of Becca, taking the opportunity to study it closely. Becca had a sweet smile, and kind eyes. Certainly there was a resemblance to Royce.

And what would you be thinking about all of this, she thought!

She raced down and out with the camera, handing it over to Royce, who snapped it open and popped up the flash. He positioned Donna-Dean next to the snowman. Gabriel dashed to her side, as if he, too, should be a part of this moment.

"Now let me get you two," Randa said, eager to capture the image she carried in her mind. She took several of what Donna-Dean refered to as "pitchers," juggling the prints as the camera spit them forward after each snap.

Later, inside by the fire, they spread the Polariods across the coffee table. Royce and Donna-Dean thought they were wonderful. They each declared the snowman the best one they had ever seen.

Donna-Dean remarked that her Daddy never did let her see the pictures he took.

Royce shook his head from side to side, while trying to keep his cool.

Randa began to help Donna-Dean get out of the layers of warmth they had concocted for her. She laughed at the way Royce had put his thermal undershirt on her and safety pinned it across her back.

They quickly redirected Donna-Dean's attention to "catching up" school work. When she had completed four workbook pages, they drilled her on spelling words. Royce pretended to misspell every word, so they both could correct him.

Later they drove into town to pick up food at the drive-thru window at the Toot-N-Tell Barbecue, returning to the house as the sunset cast a red, fiery glow across the ice-glazed roadway. It seemed like they were driving into a volcanic lava flow. The fading sun formed a backdrop in the distance, changing trees, barns, and houses into black silhouettes

After their dinner, Royce left them to go upstairs to make some calls. Randa headed Donna-Dean toward the shower, with the ultimate goal of getting her to go to bed.

The house seemed still and empty, it's usual feeling at this time of night. Royce stretched himself back into the big leather chair before his roll-top desk. Now's the time to get down to business, he coached himself. Time to set the wheels in motion.

He found himself distracted from the pain in his fingers, not only from Brodies's medicinal potions, but from the master plan that had been spinning wildly in his head.

It had taken a multitude of telephone calls to map out, explain, check and recheck instructions. Francine had often chided, "Sheriff, if you ever have children you must surely name them Check and Recheck!"

But, in the whole scheme of things, he had to make sure, doubly sure, everything would come down the way he wanted.

CHAPTER FIFTY-NINE

"Shit."

Royce slammed down the phone, violating one of his very own office rules.

"See. He's gettin' the way he always gets," Danny said.

"I said I would do one press statement. Only one. None of this calling me morning, noon, and night for an update. This case isn't going anywhere. Not yet."

Danny raised Royce's coffee mug toward the ceiling light and determined it to be clean enough for the last cup of sludge from the bottom of the coffee pot.

"He always wants us, or rather you, to hurry up and feed him something," Danny said.

"Coltan Baird is an old-money, third generation newspaper editor of the *Brandensburg Herald*. Imagines himself to be a real news hound. Only around here there's just not much to hound. At least not the kind of stuff he can string out to the big boys," Royce smiled. "What did you promise him?"

"In the morning. In the hallway out there. By now he's called all of his media buddies down in Knoxville so they will probably be here. I told him to put the word out that you will do one press thing. One. And it will be short and sweet."

"Cut and dried," Royce said.

"You gonna tell about the mother? How she was all sawed up like that?"

"Coltan knows when I'm dodgin'. If I say "no comment", they will all chew on me until I give them something that can be blown all out of proportion. I'll just read what's in the Medical Examiner's report. I'll try to indicate some of that should be off the record . . . pending this investigation."

"You want to have the Medical Examiner there?" Danny asked.

"No. I don't feel like being that accommodating. Why don't you call J. W. Hammett. He can do his District Attorney act for them."

"What about her tongue being up inside her like that?"

"It's a part of the medical report, Danny." Royce noticed a disparaging pout cross the deputy's face.

"But . . . maybe I can side step around it," Royce offered.

"Make one of those purty speeches. Dance all around the facts. You kinda know how to tell, but don't tell," Danny brightened at the thought.

"Yeah," Royce laughed. "In a way, it's like talking to a jury. You want them to hear the right things. That's why we'll type up an official statement that might help them separate the history from the hype."

"Good deal, chief."

"You know," Royce said, "I can remember my grandmother would cut stories out of the newspaper about people she knew. Back during the depression people would lose their farms and commit suicide. There were hangings and shootings. People would jump off the river bluff over here. Maybe one or two a month.

"My grandmother claimed she knew most of them, and she would put their news clippings in the family Bible. She believed that was a way of blessing their souls."

"No foolin'," Danny said.

"That Bible was a history book of this county during the '30's." Royce added.

"No foolin'," Danny repeated.

"No foolin', Dan." Royce tipped the coffee mug toward his friend, hoping he had, for the moment, brought him away from the thought of Rowena Silcox's tongue.

CHAPTER SIXTY

This Monday morning had a different feel. Randa was coming out of a dream world where crime, motherhood and romance had whirled her for several days. Donna-Dean was going off to school in her new Walmart jumper, facing her first day back into reality. Royce was nervous over facing the press, and over his impending plans to stir the fires of this investigation. He had been very secretive about things, and had convinced everyone he would be at his office buried in mountains of paperwork all day.

They left for school before sunrise, driving thru McDonald's for breakfast to go. Randa and Donna-Dean ordered extra to take for lunch. Donna-Dean seemed happy. She had no questions about David-Jack and made no inquires about the day ahead.

Royce told her that one of the deputies would be staying with them at school. She did not ask why; she had become quite content with this odd variety of care givers.

Houston was sitting in his patrol car in front of the school. Miss Mattie was inside struggling to get the oil stoves up and running. Royce walked them up the steps that were still covered with snow. Randa reminded herself of the bag of salt in the storeroom.

"Y'all have a good day," Royce said. "If I can't pick you up at three, someone else will be here to take you home. Houston will be here all day. Give him some teaching to do, he's a smart fellow."

Royce lifted Donna-Dean up onto his hip.

"Have a good time today, Miss Barbie. Do some good work. Get caught up on some of that work you missed. I'll see you this evening."

Donna-Dean hugged his neck and told him to "be good." He put her down and pushed down on the long cross bar that opened the school door. Donna-Dean ran down the hallway looking for Miss Mattie. Houston was close behind her.

Royce took Randa's hand.

"You have a good day, too. Try to get caught up on some of that work you missed," he gave her a kiss.

"And, you be good," she joked tugging at the front of his long, black prairie coat.

He watched as she went inside. He began to regret what might lie ahead in the long hours before he would see then again.

Fighting an urge to call them back, to take them back home to his warm fire, he pulled the bar handle to close the door. Had letting them come back to school been the right thing to do? He worried all the way back to Brandensburg.

CHAPTER SIXTY-ONE

Royce coughed. That was always a good opener, he thought. Harumpf your way on stage. Worked as well as anything to get their attention.

Danny had brought a rickety, wooden podium from the courtroom upstairs to make what he proudly called a "pulpit" outside the office doorway.

When they saw Royce come out of the office, the dozen or so media brought their attention up from fine tuning their instruments, leaving their sound checks, one-two, one-two, echoing across the marble floor.

The cameraman from W.B.I.R. in Knoxville, hoisted his rig up onto his shoulder. Royce overheard him say to his female reporter/ sidekick, "come on pretty boy, show us what you got," as he drew a focus.

The reporter's face changed from comedy to tragedy as she realized that "pretty boy" had heard the snotty remark. She flashed a cheerleader smile at Royce, as she elbowed an "Ow!" from the cameraman.

Spreading a few papers across Danny's pulpit, Royce gave them a meaningless "Good morning," and flashed a political smile they seemed to be waiting for.

"This will be a brief announcement of this situation," he began.

They all seemed to be inching themselves forward, trying to edge past their competition. Television always edged in and around the print media.

"I won't take any questions at this time. We have prepared a handout sheet for you. About all I can lay forth is the who, what, where, and when. Obviously, I don't know the "why.""

He smiled. They were not amused. The five "w's" were the basis of their business.

"I will remind you that this is a high profile investigation, involving many state agencies and criminalistics teams. Obviously, I will not discuss any of the key elements of this case at this time.

"Last Wednesday afternoon, I responded to a call from the 3 Springs community school. One of the students had been told by her mother not to come home when school was out. After a lengthy wait for someone to come for the child, I drove out to the home suspecting this might be a case of child abandonment," Royce paused, offering them a chance to catch up.

"It was approximately 5 p.m. when I got to the home. No one appeared to be at the residence. Upon investigation of the premises, I discovered the older child of this family, fourteen-year-old David-Jack Silcox, dying from a blow to the head, as well as a massive abdominal wound, apparently from having been struck with an axe. The boy had lost a great deal of blood, and was very close to death when I found him.

"The Medical Examiner has determined this boy died from blunt force trauma, and from literally bleeding to death." Royce paused, maybe they would think his silence was for dramatic effect, rather than to collect himself from the memory.

"On Saturday, we discovered the body of the boy's mother, Rowena Maylene Silcox, age 42, in the root cellar beneath the kitchen floor of the residence. The decapitated body had been put into a cedar chest, and someone had attempted to bury this chest into the ground."

The media seemed nonplused. Callous, at least to the verbiage. Royce bet himself they would love to get out there to the crime scene to soak up the color.

"The forensic team from the Tennessee Bureau of Investigation has been assisting my department with this crime scene. They have today completed their preliminary investigation. Until we have processed the physical evidence obtained from the scene, any thought my office may have as to a suspect would be very speculative and tenuous.

"We are, at this time, trying to locate the husband and father, Robert Allen Silcox. We have a flyer showing his photograph attached to the handout sheet. Mr. Silcox is 47 years old. He works at the Allied Zinc mine, and was last seen there on Wednesday morning. We would appreciate your using the photograph along with a request for the public to contact our office if they have any knowledge of his whereabouts."

Royce anticipated their shouts of "Sheriff?" and there were several.

"Again," Royce raised his hand, "I will remind you that based on the preliminary investigation, I cannot make any speculation as to a suspect, or possible motive for these murders. I will say that this is the beginning of an on-going, intense investigation. And, if and when I have anything further to say, you will be notified."

Cameras snapped and flashed, their motor-drives purred. There were restless shufflings until someone's pager sounded, frustrating the W.B.I.R. cheerleader who almost sprang on the lowly print media who had received the page.

"Thank you." Royce retreated quickly back into the office, and turned the proceedings over to Danny who anxiously stepped over to guard the door.

"That's it," Danny announced, as he folded his arms across his chest. "Y'all can go now."

CHAPTER SIXTY-TWO

The morning had gone well, Randa thought. The children had welcomed Donna-Dean back, as if she had only been out for the flu. Miss Mattie had coached them well on their do's and don'ts.

When someone said they were sorry about David-Jack, Donna-Dean had no reaction. She simply did not know how to respond. She was burying this deep inside, and Randa decided that was okay . . . for now.

Math work sheets and reading exercises were her assignments for the day, and Randa let Houston supervise this make-up work from their back row seats in the corner.

The rest of the class seemed fascinated by Houston's presence, and Randa promised to let him speak to them about his job as a deputy at the end of the day. The girls were interested in his having ever killed anyone, and the boys were interested in his patrol car.

Sometime after lunch, Randa thought she saw a swirl of blue light splash across the front of the school. What now, she wondered.

Soon there was a pounding on the school door. Houston crossed the classroom to go into the foyer alongside Miss Mattie.

Dead silence fell across the room. Randa recognized a familiar voice.

Houston returned to the classroom doorway, "Miss Randa, can you come here a minute."

Miss Mattie came in to quickly get the children back to their work. Jake was in the foyer, stomping snow off of his feet.

"Miss Randa, I need you to come with me. I need to take you over to your trailer."

"Wh . . . ?"

"It's on fire. Your trailer . . . it's on fire!"

From the school steps they could see the billowing black smoke a mile away. Randa's heart sank. She felt a bone-chilling weakness.

Jake gunned the patrol car, and they peeled out of the school driveway up onto the blacktop.

"Where's Royce?" she asked.

"They're tryin' to find him," Jake lied, hoping she wouldn't ask again.

"I'm going to stay here with you," Jake said as they pulled off to the shoulder of the road across from the commotion that was going on in Randa's yard. "I'll help you do whatever you need . . ."

"Where's Royce?" she asked, as she got out of the car. The volunteer fire department was there, doing what their antique pumper truck and three elderly men could do. The front part of the trailer was already gone.

Randa remembered her homeowners insurance. She would have to call the agent. At least she had the thing paid for. She would ask Jake to go up the road to find Mr. Howard Frakes who leased her the land for $100 a month.

They watched the flames rise high over the flat roof, searing into the aluminum. The furniture had quickly gone to piles of ashes. Suddenly she realized she was as lost and homeless as Donna-Dean.

Where's Royce, she thought, looking over her shoulder hoping to see him come walking up with that long, elegant stride of his. Surely he knows this is happening.

"Jake?" she shouted above the roar of the pumper truck and the men shouting directions to each other.

"Do you know how to reach Royce?"

"Can't get to him right now. He'll be here soon as he can. You need to get back inside this car. It's too cold to stand out here in all this freezin' water."

As Jake opened the patrol car door, the dispatcher was shouting alphabet codes with a panicked urgency. Jake held Randa back and leaned across the passenger seat to pick up the handset.

This is some sort of distress call, Randa thought. Jake had a look of shock on his face. Before she could once again ask "Where's Royce?," he was shoving her into the car seat.

Once again, they peeled away onto the blacktop.

CHAPTER SIXTY-THREE

"I am so hungry!" Danny whispered.

Royce squirmed himself around in the Silcox ditch.

"Wish I'd had some breakfast."

"Shh," Royce hissed over his shoulder toward Danny.

"Well, my guts are growling!"

Royce turned to look at Danny, and mouthed a firm "hush."

"Can I smoke?"

"No. Stop whining. You're going to blow this whole thing," Royce warned.

The two had been lying in the muddy, snow-filled ditch across the road in front of the Silcox house for well over an hour.

Royce had set his trap early this morning, hoping to lure Robert Silcox to his leaning mailbox, to pick up three manilla envelopes hanging from the rusty flag. Royce had replaced the pornography with wads of paper towel. The photo contact sheets were filed away in Royce's evidence box.

Only a few vehicles had passed. A truck or two.

No one had seen the two of them behind the waist-high weeds and cattails that grew along the shoulder of the road.

"Hey," Danny poked Royce. "Yonder . . ."

Royce stretched his head toward the distant curve in the road and saw the rusted-out, Dodge truck slowing its speed.

"Betcha that's him."

"Be still and quiet. Let him take the bait," Royce cautioned.

Silcox pulled up to the mailbox. The truck's muffler jiggled a dance to the rhythm of the rough idle. A blue smoke streaked out of the tailpipe. Needs a ring job, Royce thought.

Suddenly the gasping engine stopped. All was quiet. Royce smiled at the loud rumble coming from Danny's stomach.

Silcox set the hand brake and jumped out, making a run across the road up the lane toward the house, taking advantage of the patrol car being gone for the first time in days.

A quick signal to Danny and they were up and out of the ditch, eager as hounds after quail.

Royce angled his run out through the woods, parallel to the lane, staying several lengths back from Silcox, who was clumping hurriedly along toward the house, looking back over his shoulder and stumbling into the ruts he had made with his junkyard truck.

What's he after, Royce thought? You demon! Royce shot his thoughts to the back of Silcox's head. What did you leave behind?

Silcox ran toward the picket fence row, tapping his hand along the picket points as if he were counting them.

Ah-ha . . . that's what you're after, Royce thought back to David-Jack's scribbling in his Big Chief tablet about money being buried under the fence.

Silcox stopped, jerked the fruit jar off one of the pickets, and pulled the weathered board loose. He began to dig with it.

The bastard's come back for his money, Royce thought as he motioned for Danny to go toward a tree to the right to act as cover.

Royce glanced at the splint on his left hand. Randa! Oh God . . . the trailer. Jake would be picking her up about now. Shit! He needed to be there with her. But this would, no doubt, be the one and only chance to grab this son-of-a-bitch.

Silcox dug quickly. Frantically. Trying to get in, get the goods, and get out. The dull picket was slow digging through the frozen ground. Silcox dropped down onto his knees pawing into the hole to jerk forth a Mason jar stuffed with bills. He moved to the next fruit jar-topped picket that marked the grave of another bank roll.

Royce waited, impatiently, as Silcox retrieved a second and a third jar.

Go . . . now.

With one move, Royce stepped out into the clearing, pulling his gun from his holster. Using his splinted hand for support, he raised the weapon to shoulder level.

"ROBERT SILCOX! Step away from the fence with your hands over your head!"

Silcox remained crouched over the money jars.

"Stand up, NOW! Turn around with your hands up high," Royce shouted.

Silcox began to move, slowly, as if he were going to obey Royce's commands. He moved a hand inside his worn corduroy jacket and spun around firing his gun toward the sound of Royce Hawkins' voice.

The bullet hit, and hit hard. Danny couldn't believe his eyes. Royce dropped down to his knees, then face down onto the ground.

Silcox ran forward to watch the sheriff writhe in pain. Danny moved in, cautiously.

"Well now, Big Man, look at you," Silcox walked around Royce to avoid stepping in blood.

"Y'know, I could jist chop you up. Jist like I did with her. Find some big ole box to stuff you in. Maybe chop up Donna-Dean and throw her in thar on top of you."

Danny crept closer . . . stepping quietly. Royce would want him to be quiet.

Silcox put his muddy boot across Royce's neck and pointed his gun down to Royce's head.

"Let me jist help you out here, Sheriff. Git you out of your misery . . ."

Danny raised the shot gun and fired. The charge hit Silcox shattering the side of his head, blowing brains out across the snow-covered ground. The body dropped like a bag of sand.

Danny ran to Royce.

CHAPTER SIXTY-FOUR

The bullet seared a bolt of pain into his right side, just above his belt. He had gasped at the impact; not a scream of pain, but rather a sucking heave at the shock. He was losing blood. It seemed to be pumping out of the hot hole like lava flowing down into the valley of the shadow of death. I shall fear no evil, Royce thought, for the Lord Thou art with me.

He was afraid to breathe. It seemed easier to take little gruntings of air.

He nestled his cheek down onto a sloping mound of cold mud, and let his mind wander away from the bloody trench he had wallowed out for himself.

So . . . this is what it's like to "bite the dust," only in this case it's mud, Royce thought. He hadn't tasted mud since Becca had served him a mud pie on top of a maple leaf when they were kids.

He remembered the playhouse she built every summer under that big tree; sprawling roots from its trunk spreading across the ground to separate her make-believe rooms. God, where did that memory come from.

Through the buzz in his ears he could hear Danny's shouting to the dispatcher "Officer down, repeat OFFICER DOWN!"

They would all know what to do. Maybe.

For a moment Royce dreamed the people in his office were like clowns, springing forth out of a clown car . . . each of them eager to do their particular trick just right, for this would be their moment in the spotlight.

Hurry guys, he thought.

Mud began to cake on his eyelashes and eyebrows. If he could move his good hand up from below, he would wipe the stinky stuff away. Something warned him not to do that.

His splinted hand was buried under the weight of his left leg. He squirmed around, easing it out to the side.

"You hang on now, chief. It'll take them a few minutes to get here. You hang on . . . not gonna let anything happen to you . . . no siree," Danny said in a terrified babble. "Now Hannah would be all over me if something happened to you."

He reached down to pull the collar of Royce's coat up, and cupped a hand gently onto the back of his friend's head.

Royce began to try to say something. Danny moved down to look in his eyes. "You be still and quiet now . . . like you wanted me to do awhile ago."

"Randa . . ." Royce mumbled.

"Yeah . . . I've got Jake bringing her."

"Hurry, Danny!"

CHAPTER SIXTY-FIVE

"I've got to be honest with you now, Miss Randa," Jake began.

Her heart sank to an even lower depth.

"We've been working over at the Silcox house this morning. We pulled down the crime scene tape and set up a stakeout, a sort of trap, out in front of the place hoping Silcox might be interested in getting his mail today.

"Sheriff even hung some big ole stuffed envelopes out there onto the mailbox. You know, as bait. Then the call came in about your trailer.

"Sheriff believes Silcox may have set the fire thinking everybody over there at his place would jump in their cars and come runnin' over here . . . which we did . . . all except two . . . Sheriff and Danny."

"You mean you left them there alone? Are you crazy? I don't know a lot about your work, but that sounds just plain crazy to me. Against a maniac like Silcox?"

"Sheriff'll take care of Silcox, I betcha," Jake said.

Randa looked at him with doubtful eyes.

"He wanted me to bring you to your trailer, and stay to help you."

"What does this call mean?" she asked.

"I don't know," he said sheepishly.

"Yes you do!" she shouted.

As they approached the Silcox house, she brought her attention quickly from Jake to the action in the road up ahead.

An ambulance was positioned across both lanes of the narrow highway, its lights swirling, back doors open . . . waiting. Around to the side, a white-sheeted clump lay across the double yellow line.

Others were arriving now; T.B.I., a car marked Medical Examiner, neighbors. People seemed to be in individual groups, each discussing their relevance to the situation. All of them ignoring the white clump in the road.

Jake whirled the blue lights on top of the patrol car as they pulled around the ambulance up into the Silcox lane.

"Hold on," he said over his shoulder to Randa as he stepped out of the car.

Two medics ran up to him, giving instructions and pointing directions.

Where in the name of God is Royce? Randa whispered to herself.

Jake opened the car door to say, "Stay right here, I'll be back in a minute."

Moments later, Danny came running through the slushy snow. He opened the car door next to her and bent down in a half squat, almost kneeling. Randa grabbed for his hand.

"Something's happened," Danny began.

"Where's Royce?" she shouted into his face.

"We got Silcox," he pointed to the white sheet in the road.

Randa couldn't help having a sense of relief. How odd to have a feeling of exhilaration over someone's death. They would be free now. No more guard situations. Donna-Dean would be free to live her life unharmed.

"But . . ." Danny reached out to touch her arm. "Silcox was able to fire off one shot . . . it hit Royce in the lower part of his chest. The medics are up there gettin' him ready to load into this ambulance. He wants to see you."

Randa jumped out of the car, almost knocking Danny over backwards. She began to run up the lane mumbling, "Oh, my God in Heaven! Oh, my God in Heaven!" Danny hurried behind her.

"Lord . . . don't do this to us," Randa whispered. "Please don't take this man, now that you've brought him into my life . . . into this child's life. Please help him."

The shock was numbing. Her tears almost froze onto her face. Danny was beside her now. He steadied her with his arm as they ran through icy brush.

She saw Royce. Face down. The medics were hovering over him trying to get him stable enough to move onto the board they would use to lift him. They had cut his black prairie coat away from his body, not realizing that the previous evening he had wrapped her in it to watch the snow.

Randa tried to see if he was moving; a foot, an arm. Nothing. They had probably warned him to lay still.

"What happened here, Danny?" she asked.

"Beatin-ist thing I ever saw," Danny hurriedly told the story realizing he would soon lose her attention.

"Where was his vest? Danny, you know he always wears that bullet-proof vest?"

Danny jerked open his jacket.

"He made me wear it. Had a big fit for me to put it on. For Hannah," Danny's voice cracked. "He joked about not being able to handle her if I got shot."

In a moment everyone stepped back to allow Danny and Randa to walk toward Royce. Danny pushed her out in front so Royce could see her. She knelt down into the mud and leaned in to him.

"Royce . . ." she whispered to his closed eyes. "It's Randa," she took his cold, muddy hand in hers. He opened his eyes. They were weak . . . too weak, she thought. He struggled to look up at her.

"Sorry . . . about the trailer," his voice sounded as if it belonged to a space alien.

"I . . ." he trailed off.

Randa raised herself up as the ambulance crew moved in to turn Royce over.

"Tell them I'm going with him to the hospital," she said to Danny. "They need to contact Brodie Caldwell."

"Don't worry about Donna-Dean. I'll get her after school and take her home with me," he offered.

"You might ask Miss Mattie if she would keep her tonight."

"Now you know Hannah would be very mad at me for that."

"Danny, don't you dare tell them about Royce . . . not yet. And don't tell Donna-Dean about her daddy. I just don't know what to say to her about all of this. I'm not sure what to say to myself."

One of the medics shouted, "On my count . . . one . . . two . . . three," and they lifted Royce. The move across the yard was carefully orchestrated.

"Say a prayer for him, Danny," Randa said

"Oh, I've been doing that since he hit the ground."

As Randa waited for them to position Royce in the ambulance, she heard his familiar groans of pain. She wished this were as simple as a smash from a rat trap.

Danny had begun a heated negotiation over Randa riding with them in the ambulance. His argument was rooted in the thought that Royce would want her to be with him.

One of the medics offered her a hand up into the roaring beast that would soon race them down the highway toward Brandensburg.

CHAPTER SIXTY-SIX

Inside the ambulance, Randa inched herself past all sorts of built-in equipment. Knobs, levers, and suspended things poked at her back.

The one medic who would ride in a swivel chair at Royce's head, found her a place to sit on a cushioned bench to the right, and motioned for her to buckle the seat belt. The doors were slammed shut at the tip of Royce's muddy boots.

They had anchored him on to the board with some sort of head-band type apparatus. Randa leaned down to just above his ear. "Royce . . ." she gripped his arm, feeling for a sign of life. "I'm going to stay with you. Hold on now."

She leaned closer. The medic was pulling an oxygen mask away from its storage place on the wall. She noticed Royce had tears in his eyes.

"I want you to know . . . I love you," he said as the oxygen mask came down across his words.

"I love you too," Randa said. "I've been waiting for just the right moment to tell you that."

She drew his good hand close to her, and pushed the mud spattered ringlets of hair away from his face. The oxygen seemed to work magic. His eyes became clear and his breathing more settled.

Lord, please don't take this man . . . this good, loving man, Randa thought. You've got millions of good men up there, you don't need this one. Please leave him here. He's mine.

"Is he your husband?" the medic asked.

"I'm working on it," she replied. Royce gripped her hand tightly, as if to say 'I heard that.' She smiled knowing that he would not remember any of this.

In the background, someone, somewhere was radioing ahead "Transporting County Two . . . . repeat County Two is down, and we are transporting . . . 32-year-old, male, stabilized en route. Requesting Dr. Brodie Caldwell receive us in the E.R. portico."

Randa assumed County Two was their term for the County Sheriff . . . County One was possibly the Mayor. At any rate, they had just answered one of her burning questions. In their brief time together, she had not learned how old he was. 32 . . . how perfect.

In what seemed like only moments later, they roared under the canopy at the emergency room entrance to the hospital. Brodie was there, as the ambulance doors were swung open. He reached a hand in to help her down.

"This is it, Brodie," Randa said.

The two of them stepped back, allowing the medics to slide Royce out into the cold air. Brodie hovered over him and put a reassuring hand on his brow.

"The dispatcher said the wound was in his chest. Which side?" he asked Randa as the medics quickly sped Royce into the building.

Randa juggled the question in her mind. Right . . . left . . . his right facing me . . . facing you, what?

"It's his right side. Not his heart side," she stuttered her reply.

"Brodie?" she grabbed the sleeve of his lab coat. "Don't let him die."

"I'll fix him up," he promised.

"He and Danny were in some sort of shootout with Robert Silcox. Danny shot and killed Silcox."

Brodie stepped over to Royce and removed the oxygen mask. He used his pen light to shine across Royce's eyes. As he put his fingers under the jawline to find the pulse, she saw that familiar smile inch its way across Royce's face.

In his best alien voice, Royce said, "Hey, Bro."

CHAPTER SIXTY-SEVEN

If one more nurse asks me if I'm okay, I may slap her, Randa thought. The hospital staff had quickly realized that she was some sort of interested party in Royce's life.

"I'm fine," she tried yet another version of her smile to Brodie's nurse, thinking she should be nominated for an Emmy for keeping her cool with these E.R. people.

Randa watched Danny take charge, as Royce would have expected him to do. He was explaining, directing, making decisions, calling people and finding time to console her all the while. Now, he was with Royce and Brodie in the exam room.

Randa had positioned herself at the far end of the waiting room to sit in silence. Danny came to find her, followed by an older gentleman.

"Miss Randa, this is Judge Preston Ferrell. He would like to meet you," Danny stepped away to allow them privacy.

"Miss Stratton . . . Randa," he clasped both of his leather, baseball mitt hands around her hand, "I am so glad to meet you. I want to thank you so much for all you have been doing."

"You're very welcome."

"I've just spent a few minutes with Royce. He had them call me over here, and I was surprised to hear what he was struggling to say. Maybe you can fill me in," he began to pull off his long, camel overcoat to sit in the chair beside her.

"He's terribly worried about two things . . . you, and the little girl. He's begging me not to put her into foster care. But, to tell you the truth, he's not going to be able to care for her."

"I will take care of Donna-Dean," Randa vowed. "And, I'll take care of Royce."

"Well, he tells me you pretty much need some care yourself, at the moment," Judge Ferrell smiled.

"At the moment, I am as homeless as Donna-Dean, but I will be making some tentative arrangements with Miss Mattie Carnes, my teaching partner, for . . ."

"Royce says he wants to adopt this child."

"Really."

"What do you think about that?"

"I could tell that might have been in the back of his mind. And, if you were to take her away now, while he's down, that would be a terrible blow to him."

"I just don't . . ." the Judge began.

"Royce has showered this child with a kind of love she's never had. She has soaked up his every word, and every hug he has given her, over these past few days. She has never had anyone hold her, and rock her, or read to her, or dance around with her in their arms, or to even play in the snow with her. She has been starved for this kind of attention," Randa explained.

"You know that I warned y'all about getting involved," he smiled.

"But," she pointed a finger to his face, "this so-called involvement has been some sort of destiny."

"How's that?"

"Royce and I are two lonely people who have had an opportunity to meet over this child's situation. I'll admit that we have been emotionally caught up in this from the beginning, but who's to say that our emotions are not genuine. I think that after only four days, I have been able to see this man's heart and soul. He wears them right out there on his sleeve. He's quite a guy."

"He is that," Judge Ferrell laughingly agreed. "He's some sort of handsome prince of the mountain around here, and we're all blessed that he came back home to us. He's smart as a whip. He's sharp as a tack. He's sly as a damn fox when he needs to be. But, should he take on being this child's father?"

"I don't know how the legal system views fatherhood, or what you usually require to make that decision," Randa said, "but it seems to me that any old Joe out here can, technically, be a father. Obviously, Mr.

Robert Silcox didn't meet anyone's standards for being a father, but he was blessed with the opportunity."

"Legally, the first drawback for Royce is that he is a single man. Secondly, he has a dangerous job . . . validated by the fact that he's lying in there with a gunshot wound. Now this child is going to be disturbed over that."

"Judge . . . I can't lay a case here without Royce. I'm ready to attest to the fact that you could not find a more loving home situation for this child. Whatever her needs might be for the rest of her life, he would gladly meet them."

"Honey . . . I'll tell you that I've known Royce Hawkins for years. You've discovered what the whole town knows. He's a sweet, Christian man who can accomplish anything he sets out to do. I'll do all I can do on his behalf, and that's what I've promised him in there."

"Would you please let Donna-Dean stay with us until he gets back on his feet? I don't think he could take losing her, now," Randa said.

"You are both well-educated, mature adults," he continued. "And you both have the sense to realize this child is not just a kitten you've found on the side of the road. I just want your decisions to be based in reality, rather than in the fantasy of creating a beautiful dream life for her."

"Wouldn't that be behind anyone's desire to adopt a child . . . to give that child a beautiful life?" she gave him a quizzical look.

"Well, you have to know that you are not creating a false commitment. For all of you, this might seem to be the perfect answer to the problem right now. But, what will your feelings be in about seven or eight years from now, when this child is in her teens and facing some of the problems she may suffer from this abusive relationship she's been in?" he asked.

"Royce is a careful thinker and planner; in fact he doesn't leave a stone unturned. The threat of losing her any day has put pressure on him to think things through quickly. Would this decision have been a better one, or a more sincere one, if he had made it after months of thought?"

"No, not particularly," he said.

"You have to consider, too, that if you take her away from him now, that will be another loss she will have to deal with."

"And, where do you stand in this picture?" he smiled at her.

"Well I'm hoping to be there . . . to help, however I can."

"Do you think he wants . . ."

"Hold on," Randa interrupted, "only he knows what he wants," she smiled.

"It seems to me that Royce has been lucky enough to have two ladies fall into his life all at once."

"It's as simple as that, Judge," Randa smiled.

"I have tried to relieve his fears," he continued. "I've told him that I won't make a change with Donna-Dean. I'll let him get all patched up and get on the mend, and then we'll sit down and talk about the legal stuff. So . . . you can reassure him that I will handle this with the social workers. I think they are trying to make sure there is no family for her out there. Just don't tell him he's a father . . . yet."

"I would be more than glad for you to be the one to give him that news, when the time comes," she said.

"In the meantime, you have your work cut out for you taking care of the two of them."

"Right now, I'm truly concerned about him," she admitted.

"He had tears streaming down his face the whole time he was struggling to speak to me. I don't know if he was in a lot of pain or . . ."

"This has all come down pretty hard on him," Randa said.

Brodie approached them from the hallway, followed by Danny.

"I must go now, Randa," the judge said, taking his cue to leave. "It was a pleasure meeting you. I'll keep all of you in my prayers. If I can help in any way, just give me a call," he reached over to pat her hand. "Brodie," he said as he pulled on his coat, "I know you'll take good care of Royce for us."

Danny walked away with Judge Ferrell, toward the automatic doors leading outside.

Brodie offered Randa his hand.

"Would you like to see Royce? He sure would like to see you."

"How is he?" she asked.

"I've got him stabilized. I've given him a powerful pain killer, so he's pretty mellow now. He may close his eyes while you are there, but that doesn't mean anything," he explained as they walked toward the exam room.

"The bullet has done some internal damage, to the back side of his lung, in and around his liver. He has some internal bleeding that has to be stopped. Since this involves damage to one lung, the other lung is compensating.

"I have made the decision to transport him by Life Flight to the University Hospital in Knoxville. I've chosen a lung specialist there, who will be ready to get him into surgery as soon as we get there. Life Flight will be here in about an hour. Do you want to go with us?"

"Yes."

"We'll need to be ready as soon as they get here, so if you need to make any arrangements, maybe you should do that now. I've told Royce everything and I believe he understands. He can't seem to stop crying . . . I think he's scared," Brodie said.

"How bad is this? We aren't going to lose him, are we?" Randa asked, fearing his answer.

"Well this surgery isn't anything for me to take on. I'm out of my league here, so that's why I want to get him on down to Knoxville. I'll know more after they have had a chance to make an evaluation. I'm going to assist in the surgery . . . I'm not going to let anything happen to him."

Randa walked into the room. Royce was positioned on his side. An oxygen line fit snugly into his nose, and an I.V. rigging had been inserted into the vein on his right hand.

Brodie had removed the muddy splint on his broken fingers. The white tape shown brightly as the hand lay across the covers.

"Royce . . . ?" she said softly, leaning down to his face. His eyes remained closed. Tears ran down each cheek.

"Royce?" No response. She looked at Brodie.

"Royce?" Brodie said, reaching over to massage his patient's shoulder. "Come on back to us, bud . . . Randa's here."

Royce opened his eyes slowly, but he seemed to be far away in another galaxy. She stroked his hair back from his forehead.

"He'll be with you in a minute, just keep talking. He can hear you." Brodie left them alone. The ticking of the I.V. machine seemed to fill the silence.

"Royce?" she said. "Don't cry . . . everything is going to be okay. I'm going to stay with you. I won't leave you," she said hoping for a response.

"I love you," she continued. "I love you," she said a bit louder as she pressed his good hand three times, in a sort of touch language.

He rolled his eyes toward her.

"Don't cry. You've got to gather all of the strength you can."

He looked helpless and defeated. He could not glance his eyes much higher than the top of the bed railing.

"Don't worry about me, or Donna-Dean, or Gabriel. We've got arrangements made," she lied. "I'm going to stay right with you during all of this. You are all that matters to me."

"I love you," he said hoarsely. "I've loved you for a long time."

She smiled at his misconception.

"Well, it took you long enough to tell me," she smiled down at him.

"Since our first date," he said, the hoarse whisper weakening.

"We've only had one date," she said raising his hand up to kiss his fingers.

"It was that one," he drifted back to sleep.

"You rest now . . . I'll be right here."

CHAPTER SIXTY-EIGHT

Danny made the suggestion that he get Randa's Jeep out of the Sheriff's Department impound lot, and drive it down to her in Knoxville. He said would get somebody to follow him in the patrol car, and they could offer Brodie a ride back to Brandensburg.

That all sounded like the right thing to do. She could tell there was a numbness to her response.

"Whatever, Danny. Whatever," she found herself not really caring who did what. Only Royce mattered.

Danny had continued to help greatly. He had spoken to Miss Mattie and the two of them had mapped out plans for the care of Donna-Dean, including explaining to her about Royce.

Danny said he would be going to Royce's to get Donna-Dean's clothes and did she want to go with him to get clothes for herself.

Why . . . she thought. Why does he keep saying clothes, clothes. This isn't a vacation I'm going on here, Danny. Clothes are of no concern to me now. She simply could not pull her mind away from Royce.

The waiting room people ran to the front windows when Life Flight arrived, landing within its circle on the parking lot.

"Oh God," she said to Danny.

"They are getting him ready to board, now," Danny said leading her toward the exam room. As they neared the doorway the medical team pushed their gurney, with Royce strapped to it, out in front of them.

"Hey . . ." she leaned over him. "I'm here. Who would have thought you would be taking me on a helicopter ride."

Royce looked up at her with surprising clarity. "Let's go get this done," he said.

"I love you. Donna-Dean loves you too. She would want you to know that."

The medics stepped around her to reposition the gurney to move it quickly down the hallway.

Brodie came up to grab Randa's elbow. He had changed from his hospital scrubs to real clothes, topped by a trench coat.

Clothes. Again the focus of her mind seemed redirected to clothes.

As they stepped in behind the gurney to follow the medics out across the parking lot, Brodie said, "I've asked him if he wants me to call his sister. He said no. She sure will be mad at me if I don't call."

"She loves him and she needs to know. Call her. You can tell both of them that I made you do it," Randa said.

They waited outside the automatic doors and watched as the Life Flight team sped out across the parking lot. It seemed like an eternity before they motioned for Brodie and Randa to come forward for boarding.

Inside, the helicopter was a medical madness. Shouts from one person to another, arms reaching back and forth across Royce. Three entire bodies huddled near his head, doing something with oxygen.

As the rotor above them revved itself to the fullest, the helicopter seemed to lunge forward like some sort of animal trying to raise itself on trembling legs. From where she was strapped in place to the side of this whirling machine, Randa could reach out to touch Royce's foot. She held it hoping, somehow, he would know it was her.

Brodie made several moves out of his seat to check, and recheck Royce.

"He's doing well," he yelled his report to Randa.

Good, she thought. All else is a nightmare.

CHAPTER SIXTY-NINE

My mind is so tired, Randa thought. It's come from some maddening overdrive, down to a hollow numbness. I need to sit . . . here, in yet another hospital waiting room. Bend and sit, she coached herself. Breathe. Blink. Swallow. Concentrate.

So much to think through. A year's worth of emotions had been packed into a few hours on the clock. The trailer, burned . . . gone; Robert Silcox, shot . . . gone; Royce, shot . . . gone now into a life or death surgery.

And somewhere back in the midst of this day, he had told her that he loved her. Imagine that!

She leaned her head back against the cold, concrete wall behind the waiting room chair. Be still and quiet. Try to relax mind, body, and soul.

*   *   *

It was Saturday afternoon. The lake was glistening, clear and blue under clusters of big white, puffy clouds. The setting was perfect, as if she had ordered and paid a great deal of money for it like everything else. After all of their worrying, and what ifs about the weather, it was a perfect day for an outdoor wedding.

Her dress was wonderful. After changing her mind so many times, she now felt she could not have made a better choice. If all else fell apart today, at least she knew she would dazzle them all in this dress with its long, scalloped train.

She dressed in the guest room where she and Donna-Dean had slept when they first came to stay with Royce. Becca had helped her get into her new undergarments and the long slip with layers of crinoline that would make her dress stand out. Her hose were antique white, one leg topped with the blue garter that had been one of Becca's gifts in the wicker bride's basket she had fixed for her.

Earlier, they had worked to get her hair pulled back into a french braid. Becca had a knack for that sort of thing. The crowning touch was the circle of flowers headband with the veil falling off to her shoulders.

Becca checked and re-checked everything. She seemed to be very excited to be Randa's Matron of Honor, and she looked quite beautiful in her long, teal blue bridesmaid's dress.

As they gathered to walk out of the french doors. Becca gave her a big hug and handed her the bridal bouquet. Derrick stepped proudly to her side. He was handsome in his morning coat tuxedo . . . its cravat and vest covering his paunchy belly. He seemed teary-eyed at giving her away.

"You are so beautiful," he said. "It just takes my breath away." He tucked her arm around his elbow.

Becca preceded them out the door as the wedding music began. From the patio they could look out over the wedding guests who had been cordially invited to attend. The ceremony would be in a grove of pine trees near the boat dock.

As Derrick led her to the top of the stone steps, Donna-Dean stepped out to follow behind Becca. She looked so cute in her matching teal blue junior bridesmaid's dress. All morning she had carefully practiced walking down the steps in her new "heels."

When Randa stepped down onto the first tier of steps, she looked back over her shoulder. Royce was standing back there, by himself, leaning over the foot he had propped up on the patio wall. He gave her a nod, and tipped his Smokey-the-Bear hat at her. He knew she would like that.

She turned her attention back to Derrick, who seemed to be hurrying her on down to the next step. Don't fall, she reminded herself as she looked ahead to the minister.

She tried to look at the guests. Everyone was there. She had been afraid no one would come. Miss Mattie was in her new outfit she had bought for the occasion. Danny and his wife were there. Hannah looked lovely in her dress. She had been given the job of holding reign on Gabriel, who was sporting a black bow tie around his neck.

At the altar her groom stood facing the lake. Shouldn't he be facing me, Randa thought? Somebody should tell him to turn around toward me.

As they approached, Randa looked to the groom's side of the aisle. How odd. Mr. and Mrs. Silcox were standing there. They decided to come after all, she thought. There had been a big to-do over whether or not they would be able to make it.

As the Wedding March blared from the boom box placed near the minister's feet, Derrick and Randa came alongside the groom. Derrick carefully took Randa's hand and offered it to . . . after several embarrassing seconds passed, he finally turned around toward her . . . it was DAVID-JACK SILCOX!

"Randa . . . ," Brodie said softly.

"Randa . . . ," he said again, gently shaking her shoulder. Randa jerked herself awake, jumping up in the waiting room chair where she last remembered leaning her head back against the wall and closing her eyes.

"The surgery is over . . . he did great," Brodie announced. "Everything looks good. He'll be in recovery for a couple of hours. Randa, don't you want to go home and come back down in the morning?"

"No . . . I'll stay," she said, hoping to the Good Lord in Heaven that Brodie had not been able to see her dream.

CHAPTER SEVENTY

Randa watched the woman from the moment she came through the automatic doors. Someone new to stare at. This one had a long, elegant stride that drew every eye. Her purse hung from a gold chain and thumped her form-fitting jeans stuffed inside her black leather boots.

A sweet, delicate face was cuddled into a curly, woolly, stringy-type hot pink jacket. Randa thought of the chenille bath mat she had grown up with in her mother's house.

Someone in the chair by the Coke machine cattily muttered, "Snow bunny."

Oh no, Randa thought. When had Brodie made the call to Becca? How long ago? Would she have been able to get a flight and be here by now? Surely not . . . not this . . . not yet.

Randa strained to hear what this woman was saying to the nurses at the waiting room desk. One of the nurses picked up the telephone to make a call, and was soon passing the receiver over the counter to the snow bunny. The roar from the sick and hurting humankind waiting their turn to be treated made it impossible to hear what she was saying on the phone.

Randa continued to watch as this mystery lady returned the phone to the nurse. Now she walked over toward the double doors leading to the exam rooms. The heels of her leather boots made a prissy trip-trot, trip-trot sound with each step she took. She turned and faced her audience now, and lifted her eyes to return their stares.

In a moment, the double doors swung open and she stepped quickly into a big bear hug from Dr. Brodie Caldwell. His head seemed to be buried in the fluff of the stringy hot pink jacket.

A panic attack bolted its way through Randa's tired mind, planting the idea to run away, go, get out of here. Where did Danny say he had parked her car? Lot A. Go . . . quick. They'll never miss you.

As she dug in her purse for her car keys, Royce said, "Stay." A clear voice . . . not that raspy, alien voice he had when he came here, but his same-ole-self voice rattled through her gray matter asking her to, "Stay."

He would be hurt if I left, she reasoned. He would cry. Leaving would not be good. Stay and face the music, whatever the tune.

Things would be different now. Besides Donna-Dean, this was the other woman in Royce's life. Could she affect their relationship? This new love they had discovered might not be strong enough to withstand any strong winds blowing in from Colorado.

Randa moved to another seat across the waiting room, far from the double doors. Maybe I could send a note in to Royce telling him I will be back tomorrow, she pondered. No. That wouldn't work. Somehow she knew he would be hurt. Or, maybe not. Now that "she" was here, he might not mind at all. No . . . the voice in her head argued.

The child in the arms of the woman next to her, began to scream . . . in pain, or in temperament. Shut up, Randa thought, I'm working on a mental conflict here. She grinned at the image of the teacher within thinking a child should "shut up."

Soon, the double doors opened for nurses to push out a patient in a wheel chair. Brodie was following behind them. He looked around the waiting room, searching for her. Oh God, here he comes.

"Randa?" he said. "Let's go to the office back here." He held out his hand to lead her. All of her fellow waiting room onlookers stared at them. She could imagine what they were thinking about this doctor holding her by the hand, leading her away. She would like to have told them she didn't need this doctor . . . she had a sheriff waiting for her back there.

Pulling a chair up close to the desk, Brodie said "You are worn out, I can tell. It's been quite a day. But, we've all made it. We've saved our boy."

"Thank you for being such a sweet friend to him. I know he thinks the world of you," Randa said.

"I'll have to admit, I was a bit worried. This could have done him in."

"You've saved his life."

"I think that honor will have to go to Danny," Brodie said.

"Oh God. Yes." Not once had she thought to thank Danny.

"I'm going to let you go in to see Royce. Now . . ."

Randa gave herself a mental note to hold on tight . . . something was coming.

"Becca has just gotten here. She's in there with him."

"Oh, well I shouldn't go . . . ." Randa stammered.

"Before I took her in, I spent quite some time explaining things. I've told her what I know about Donna-Dean, and the murders, and how this shooting came about. Of course, Danny will want to talk with her."

"How did she take it all?" Randa asked.

"Well, like all of us, she was a little overwhelmed."

"Royce has told her about you," Brodie smiled.

"Uh oh," she said.

"He's still under some powerful pain medication, but you seem to be what he wants to talk about. He was very proud to be telling her about how you two met and . . ." Brodie touched her arm. "He's told her that he is in love with you."

"Uh oh," Randa repeated.

"Now . . . don't worry . . . he knows how best to handle Becca. He knows she appreciates honesty. He's selling you like a used car salesman would sell a pink Cadillac," Brodie laughed.

"I don't know if he should be jumping ahead of himself like that," Randa said.

"What do you mean?"

"We've only known each other for what . . . a week now! That's going to stick out like a sore thumb with Becca. Because he was shot, she may think he was sort of forced into these feelings."

"Randa, this is Royce. I think you know he wouldn't force himself to say anything he didn't mean."

"I'm not saying he didn't mean it. In fact, I'm praying to Almighty Jesus that he won't change his mind."

"I don't think that will happen," he said. "Now what do you think about meeting Becca? Now. Right now. Are you ready?"

"I look like hell," Randa said.

"So do I. So does Royce. We've all spent the day in the Twilight Zone, or Oz, definitely somewhere over the rainbow."

"Okay. I'm ready. Let me jump into the deep end of the pool. This awful hair and sweaty clothes will make quite a first impression."

"Royce has already painted quite a beautiful picture of you. I think that will be what she will always remember . . . I know I will," he reached out for her hand to lead her down the back corridor to the recovery room.

CHAPTER SEVENTY-ONE

The hot pink jacket lay on the chair by the bed. Becca was wearing a white blouse topped with a suede vest. She stood at the head of the bed, when Brodie opened the door.

"Randa." Becca came toward her with her hand outstretched. "Royce has told me so much about you."

Randa expected a wimpy, socialite's hand shake that would rest like a cold fish in her palm. But, no, this was a forthright glad-to-meet-you grip.

"You'll have to excuse the way I look . . ." Randa began.

"Thank you for taking such good care of this guy," Becca smiled what seemed to be a genuine smile as she pulled Randa over to Royce. Becca stepped back alongside of Brodie. Randa looked down to meet Royce's smiling eyes.

"Hey . . ." she whispered.

Royce reached a weak hand up to the bed rail for her to hold.

"How are you?" Randa asked.

"I feel like something has gone straight through me."

"It did. It was a bullet," Brodie said as he stepped over to adjust a heart monitor and shine his pen light into Royce's eyes.

"Brodie . . . you keep doing that! You're going to make me go blind. Why do you keep looking at my eyes?" Royce fussed.

"He's back!" Brodie announced.

CHAPTER SEVENTY-TWO

Becca came out of the room followed by Randa.

"He's told me quite a story," Becca said laughingly. "Quite a fascinating story."

"It's been an adventure," Randa admitted. "One that doesn't seem to end."

"He says that he loves you, Randa," Becca got right to the point.

"And I'm flattered by that," Randa admitted.

"Love doesn't come easy for Royce," Becca said.

"These past few days, since we've met, have been packed with lots of emotional things. Especially involving this little girl," Randa explained as they walked toward the waiting room. "Maybe everything, including getting shot, has made him a little vulnerable."

"Oh, I believe he means it. Especially since he's told me. It's just love at first sight . . . buried in this horrible crime," Becca said, patting Randa's arm.

Randa gave a sigh. This was going remarkably well.

"I truly care for him, too. And I would love to do cartwheels down this hallway because we have declared our love for each other. But, I don't have the strength. I'm so tired I could drop," Randa admitted.

Brodie walked up behind them, hearing her last remark.

"Why don't we all go out and get a decent supper, and I'll try to talk you into going home to get some rest?"

"What home, Brodie?" Randa said.

"Well, go to Miss Mattie's," he added.

"Did Royce tell you this Silcox man burned out Randa's trailer this morning?" Brodie said to Becca.

"Oh my Lord," she replied. "Why don't you plan to stay on at Royce's . . . with me? I don't want to be there by myself," Becca offered.

"Thanks, but I really need to be with Donna-Dean. She needs to be told about Royce, before she hears it from the other children at school."

"Bring her on back to Royce's with you. I would love to meet her. And, I want to visit with you as much as I can while I'm here. Royce would like that," Becca pleaded.

This sounds too good to be true, Randa thought. There has to be a hitch in here somewhere. Was it truly possible that this woman was as sweet as her brother?

"I'm torn between what I want to do, and what I need to do. My mind tells me to do one thing, and my heart tells me to do something else," Randa said.

"Let's go eat," Brodie whined.

"Maybe I'll stay here with Royce. Y'all could bring me something to eat."

"Randa, you need a good hearty meal. I'll bet you haven't had anything to eat all day. Royce is going to be fed intravenous sugar water. He's on a sedative that will soon convince him he's in Paris, France having filet mignon. Then he'll be going back to sleep," Brodie explained.

"Okay, you win. But, I think I want to follow you in my car. If I get a spurt of energy, I want to stop by the mall to get a few things. Maybe I can think more clearly when I get out of here. I need to go back in there to say goodbye to Royce."

Randa stepped away, leaving Becca and Brodie staring after her.

When Randa came through the recovery room door, Royce was raising himself up on one arm, then trying to rise up into a sitting position.

"Hold on, don't try to do too much," Randa warned.

"I've rolled all around trying to get comfortable."

"Royce, I think I will go with Brodie and Becca to get something to eat," she said.

"Okay, but don't forget to come back," he smiled. Randa could see he was quite sedated.

"You have a good nap," she leaned down to kiss him softly and to stroke his forehead for several minutes until he was sleeping.

He has curly hair, she thought. Must be from all the time it spends under that Smokey-the-Bear hat.

CHAPTER SEVENTY-THREE

"Let me make two quick phone calls, then I'll join you," Randa begged of Brodie who was jingling Becca's rental car keys in front of her.

At the pay phone, she dug into her purse to find change and her phone card. Miss Mattie soon answered, quite eager to hear the news from Royce.

"He's in the recovery room. Everything went fine. His sister has gotten here from Colorado," Randa hurriedly spilled out as much as she knew. "How's Donna-Dean?"

"She's been hysterical. I think I will call Danny to come help me with her. He offered to do that if I thought I needed him."

"Let me talk to her," Randa asked.

After some shuffling of the telephone, Donna-Dean said, "Miss Randa? Where are you?" she cried.

"I'm here at the hospital. Sheriff Royce was hurt today and I had to bring him to Dr. Brodie to get fixed up. He had to have an operation."

"You gotta bring me there too," she shouted.

"You need to stay with Miss Mattie until I can get back there. You wouldn't want me to leave Sheriff Royce right now. I want you to settle down and help Miss Mattie take care of you. Sheriff Royce would want you to do that. I'll get there as soon as I can leave him, okay? Let me talk back to Miss Mattie," Randa said.

Mattie was back on the phone.

"Randa, you know you're both welcome to stay here with me for as long as you need to. Can you get here tonight, to get some rest? I know you must be exhausted."

"I can't leave him . . . not yet. They are going to get him to a room later on tonight. I think I should call Danny. I'll have him get back with you. Mattie, you will need to keep the children from talking to Donna-Dean about this shoot-out with her daddy . . . at least for tomorrow, until I can get with her to explain things. I'm not sure what Royce would want me to tell her," Randa said.

"Sure, honey. You just try to get some rest. Hospitals can get you down when you're just waitin'," Mattie said.

"Thank you for helping us. I know it will mean so much to Royce. I'll call Danny right now," Randa promised.

Moments later she rang Danny's home telephone and soon he was fighting Hannah for the receiver.

"How's he doin'?" Danny asked.

"He's just coming around, sort of. He's come through the surgery just fine. I don't want to leave him, Danny. If I do, I'll be a nervous wreck."

"I imagine," Danny said.

"Mattie is having some difficulty with Donna-Dean. It makes me wish I could be in two places at once."

"I was planning to go over there and get Donna-Dean and bring her here with us, at least for this first night away from y'all. We'll tell her we're having a slumber party . . . and we will. I'll drive her back over to school tomorrow morning."

"Danny, that's wonderful. How sweet of you to do that. She may need to have her clothes from Royce's. You might stop by . . ."

"Whoa . . . I'm one step ahead of you . . . I need to go by to feed Gabriel. I'll take Linda and Hannah, and they can get whatever she needs," Danny said.

"Danny . . . Royce's sister is here."

"She is . . . well, I'll bet he was tickled to see her."

"Yeah, tickled . . . we're tickled," Randa found herself muttering. "Thanks, Danny, for all of your help. If you need Donna-Dean to talk with me in the middle of the night, just call here and ask for Royce's room."

"Okay."

"Danny . . . ?"

"Ma'am?"

"Thank you for saving Royce's life."

CHAPTER SEVENTY-FOUR

Outside the hospital, the cold air blew in crisp gusts across the parking lot. Brodie and Becca walked with Randa to find her Jeep Cherokee, then Randa drove them over to Becca's rental car parked in the 'Doctors Only' parking area near the front of the hospital.

They voted to eat at a nearby O'Charley's restaurant, because Becca remembered their caramel pie.

Randa seemed lost in time and place; actually free, for the moment, from everything . . . but rush hour traffic. It felt good to be sort of floating, in suspension, from worry over Royce, or Donna-Dean, or from what had burned and could never be replaced in the trailer.

At O'Charley's she considered ordering two, or possibly three Strawberry Daiquiri's at the bar, but decided they would make her instantly high. She chose to intoxicate herself on a prime rib dinner, then joined Becca for a round of caramel pie.

The food did give her a power boost. She enjoyed the company, although feeling a bit like a third wheel with these two old friends who were reveling in the life and times of Royce Hawkins as if he were a movie star. But, what else would these two have in common with me, she thought.

They were right in assuming she would be interested in Royce stories. She tried to stifle the feeling that she would rather be hearing these memories from the man himself. If only he were here. It would be point . . . counterpoint.

The mental picture of Becca dressed as Cher, accompanied by little Royce dressed as Sonny Bono, singing "I Got You Babe," for Becca's 6th grade talent show was enlightening.

"Mama ordered those wigs for us from an ad in the back of a movie magazine," Becca laughed. "I remember doing Cher very seriously. Royce just wanted to act like a nut."

I'll file that tidbit away to tease him with someday, Randa thought.

"Do you remember when Royce and I used to make prank telephone calls?" Brodie asked Becca.

"Oh yes. You would dial up some little old lady and very politely ask, 'Is your refrigerator running?' And after she answered 'yes,' you would say, 'Well, you'd better go catch it!' Or, Royce would call all of the grocery stores in town to ask, 'Do y'all have Prince Albert in a can?' They would answer, 'Yes' and then he would say, 'Well, you'd better let him out'." Brodie chuckled between sips of coffee.

"Then there was the summer we went around closing things up in people's mailboxes," he added. "Field mice . . . a cat . . . a rubber snake."

"That was my best friend's cat!" Becca slapped at Brodie's shoulder. "Her family didn't appreciate that at all, and it nearly scared the postman to death."

"Royce should be here to defend himself," Randa said. "I'll bet he would have some stories to tell on you two."

Becca asked Brodie if Royce was still making raids on the prostitution ring operating out at the Bunkhouse Truck Stop.

Brodie laughed. "That one just before Christmas is the last one I've heard him talk about. He arrested Tangee for about the fortieth time."

To Randa he explained, "That's the one who always flings herself all over him, and usually vomits in the patrol car while he's driving her in to jail."

Hmmm . . . Randa thought. More ammunition to tease him with. Randa's mind turned briefly to her brother Derrick. If she were relating stories about their years together, would her eyes sparkle, and fairly radiate love and respect, as Becca's were doing with these recollections of Royce? Would there be any fun times to recall? Probably not.

Derrick grew up secluded in his upstairs bedroom, while she was assigned to the walled-in side porch on the front of the house. They had met at the kitchen table to eat, and occasionally fought each other over who would get to use the bathroom first. They seemed to have one common thread running through them; they had both dearly loved "Mission Impossible."

Derrick had seemed to draw closer to her during their adult years, probably as a result of his therapy. They had formed some sort of makeshift bond when her mom fell ill. He had needed her help so badly she dropped out of college for two semesters. They were good friends now, but would never be soul mates as obviously Becca and Royce were.

"Randa, you are going to go to Brandensburg with me tonight, aren't you?" Becca broke into her thoughts.

"I can't go tonight . . . maybe tomorrow night, if you will extend the invitation?" Randa replied.

"Sure, but don't you think he will be okay tonight?" The question seemed more directed to Brodie.

"He's asked me not to leave him," Randa interjected, "and I've promised him I won't."

The statement fell across the table as if it had been dropped from the waitress' tray; landing hard and washing across to Becca. She seemed disappointed. Her spirits seemed to fall. "Do you want me to stay, too?"

"I was hoping to catch a ride home with you," Brodie pleaded to Becca. "Remember I came down on Life Flight. If you'll take me home, I'll tell you how I'm contemplating my second divorce."

"Bro . . . dee!" Becca's attention was diverted. Brodie shrugged, sheepishly.

Later, in the parking lot they promised Randa to see her early in the morning. Brodie said Royce would be assigned to a room, probably by the time she got back to the hospital. They would stop in to check on him before they headed "up home."

"I'll make sure the nurses have your name as his 'significant other.' That's hospital talk for a person who is going to be assisting the patient. You're not a spouse, or a relative. You're an 'other'. They'll let you sleep on the pull out bed in his room, and use the shower if you want. Now get some rest, and let Royce get some rest, too." He stepped over to hug her. "Thanks for coming down on Life Flight with us."

"Well thank you, Sir, for bringing him back to us," she whispered. "You're not really going to get a divorce, are you?"

"Maybe Becca can talk me out of it," he winked as he got into the passenger side of the car.

Becca, bundled in her hot pink, stringy jacket, waved a quiet goodbye as she slid in under the wheel of the car.

As they backed away, Randa breathed a deep sigh. Freedom . . . for however long it might last, a quiet, settling freedom.

CHAPTER SEVENTY-FIVE

The move from the recovery room had left Royce restless and anxious. He had asked the nurses not to give him a sleeping pill until after Randa got back. But, Brodie had written specific orders for it to be given at nine o'clock. The pill made him feel like he could climb Mt. Everest, and yet so groggy he could barely keep his eyes open.

Randa found her way to the new room at 9:30. She quickly dug through the shopping bags full of things she had bought at the mall, to find the hunter green velour robe she had bought for him. She spread it across the top of the hospital bedspread, then showed him the package of matching pajamas.

"Tomorrow," he muttered rubbing his hand across the soft velour.

"And . . ." Randa said, "This is a present from Donna-Dean." She produced what the box called a Baby Boom Box; a portable radio that was a miniature version of its namesake.

Randa loaded its batteries and dialed around to find his FM oldies station. Recognizing Elton John's "Crocodile Rock," she turned the volume down low and set the radio on his bedside table.

The music seemed to be a magic potion for soothing his soul. Like pulling the thorn from the lion's paw, Randa thought.

She told him she needed to find the shower, put on a sweat suit she had bought for herself, then she would find that pull-out bed Brodie had told her about.

"Guess you might say this will be our first night to sleep together," she laughed to herself, knowing he probably had not heard her.

"Somehow I imagined that would be different from this," he said, as the sleeping pill took him dancin' and prancin' with Elton.

At 2:30 a.m., in the wee hours of the morning, an old lady across the hall began to scream. Randa popped up from the pull-out bed, and immediately looked to see if the sound had awakened Royce. He was beginning to stir.

The screams turned to shouts that brought the nursing staff running from each end of the hallway. Randa giggled as the lady claimed they had lost her false teeth and she wanted them to call 911!

Royce rose up on one elbow . . . fully awake. "What's going on?"

"The lady across the hall must be having a nightmare," Randa said.

"How are you doing over there?" he said, peering through the bed rail the nurse had insisted must be kept in place for the night.

"I'm fine. Are you remembering that Becca will be here early in the morning? You two need a day to be together. Maybe I should go home," she said.

"You and I need to be together," he said wistfully.

"We'll have our days together . . . peaceful days, when we can get back to a real life. Maybe you will ask me out on another date," she suggested.

They both fell back to some semblance of sleep, passing the night away until they were awakened by the bustling noises from the hospital nurses station. The 7 a.m. shift change brought a flurry of activity from the nurses going off, as well as the ones coming on for the day.

CHAPTER SEVENTY-SIX

"Don't leave me," Royce said as Randa helped him sit up on the side of the bed.

"I won't," Randa said pulling on his arm as she edged her shoulder under his.

"I mean . . . ever."

"What are you talking, now?" To Randa's surprise, he began to rise up on wobbly legs.

"I don't want you to ever leave me," he repeated.

She looked into his eyes. A twinkle was trying to work its way through the weakness. Somehow this was an odd gaze, it surrounded her like a warm embrace. She felt herself blush.

"I'll bet you say that to all the girls," she joked.

"There's only one reason I want to stand up," he said tugging to get her around in front of him.

"What's that?"

"I want to hold you in my arms . . . if I can muster enough strength."

"Sure." She snuggled quickly to his chest. His body felt frail and jittery beneath the hospital gown.

He leaned heavily on her, the I.V. line pulling his hand in an odd position.

"Now that I'm drug free, I want you to know that I am fully aware of how many times I've told you that I love you. I remember each time . . . I do," he insisted.

"I remember each of those times, too," she said.

"I do love you. I want you to know I'm quite serious about that, whether I'm facing death or not. You do believe me, don't you?" he worried.

"Yes, I believe you. And I love you, too. Do you remember the times I told you? Some of those times you were off out there in another universe somewhere," she said.

"I . . ." he began. Suddenly, the door swung wide and Brodie appeared.

"What are you doing?" he blustered.

"And he's the one with the medical degree," Royce whispered to Randa. "A little touch therapy, I suppose," he quipped back to Brodie.

"You should have called the nurse."

"I didn't need a nurse. This is the one I needed," Royce said.

"Uh huh. Do you want to go up to I.C.U. . . . see what sort of torture devices they've got up there?" Brodie threatened.

"No . . . no sir . . . I don't," Royce sat down quickly on the bed.

"You shouldn't get up just yet. Maybe later on tonight. I'm surprised you didn't faint." Brodie continued to scold. "Now, if you want to head home in about three days, you're going to have to take things slow and easy."

"Don't get your hackles up, Bro. I just stood up to . . . uh . . . stretch my legs. I wasn't going to take a step."

"Well, I'm glad to see you at least felt like trying to stand. It's just too soon."

"Why do I feel like I've been sawed in half?" Royce asked.

"Because we had to take a slice out of you to get back in there to your lung. You'll have a pretty good scar over here," he pointed.

"Brodie, I need to get back home as soon as I can," Royce said.

"Don't start. You've had major surgery and that just takes something out of you. Your body and mind need the recovery. You don't need to get yourself back into a stressful situation."

"I've got things waitin' on me that I have to handle myself; things I can't bump out of my mind. I'm fixed now. You've done a great job gettin' me back together."

"And you can't undo that good work. You can't have a set back. You can't get any infections going. Now, later on I'll let the nurses give you a bath," Brodie smiled.

"Oh God," Royce said, quickly grabbing Randa's hand. "Don't leave me, ever," he said.

"I won't," she promised.

CHAPTER SEVENTY-SEVEN

The nurses brought what Royce called his "brown" breakfast at 8 a.m. Randa helped him get positioned to eat from the rolling tray table. Brodie had promised him real food today. When she removed the dome-shaped, metal cover it was the same liquid diet as the previous meals.

"I guess I'm supposed to imagine this beef bouillon is a stack of pancakes with a side of hash browns," he said.

"You know, I've been thinking," she began her careful approach. "I probably should go back up to school this morning. Donna-Dean needs some help in understanding all that has happened. I need to talk with her before she hears things from the other children." She took his hand. "Do you think you would be okay here, if I do that?"

"Yeah," he said softly, looking into her eyes with that powerful gaze. "I know she needs you."

"I don't want you to think that I am breaking my promise not to leave you."

He squeezed her hand. "I'm really going to miss you."

"Do you think you would feel up to seeing Donna-Dean this evening?"

"Sure," he smiled.

"Just for a little, short visit. I'm sure it would ease her mind to see you."

"Can you come down as soon as school is out?" he asked.

"We'll try," she promised. "Can you go back to sleep now?"

"I don't know."

"Now don't worry about me leaving . . . you know I'll be back . . . and you probably know that I'm going to be a total wreck all day thinking about you," she smiled.

"I'm missing you already," he said pitifully, as she bent down to kiss the top of his curly hair.

CHAPTER SEVENTY EIGHT

Randa prepared for her hour-long drive up I-40 in the pouring rain. The nurses had been in and out of the room several times during the night to do various things to Royce, and he was totally worn out. The breakfast bouillon made him sleepy, and he was vaguely aware of her kissing him goodbye when she left. It was good that he seemed more interested in sleep.

An hour and a half later, she sped through the valley just as morning sunlight cracked open the dark, jagged clouds. The rain had slacked off now. She was glad it had followed her all the way from Knoxville. It had kept her alert and focused.

The road led past her burned trailer. There it was in a big, black crumbled pile. She decided to let herself cry over it. Big tears formed floating prisms across her eyes. This had all really happened, yesterday morning. It was not a dream. She warned herself to get a grip, as she wiped away the tears from her face on her coat sleeve.

At school, she hurried up the steps into the building, remembering that Royce had given her a kiss right here at this door, just hours before all hell broke loose.

Juggling three shopping bags from Towne West Mall onto one arm, she slammed down on the bar to open one side of the double doors. There was that smell . . . somehow a refreshing reminder that life here had gone on.

Randa appeared in the doorway as Miss Mattie was conducting a spelling bee. All of the children were lined up across the front of the blackboard anxiously awaiting their vocabulary word.

Mattie's face beamed her happiness at Randa's return. Donna-Dean ran quickly from the group to grab Randa around the waist. Mattie waved them on toward Randa's office down the back hallway.

"Donna-Dean, I need to explain to you exactly what has happened with Sheriff Royce. He was shot by your daddy . . . and then your daddy was shot by another officer. Your daddy was shot dead."

Randa waited for a response. There was nothing but eye movements here and there, to avoid Randa's quizzical stare.

"Oh," Donna-Dean said.

"Sheriff Royce had to be taken to the hospital in Knoxville to have an operation, and he's going to be just fine. He wants us to come down there to see him after school. Do you want to go?"

"Uh huh," Donna-Dean used David-Jack favorite response.

"He's anxious to see you."

Randa sat the three bags on her desk in front of Donna-Dean's curious eyes.

"I bought you a dress."

Randa pulled out what the saleslady had called a ballet length, velvet dress with a lace collar, and a sash that tied in the back. Another bag held a white slip with lace across the bottom.

"You got me a princess slip, too?" Donna-Dean shouted.

"And panties, and those cream-colored tights like Hannah wears," Randa spread the things across her desk.

"My ma never would let me have a princess slip. She said piss-ants didn't need princess slips."

"Well, she was wrong, Donna-Dean. You never have been, and you will never be a piss-ant. In fact, there is no such thing as a piss-ant. That was just a mean thing for your ma to say to you."

Donna-Dean's eyes sparkled as she spread her hands across the velvet dress.

"I bought you some new shoes," Randa said. "I had to guess at your size. I hope they fit." Randa took the top off of the shoe box to display one of the black patent leather Mary Jane's with a grosgrain bow across the toe.

"Why'd you git me these thangs?" Donna-Dean asked.

"Because you are a special friend of mine, and I thought you deserved to have a fancy outfit. I thought maybe you could get all dressed up to go see Sheriff Royce. But first, you and I have to do a real good job at our school work today. Do you think we can remember how to do school?" Randa asked.

"Maybe we can 'member'," Donna-Dean smiled, as she headed back to the classroom, seeming to totally ignore that she had been told the news about her daddy.

CHAPTER SEVENTY NINE

Becca settled herself into the leather chair beside Royce's bed, and propped her feet up on the edge of the covers.

"We had a bad storm at the house last night. I let Gabriel sleep at the foot of my bed. He doesn't like thunder and lightening, does he?"

"He's a very good actor," Royce said.

"Are they going to let you get up today, maybe let you sit up in this chair for a while?"

"I don't know. Brodie seems to have a plan he's following on that."

"Brought you some clothes. I didn't know about your shaving gear. I couldn't find anything in your medicine cabinet. John uses one of those battery-operated shavers."

"I've been meaning to try one of those," he said.

"I'll go get you one. I was going to get you a robe, but it looks like Randa was one step ahead of me."

"Now don't go letting that jealous streak come out," he warned.

"Just kidding about the robe. It was very thoughtful of her to do that."

"She's a very thoughtful person," he said.

"I think she has impressed me. Now, I really do want to go get you a shaver. Can you think of anything else you need?"

"Yeah. There is something else. This will surprise you," he said.

"Okay. Surprise me."

"First, I need for you to find my wallet in my pants wherever they are. I did wear pants in here . . . or maybe not. I had pants on when I got shot. I need to find my credit cards. You'll need money."

Becca searched the drawers beneath the night stand. Pants were not there. She checked the drawers beneath the sink. Pants were not there. The only remaining place was the top shelf of the closet by the door. They were there, inside a plastic hospital bag. The wallet had been stuffed inside his boots, and covered around with the blood-stained uniform shirt they had cut off of him.

"Are we going to save this?" she asked.

"No."

"I've brought your underwear and undershirts in the bag over there."

"Thank you, momma," he said.

"Well, sometime during this week, I thought you would feel like wearing underwear."

"Who says I'll be here a week?"

"Brodie."

"Yeah . . . well, I can make him re-think that."

"You can, can you? He saved your life, you owe him this one."

"He knows I want to get back home."

"He knows you want to get back to work. You're on his turf now. You got yourself over into a world where he's sheriff, and you're in his jail. His prisoner so to speak," Becca teased.

"I want a new trial," Royce pouted.

"Here's your wallet. What do you want me to buy?"

"I want you to go somewhere and buy a boy's suit; a nice dark colored suit, with a shirt and tie. Get it to fit a fourteen-year-old boy. I want it for David-Jack. To bury him in."

"Royce . . ." Becca grabbed his hand.

"Don't argue with me. I've been thinking that I'd like to do that for him."

"You are a sweet man, Royce Hawkins," Becca said.

"He died in my arms. You can't imagine what that felt like. I was too late . . . couldn't do a blessed thing for him. So, this is something I can do. I'd like for him to have a decent funeral. Brodie has talked the Rotary into paying for it."

"I'll get something real nice. Do you want a white shirt?" she asked.

"Whatever you think will look good with the suit. I'll bet he didn't have a suit of clothes to his name," Royce said.

"Probably not."

"Oh, Becca, there's something else."

"Another surprise?"

"Yeah. May as well lay this one out there on the table. I've been doing a lot of thinking about Donna-Dean.. . . you know, long range thinking, about what's going to become of her. She needs a good home. Good people to love her."

"No, Royce. There is absolutely no way I can take her. John would just have a fit, if I brought this child home with me. It was nice of you to think of us, but no . . . we're just not in the market for a child."

"Hold on, girl. It's not you I'm thinking about. It's me. I'm thinking about giving her a home. Me and Gabriel. What do you think?"

"Oh . . . Lord . . . Royce . . ." she stammered.

"Wait till you meet her, Becca. She's a cute little thing."

"My goodness, don't you think you're getting a little caught up in all of this? They'll find a good home for her," she said.

"I don't want anyone else to get her. That's why I've made up my mind," he said.

"But . . . why?"

"Because I know the kind of life I want her to have."

"She needs a mother, Royce."

"She'll have a mother, someday. I read someplace that the best thing a father can do for his child is to love its mother."

"But Royce, think. You have to find a wife for you, not a mother for her! You've got your priorities all wrong."

"No, I haven't. It's just that a race is on to keep Donna-Dean from being placed somewhere in a foster home, or to be put in the State Children's Home in Sevierville. I don't want her to have to go through that."

Becca looked at him and shook her head slightly. "You're a sweet man, Royce Hawkins." She got up from the chair to pull on her hot pink jacket.

"Have you thought about her as a teen-ager? What if she has a lot of trouble dealing with the things her father did to her?"

"Yeah, I've run that one up the flagpole. Hopefully by that time she will realize how a good father can overcome a bad one. And even before then, if she needs counseling, or whatever, we'll deal with it."

"What if you have other children come along . . . I mean your birth children . . . not other wards of the state children?"

"Don't you think I could love and take care of a whole houseful of children? Fact is, I might could turn that house of mine into an orphanage."

"What if you are called out to run the roads in the middle of the night? You can't just go off and leave a child with Gabriel!"

"So . . . we're covering all of the 'what ifs'. That's okay. Keep 'em coming. You can't come up with one single thing that I haven't worked out," he said.

"Sweetie, my questions are undoubtedly the ones you will be asked by the powers that be. You have good sensible answers. Your defenses are up. It seems like you have made a strong case for yourself, Mr. Attorney!" she teased.

"We'll see."

"What if you get shot?" she resumed her interrogation.

"Then this incident here has served as a training exercise, hasn't it."

"What if you die?"

"She would be my beneficiary, and you would be her next of kin. I'll will her to you."

"You sure have made a lot of decisions over this past week." They sat in silence for a moment.

"You know that statue of Davy Crockett out on the courthouse lawn?" Becca asked.

"Yeah."

"What does it say on there?"

Royce laughed. "I don't know."

"Yes, you do. We grew up climbing around on him. You've read that thing ever since you were a kid."

"I guess it says 'Davy Crockett,' why?"

"Below that. It has his motto, 'Be sure you're right, then go ahead.' That's good advice for this situation."

"I'm sure I'm right," Royce said. "Sometimes big, important matters have to be decided quickly. Fact is, over time you could talk yourself out of something by hashing and re-hashing all of the pros and cons. Might miss out on a wonderful opportunity by being skeptical."

"So, maybe your motto should be, 'Throw caution to the wind, and jump right in'." They laughed.

"That's good. You can put that on my statue," he said.

"Royce, I've supported you in just about every wild-haired idea you have ever come up with . . . and you know that."

"Does that mean I have your blessing? Could you and John handle being aunt and uncle?"

"That would be fun," Becca smiled.

"You are a sweet woman, Rebecca Hawkins Greer," he reached out and made her slap a high five across his good hand.

Chapter Eighty

"You haven't promised anything to Donna-Dean, have you?" Becca asked.

"Of course not. She's got more to deal with than she can handle right now."

"I've just never thought of you as a father. Of course, I never thought of you as a sheriff either," she joked.

"I know."

She poked a finger onto his forehead. "And, there's one other person's opinion you should consider over mine and that is . . . ?"

"Randa!" They both said the name simultaneously.

After sharing a laugh, Becca asked, "Seriously, have you talked with her, does she know your plans on this?"

"She's probably got a strong suspicion. But, I want to make sure she knows that my relationship with her takes precedent. Regardless of the outcome with Donna-Dean, Randa will be my first priority."

"So, what you are saying, pretty much is, that this is Miss Right?"

"I sure hope so. I think she's pretty much what we've all been praying for."

"Does she know that?" Becca probed further.

"As of two days ago, she knows that I love her. I don't think I should propose to her just yet."

"And when you do propose, is she going to think it's because you want a mother for Donna-Dean?" Becca asked. "She might not want to share you with a child."

"I . . . uh . . . hadn't thought about that. She would know that I . . ."

"Think on this while I'm gone," Becca interrupted. "Randa needs, and deserves to have, a courtship. If she doesn't have that before she's married, she'll never have it. You are supposed to like each other before you go straight into love. It's almost as if you've skipped a step."

Royce drew himself up in the bed. "We did 'like' each other, we just didn't dwell on it."

"I see," Becca nodded.

"The circumstances are odd," he said. "Both of them, all of a sudden, here in my life at once. I don't want to short change either one of them."

"I think you need to stop thinking in terms of 'two'. There is really only one and that has to be Randa. You know that. Don't you?"

"Yeah," he admitted.

"Do you know that deep down, your wanting this storybook family shouldn't be the driving force behind your sudden love for either one of them?" she asked.

"To tell the truth," he began "and Randa doesn't even know this . . . I think I fell in love with her the minute I laid eyes on her walking down the steps of the school, toward me in the parking lot. That was before I ever knew anything about Donna-Dean. When we shook hands, she seemed to have that 'someday my prince will come' look in her eye. And I immediately started to hope to God I could be that prince!"

"I'm probably among a minority of women, mostly those who read Harlequin romances and watch soap operas, who do believe in love at first sight. John always claims he knew immediately when he first saw me, that I was the one he would marry."

"Really?" Royce asked.

"It took longer for me. It wasn't an instant click. As you may well remember, I met John on the rebound from . . . who was that?"

"Lord knows," Royce teased. "There was a whole string of broken hearts. You left quite a trail."

"Daddy is the one who didn't like John; from the moment they met, right on up to the day we told him we were going to move to Colorado."

"Nobody would have been good enough for you in dad's opinion," Royce recalled. "But me, I always supported you in your romances . . .

no matter who you brought home. Even that Harold Proctor who wanted to be an astronaut. Whatever happened to him?"

"He died," Becca said.

"So much for being an astronaut," Royce ducked his head to avoid the sweep of her hand.

"Well, am I going back to Colorado with the thought that I might need to come back for a wedding any day now?"

"Yep. I'd marry her today, if I thought she would say yes and we could drag a minister in here. But that's probably not the right way to go about it. A bit too presumptuous on this our 6th or 7th day of knowing each other."

"I can't wait," Becca said. "Now, when I'm with her I'm going to see her as my sister-in-law. I won't be able to stop grinning."

"Hold on now. We'll scare her to death. Just be cool. Don't go telling her everything I've told you. I'm glad you're getting the opportunity to meet her, and to get to know her. If it happens, it happens, then you can plan to be a sister-in-law. I kinda thought you might be jealous of her."

"I'll try not to be like dad was with John, that she's-not-good-enough thing. If you love her, then I love her."

"That's a deal. Now, go buy me a shaver. And David-Jack's suit. Here's my American Express card. Try not to max it out!"

CHAPTER EIGHTY ONE

After school, Randa drove to Miss Mattie's house where they shared the joy of helping Donna-Dean wiggle and giggle her way into her new clothes.

Donna-Dean continued to be fascinated with the slip and related her mother's "pissant" remark to Miss Mattie, who looked at Randa over the top of her reading glasses.

"Donna-Dean, you look just like a princess in that dress. You do!" Mattie complimented her.

"Like the girls in the wish book?"

"Y-yes," Mattie answered, helping her into the new shoes.

"Do they fit?" Randa asked, kneeling down to feel for the child's toes within each shoe. "They aren't too tight, are they?"

"No. They're just right," Donna-Dean answered, pointing her toe in ballet style.

The dress seemed to give Donna-Dean a new life. Like Cinderella, touched by a magic wand making her come alive, or at least drawing her out from some dark corner.

"I'd just love to see the look on Sheriff Royce's face when you walk in," Mattie said, tying the sash in a giant bow that spread across the girl's back. Donna-Dean giggled in anticipation. "Now you'll need to sit still in the car on the drive down there. You don't want to wrinkle up your dress."

Randa loaded their bags of clothes in the car, in case Becca extended her offer to stay at Royce's. It seemed like they were two vagabonds sleeping here, sleeping there, and moving their few precious belongings around on hobo sticks. She had told herself "this, too, shall pass" so often that it seemed to be some sick joke rather than her philosophy of life.

They said goodbye to Mattie, and backed away amid a beginning snow shower.

CHAPTER EIGHTY-TWO

The snow was falling hard as Randa pulled into the parking lot at the hospital. The radio weatherman declared it was going to "stick," and that bridges and overpasses would become slippery in time for rush hour traffic.

Donna-Dean had fallen asleep and had laid her head over onto the padded car door. She had sat perfectly still for the beginning minutes of the drive, trying very hard to keep her dress from getting rumpled. The monotonous drive down I-40 had lulled her to sleep. Randa had watched as her head slowly edged itself over to prop against the door.

"Donna-Dean, wake up, we're here," Randa said, and the child jumped.

"Did I tell you that Sheriff Royce's sister is here? She came in from her home in Colorado to see him. He's been telling her all about you. Her name is Becca."

"I was David-Jack's sister . . . one time," she muttered sleepily as Randa helped her out of the seat belt.

"And you will always remember that, Donna-Dean. It's pretty special being someone's sister." Randa couldn't believe she had that particular thought, much less to have spoken the words from her mouth.

Outside of Royce's room, Randa knelt down to help Donna-Dean take off her ratty little coat. Got to get rid of this thing, Randa stored the idea away for her next shopping spree. She fluffed out the dress and re-tied the sash across her back. They gave each other excited smiles as Randa knocked on the door and swung it open.

They stepped into the room amid ooh's and ah's from Royce and Becca. Randa held Donna-Dean's hand and led her over to the bedside.

"Hi . . ." Royce held out his hand. Randa wasn't sure if the hand was extended to her, or to Donna-Dean. She decided to take the opportunity and grabbed it with her left hand. He squeezed the hand and gave it a kiss. He patted the bed indicating that Donna-Dean was to sit there beside him.

"My goodness . . . look at you. How beautiful you are." Royce sounded amazed.

"I'm a catalog girl," Donna-Dean explained. Royce looked to Randa to interpret the remark.

"A model . . . catalog fashions."

"Well, you look like a princess girl to me," he said. "I've got someone I want you to meet. This is my sister, Becca," he said.

Becca stepped over to pat Donna-Dean's hand. "Hello, Donna-Dean. Royce has been telling me all about you," she said.

"I used to be a sister," she said. Becca seemed slightly shocked by the remark and cast a glance at Royce.

"Now tell me about this outfit," he quickly diverted Donna-Dean.

"Miss Randa bought me all of the things. She even bought me a princess slip," she said, quickly pulling the dress high so he could see.

"My ma used to say . . ." Randa stepped over to help her pull the dress down and interrupt the upcoming reference to a "pissant."

"Ladies have to keep their princess slips covered up, Donna-Dean," Randa coached. Everyone smiled over the awkward moment.

"Well, Miss Randa bought me these pajamas and robe. Do I look like a catalog guy?" he teased.

"Yep," she giggled.

"See my shoes?" she asked Royce, pointing her patent- leathered toes out across the bed.

"They are pretty. Bet you could do some tap dancin' in those," Royce planted the idea. Moments later, Donna-Dean eased herself down from the bed, passed behind Randa, and began a few hops across the tile floor. Once she heard the clicks of her heels, she plopped each foot repeatedly in her own version of the step, ball change.

"See, these fancy outfits just make you women all feisty and prissy," he said to Randa and Becca.

"That's the gospel according to Royce Hawkins," Becca said nudging Randa's arm.

"Donna-Dean, you just couldn't look any prettier," Royce said.

She came running back to fling herself at the bedside. "It's snowin' agin," she said, patting his hand.

"Maybe we can make another snowman. Becca can help us. She lives out in Colorado where it snows all the time. Bet she can build some great ole big man."

"Do you hurt?" Donna-Dean asked suddenly.

He brushed her stringy hair back away from her eyes. "A little bit, over here on my side," he answered.

"You wuz shot?"

"Yeah."

"It wuz my daddy?"

"I'm not sure, it might have been," Royce hedged.

She looked him straight in the eyes, "He won't be gettin' at 'cha any more."

"No . . . he won't be gettin' at any of us, darlin'," Royce hugged her tightly.

"You think he's gonna go up to Heaven?"

"I don't know."

"Cause he'll be gettin' at David-Jack," she worried.

"No. He won't. I'll tell you why. All the angels will gather around David-Jack and hold him in their arms, like I'm holdin' you. Then they'll all fold their big ole wings over him to keep him safe, and warm, and happy. And nothing bad will every happen to him."

Becca put both hands up to her mouth to stifle her gasp, totally astonished that her brother was showing this child the compassion of a poet.

The phone gave a startling ring on the bedside table, reminding each of them that the world was still turning outside.

Becca lifted the receiver and passed it over to Royce's hand.

"Hello," he said. Donna-Dean raised herself up from his hug, and Randa helped her down from the bed.

"Hey, Danny. Yeah . . . okay . . . doin' pretty well today. Yeah, she's right here," he handed the phone to Randa. "Says he needs to talk with you."

Randa took the phone. "Hello?"

Royce watched as the color drained from her face, as she launched a string of "Uh-huh's."

"Okay. I will . . . but why . . . I mean, can't I just handle this on the phone?"

"Danny, it's snowing pretty good down here. I'd say it will take me at least two or three hours. I'll be right on," she gave the phone back to Royce.

"What's up?" he asked Danny. "Well, I'll talk to you later, thanks Dan," he edged the receiver over to Becca, who hung it up up for him.

"Sounds like you've got to go," Royce seemed concerned.

"He says it's some business regarding my trailer. He didn't give me many clues. Some guy is going to wait there in your office to see me."

"Royce, I need to go and let you get some rest," Becca said.

"I'll follow along behind them in my car. Randa, I do want the two of you to spend the night with me tonight. Can you?"

"Sure, if you don't mind waiting for us at the courthouse?"

"That's fine. I'll wait," Becca agreed.

As they were saying goodbye to Royce, Becca offered her hand to Donna-Dean to lead her out into the hallway. Donna-Dean became immediately attracted to Becca's stringy, hot pink jacket.

Randa stepped over to sit on the edge of the bed alongside Royce.

"Don't worry . . . if it had been anything, Danny would have told me." He reached out to hug her.

"Have you been up to walk today?" she asked.

"Yeah . . . walked out into the hall. Sat up in that chair to eat lunch. They said I might get a shower tomorrow. I'm really lookin' forward to that. Then, I'm going to start raisin' a little hell to go home," he promised.

"Okay. That sounds perfectly normal to me. I guess I'd better get us on the road home."

"She sure looks sweet in that dress, doesn't she? Looks like a real little girl," he said.

"She is a real little girl!"

"But she's had her light under a bushel," he laughed.

"Yes, she has."

"I sure have missed you today," he said.

For a moment she was caught in his eyes.

He scooted her aside with his good hand, and jerked back the covers.

"I'm gonna finish what I started to do yesterday, when my Doctor so rudely interrupted."

In spite of her words "stop," "quit," and "don't," he stood up and pulled her into the hunter green, velour robe to hug her tightly.

"Wow . . . it's catalog guy," she teased.

"I love you, are you remembering that?" he said.

"That's something I will never forget," she replied as he kissed her softly.

"Sorry you have to leave. Call me later, when y'all get to the house," he said. "I sure have missed being with you today."

"I've missed you too."

"Oh . . . I had Becca go out and buy a suit for David-Jack. I want them to bury him in it. Does that sound crazy?" he asked.

"No. Somehow that gives me a good, settling feeling," she said.

"Me too," he said as he gave her a kiss goodbye.

CHAPTER EIGHTY THREE

Randa pulled into the courthouse parking lot, closely followed by Becca who parked in the space beside. As they walked toward the building, Becca said, "This old place hasn't changed in a hundred years. Even these parking meters are antiques."

Lights were on throughout the sheriff's department. As they entered the door, Danny stepped out to greet them.

"Miss Randa," he said tipping his hat, but not quite as eloquently as Royce.

"Hi, Miss Becca. How's our boy look to you?"

"Pretty fine, Danny, pretty fine," she brought the Colorado in her voice quickly back to the twang of East Tennessee.

"What's going on here, Danny?" Randa asked.

"Well, we have someone waitin' in Royce's office. You can just go on in there. He's been here over three hours. I think he gettin' a little anxious."

Randa left them to entertain Donna-Dean, and walked to the familiar doorway. She knocked on the glass beneath the letters R. HAWKINS, SHERIFF and turned the knob to open the door. Sitting in the window seat . . . their window seat, where she had probably felt her first spark of love interest in R. HAWKINS, SHERIFF . . . sat her brother Derrick!

"Oh my God. What are you doing here?"

He sprang up at her from the padded seat. "What in the name of God are you into?" he squawked.

"Oh . . . I'm sorry, Derrick," she walked over to offer him a hug. "I just haven't had time to . . ." she jumped back out of his way.

"Christ, Randa! You call me up and lay out all of this crap about this child and how you . . ."

Randa quickly stepped back to close the door.

"Now just calm down," she reached out to take his arm.

"What in the hell is going on? I've called up here to that number you gave me a hundred times over the last two to three days. Called night and day. No answer, not even an answer machine. Damn, I thought you'd been murdered and laid in a shallow grave somewhere."

"Something has happened . . . and it's taken my full attention."

"Yeah well . . . I know what's happened, but not from your mouth 'thankyouverymuch'!"

Randa fell silent.

"I finally had to force it out of this little secretary out here . . . who'll probably lose her job over telling me what I should have been told by you," he stormed.

"Okay, I'm sorry. You fell through a crack. You're one of the bases I didn't cover. Frankly, I didn't give you a second thought. I haven't had the time. And, right now, I'm too tired to put up with your shouting at me."

"The only thing I remotely give a shit about, Randa, is where you're going to live. When I found out about the trailer, I wanted to get up here to help," he said as he grabbed her into a hug.

"I want to help you however I can. Do you need money?" he asked.

"No, not unless the bank burned down," she smiled.

"I think you are in shock . . . you're not reacting to this the way I thought you would."

"I guess you're right. I'm sorry I scared you. I do want you to know everything. There are parts of this story that will astound you. Just don't shout . . . my nerves are right out there on the edge," she said.

"I've rented a motel room. Can you come over there with me, to talk?"

"Well, I have Donna-Dean to take care of, and we have school tomorrow, so I really need for her to get to bed. Let me go make some arrangements. I'll be right back."

Derrick returned to the window seat and picked up the cup of Luzianne coffee Danny had provided him.

"Becca . . . my brother is here from Florida," Randa moaned. "He's not understanding about my trailer. He only knows about one fourth of this ordeal, and he is absolutely frantic. I need to talk to him. Explain things. Can you . . ."

"Bring him out to the house. You two can sit by the fire while Donna-Dean and I fix us something to eat." Becca said.

Randa wanted to hug her neck. How did she know that a comforting fire and food would work a miracle with Derrick's hysteria.

"I don't know how to thank you . . . that sounds wonderful," Randa said.

"To tell you the truth, I may have to let you or your brother make the fire. Royce says I can't make a fire worth a durn!"

Randa turned to Donna-Dean, who was now wearing Becca's ugly, hot pink jacket over her new dress.

"Donna-Dean, my brother Derrick is here, and he wants to meet you," she lied, but what the hell. Reality was beginning to be a worrisome bitch.

As they gathered their coats to follow Becca out the door, Danny tapped Randa on the shoulder.

"Sorry . . . he wouldn't let me tell you on the phone that he was here. Said you wouldn't come if you knew it was him. He got a little snippy about it, too."

"He's just upset. I haven't kept in contact with him. He didn't know where I was."

"Oh, by the way, Judge Ferrell has been ridin' me hard to come up with a next of kin for Donna-Dean. The T.B.I. has found a name in some of the Silcox belongings. Seems ole Robert has a brother."

Silence.

"Oh, really," Randa whispered. "Who is he, where . . ."

"Don't know anything yet, they're working on it," Danny said.

"You don't have to tell Royce . . . yet, do you?"

"No. Not yet."

"It would set him back, Danny."

"I do have to tell Judge Ferrell, sometime . . . some of these days . . . sooner or later, and he'll probably think Royce ought to know."

"Danny, I can't deal with this now. Too many things are ahead of that. I've got to take a few minutes out of this nightmare, to handle my own situation."

"I understand. Completely. Just wanted you to know the Judge has been leaning on me to come up with something, or else be able to rule out the possibility."

"He would have been pushing Royce to do that."

"Guess it was inevitable that somebody would be out there," Danny replied. "Now that somebody is going to be told about three deaths."

"Looks like the plot thickens. Goodnight Danny," she said over her shoulder.

Danny gave a quizzical look as he yelled "Goodnight" to the closing door.

CHAPTER EIGHTY FOUR

Randa glanced up at Royce's beloved fireplace, with its stacked fieldstone chimney reaching high into the log-beamed ceiling. She missed him and longed for him to be sitting here on the couch with his boots propped up on the coffee table.

Donna-Dean lured Becca over to her Barbie house to introduce her to Ken and his dolls. Randa left Derrick to wander around this great room, to accumulate a thousand more questions to prod her with.

Randa placed a quick call to Royce on the kitchen telephone, explaining about Derrick in a rapid-fire monologue, revealing the exhausted, aggravated, and whiny-butt side of herself, all the while, vowing she could handle anything Derrick could dish out.

As she hung up the phone, the thought of Danny's comment about a Silcox relative crept into her mind. There was something scary about that, and tragic as well.

Becca began to gather newspaper.

"I think his secret is he rolls newspaper into tight little sticks, and pushes them back up under that mother log there," she said, documenting Royce's fire-building technique.

"To use as tinder," Derrick said.

"I guess so. He always says I do it wrong. I love a fire, I just hate fooling with building it. I've told Royce he needs to get gas logs."

"I can imagine what he said about that," Randa laughed.

"Yeah, something about the frontiersmen who hauled these stones up this hill to build this chimney, did not intend for it to have gas lines running into it. To which I replied . . . but the frontiers-women would have loved the idea!" Becca said.

Derrick angled himself down across the raised hearth to put the paper sticks into position. He struck the match and soon a small flame leapt up across the back log like an orange leprechaun prancing around in the deep, dark cavern of the fireplace.

"Ah ha," Derrick gloated, as he began to search the nearby wood basket for two small logs.

"Donna-Dean, why don't you come help me fix some supper?" Becca invited. "We'll play restaurant. That would be a good school lesson for you. You can write out a menu. Miss Randa and Derrick can be our customers."

Randa smiled to herself, knowing full-well that Donna-Dean had never been to a fancy restaurant and would not know what Becca was talking about. However, ignorance was empowered by enthusiasm and Donna-Dean skipped herself along with Becca as they headed toward the kitchen.

Derrick scrunched himself deep into the leather couch, confident that his fire would take hold.

"So . . . who is this guy, anyway?" he said softly, so Becca would not hear. "It's he this, and he that, from everybody."

"Look, Derrick, I've got just about an hour left in me. I'm physically exhausted and I need to go to sleep. Mentally I'm wiped out."

"I don't doubt it," Derrick said. "you've not exactly been living the life of the spinster school teacher, now have you?"

"No . . . and I want to tell you this whole story . . . step by step, the way it has unfolded. Save your questions til I'm through, and I'll answer them all. Then we can talk about how you can help me, if you still want to. You may just want to get in your car and head back to Florida."

Randa glanced over her shoulder to make sure Donna-Dean was distracted. Becca had her seated at the counter with pen and paper in hand, the two of them were in deep concentration over what to cook.

"Well, as you know," Randa began softly, "this all started last week . . . on Tuesday, I think. Was it only last week. God it seems like an eternity ago."

She carefully retraced the sequence of events, factually rather than emotionally, in about ten minutes. She edited out a few details relating to their date, by over-emphasizing the croquet ball through Royce's truck window.

"That incident stepped up the protective custody situation. Royce brought us here, and continued the round-the-clock guards."

She used cautious judgment in editing the rat trap story. Derrick need not know that for one brief moment Royce had seen her in her bra.

She did admit that she had begun to care a lot about Royce Hawkins, and because they had drawn close to each other, she felt a need to go with him on the Life Flight, and stay with him until Becca arrived.

"If we weren't caught up in some surrealistic horror story here, I probably would want to date him," she looked to see if her mental tip toe around the subject had taken hold.

"Hmm," Derrick met her eyes. "Sounds like there might be more to this."

"I do care for him. We haven't had many opportunities to be alone, so don't even waste time arching your eyebrows," she warned.

"Now, don't go gettin' your feathers up," Derrick said.

"Well, I know the paths you take. You nose around in my business trying to gather enough facts to use against me."

"Not anymore," he said sadly. "I've had a change of heart."

"You mean your nosey concern won't be added to criticism, and lead to judgmental control to the tenth power?" she teased.

"That was my formula, wasn't it?"

"Pretty much. That's why I don't tell you anything, anymore."

"Remember I've been in a therapy group for two years. Mucho money down the drain. I'm hoping you will find that my nosey concern will now lead to support and positive validation."

"Okay. Just steer clear of giving me advice. That's our sensitive area," she said.

"What have you done about the trailer?" Derrick quizzed.

"Now, that's where you can help me. I have to get back to school, and I could use you to do the leg work for me. I've called my insurance agent, and he has already filed my claim. You need to go by his office and see what to do next. I think I have to pay a deductible, and sign some things. You may have to bring those papers out to school for me."

"Okay, I'll go there bright and early in the morning to see what's what."

"Then . . . ," she laughed and nudged his shoulder. "After that, I need for you to see how we go about getting the trailer pad cleaned off, and all the burned stuff hauled away. I can get the names of people you can call."

"That should be done soon, before we get the new trailer on its way. Now, see, you do need me to help, don't you."

"I hope you realize you've caught me with my defenses down. Just please don't aggravate the situation," she pleaded.

"I won't. This is an opportunity to show you that I'm trying to turn over a new leaf," Derrick explained.

"Uh huh," Randa said, doubtfully.

"It took losing three damn good jobs, two really great girlfriends, and you as a really great sister for me to start turning."

"Derrick, you have to make psychological changes for you . . . yourself . . . and not for other people."

"Now . . . now," he said, waving his finger in her face. "Don't give me advice, that's our sensitive area!"

Randa drew back her fist and pretended to throw him a punch, which Derrick quickly grasped her arm in mid air "So . . . now . . . tell me, who is this guy anyway?"

CHAPTER EIGHTY FIVE

At school the next morning, Randa found herself as lost and distracted as her students. For the first time in her teaching career, she simply didn't care if they "got it" or not. Her life had been turned away from her burning desire to teach.

Shortly before lunch time, the door to the school swung open and a large, burly man entered slinging rain from his greasy baseball cap onto the linoleum floor. Miss Mattie had seen him drive up and park his truck at the school steps.

"May I help you?" Mattie said, stepping toward him from her classroom door, suddenly wishing a deputy was here.

"I'm here to pick up my niece. There's been a death."

"Who are you looking for?" Mattie asked, peering skeptically over her glasses.

"The Silcox girl."

"Who are you, sir?"

"I'm her uncle."

"Just a minute," Mattie said to him as she stepped across the hall to Randa's room. Three of the children, working in their workbooks at their desks, whispered to each other about the stranger "out front." Randa sat with the others in a group reading session near the back of the room. Donna-Dean was among them.

"Randa?" Mattie motioned for her to come quickly.

"This man wants Donna-Dean. Take her to your office and lock the door. I think you should call Royce's office. This could get nasty."

Mattie quickly turned to meet one of the older boys from her room, who had been sent by the stranger to make her "hurry up."

Mattie thought for a moment. She told him to get all of the children together in the back hallway, thanking her lucky stars that this big old building had its interconnecting rooms and a maze of hallways.

"Sir, we're not allowed to give out any information on Donna-Dean Silcox. You will have to contact the sheriff's office over in Brandensburg."

He shot past Mattie, using his arm like a linebacker pushing her aside to look into Randa's empty classroom.

"Wait a minute," Mattie said. "You can't come in here causing a disturbance!"

"I know she's here. You jist go and bring her right on out here to me, and there won't be no disturbance. I'm her only kin, so I drove up here to git her. And I don't have all day, neither," his temper had pumped his cheeks to a blistering red.

"Well, I've told you what you need to do. Now, I must ask you to leave the building," Mattie ordered.

"You go tell her that her Uncle Eugene is here to git her," he shouted as amber-colored tobacco juice seeped down from the corner of his mouth.

"Uh . . . she's not come in here yet this morning. Actually she hasn't been in school since all this happened. So you should just go . . ." she continued with her afterthought, "how 'bout you wait back here in my office?" Mattie urged and cajoled him all the way down the hallway into her office, where he headed himself toward the big winged-back chair in front of her desk.

Mattie stepped back outside the door and nervously pulled it closed, throwing the old-timey bolt latch at the top.

Randa appeared. "I've locked the son-of-a-bitch in there," Mattie said.

Randa laughed to hear Mattie use the term.

"Help me push this across," Mattie urged.

They put their shoulders to a large, wooden chest of drawers, and positioned it in front of the office door. Mattie had donated this old, beastly white elephant for them to store art supplies in.

"Hey, wait, what-the-hell. Let me outta here," the stranger pulled and pushed, and pounded loudly on the door. "Let me out. I've got a gun. I'll shoot my way out," he rattled and pounded louder.

"Oh my Lord. A gun," Mattie fretted.

"Let's go . . . get the children down in the cellar," Randa said pulling at Mattie's arm.

"Wait. Randa you go, take Donna-Dean out of here. Go to my house with her, the key is under the mat," Mattie said as they moved toward the children.

"No. I won't leave you. I've called Royce's office. Somebody will be here soon."

They herded the children down the plank steps into the cold cellar. Randa looked at the frightened faces. She gathered Donna-Dean in her arms.

"Now this is going to be all right. The sheriff's deputy is on his way. He'll be here any minute now. This might be a sort of history lesson for us. This might be how the frontier people felt when they had to hide away from the Indians."

Randa smiled weakly, wondering if they had bought that.

"Donna-Dean? Do you have an Uncle Eugene?" Mattie asked.

"Yessum."

"Well, he can't just take her from school. He has to go through the proper channels. Royce would just have a fit," Randa whispered.

The minutes crept by. The children began to get cold . . . colder. They could hear their prisoner thumping loudly, probably kicking at the locked door. Shouting profanities these school children should not be hearing, although it seemed to entertain the older ones. Someone began to whine to go to the bathroom.

"Randa?" The voice from above seemed to echo its way down the front hallway.

"Randa? Where are you? The voice was now accompanied by footsteps crossing the creaking floorboards over their heads.

"Anybody here?"

"Derrick!" Randa said to Mattie. "That's my brother, he'll help us. I'm going up. Y'all just stay quiet."

She inched herself up the plank steps and pushed up hard on one side of the heavy doors. The hinges gave a loud screech as the door plopped itself flat out onto the floor.

"Randa?" Derrick continued to shout.

From the office door behind the chest of drawers, came a deafening blast of gunfire.

"Derrick! Over here!" Randa screamed.

Derrick came around from the hallway and saw her head sticking out above the cellar door. He made what looked like a belly-buster dive onto the floor, then crawled along the baseboard toward her. Randa came up out of the hole in the floor, and crawled with him toward the kitchen at the back of the building.

"What in the name of God?" Derrick huffed breathlessly.

"Welcome to the on-going Silcox saga," Randa said. "It's her uncle . . . he says. And he wants to take her, now. We've got the children in the cellar. We've barricaded him in Miss Mattie's office. We had no idea he had a gun."

"Have you called for help?"

"Yes, but it takes them a while to get here."

"I've got a gun in my suitcase in the car. I'll get it." Randa had a look of complete surprise on her face.

"What . . . I'm on the road all the time . . . you're damn straight I'm gonna carry a gun. I know how to use it, too. You go back down there with the kids."

"They're freezing to death. They can't stay down there too much longer," she said as he helped her back into the cellar. "Derrick . . . ?" He was gone, running back across the creaking floorboards and out the front doors. Silence fell throughout the building, with only the muted groans from whoever it was who had to go to the bathroom.

Soon, Derrick was back wielding the longest gun Randa had ever seen. He would later brag to Royce that it was a 357 Magnum . . . and, yes, he was duly licensed to carry it.

"Keep down there," he said to Randa, noticing that she was peering out from under the heavy wooden trap door.

"Derrick?"

"What?"

"What are you going to do?" she whispered loudly.

"I don't know . . . whatever I have to."

"Danny will be here any minute."

"Who's Danny?" he asked.

"Royce's deputy."

"Good. He can take this creep to jail."

Derrick pulled the gun up and took a double-handed grip, reminding Randa of every detective who had packed heat through the annals of television history. He moved cautiously toward the chest of drawers, keeping himself low and braced against the wall.

"Okay . . . asshole . . . so you've got a gun, have you?" he shouted. "Well, let's see, how 'bout you look out that back window in there, see that tin roof on that old outhouse back there. Well, watch this."

Derrick turned to aim through the panes of glass across the back of the building. He fired. The powerful blast blew shards of glass everywhere. The deafening sound rang in Randa's ears for several minutes. The old school building seemed to shudder in the aftermath. Outside, Derrick's bullet hit the rusty tin roof and split it lengthwise.

Randa thought about the children huddled below. What must they be thinking?

"Now, you know what kind of fire power I've got out here," Derrick taunted. "You shoot off one more shot and I will peel this door open like a can of sardines with a bullet that's got your name written all over it!"

Silence.

"I don't know what your problem is, but you can't come into a school building shootin' a gun . . . Man, they'll send you so far up the river. What in the hell's wrong with you, anyway?" Derrick continued.

"Derrick?" Randa said.

"What?" he took his eyes off of the office door to give her a glance.

"Don't make him mad."

"Mad . . . I don't give a shit if he's mad. I'm a little pissed myself," he said loudly.

CHAPTER EIGHTY SIX

Once again, Randa pulled the cellar door closed over her head and moved backwards down the steps. A dull ache in her legs told her she had done an aerobic workout on these steps today.

The children were cold and scared. "Don't worry about the gunshots," she told them, "they're just showing out."

"Swapping noises," one of the boys said.

Mattie gathered them close together in one big teeth-chattering huddle. Ever the teacher, she began to explain about body heat and how their hugging close would create warmth.

From a distance, Randa thought she heard a siren, possibly two or three.

"Danny's here!" she whispered to Mattie.

They all listened intently as the sounds came closer. Soon two patrol cars pulled into the schoolyard, their sirens winding down to a whir.

Just in time, Randa thought, it was getting too cold.

Voices quickly filled the building along with heavy, fast-moving footsteps here and there on the boards over their heads. The voices seemed to blend together, one over the other in a syncopated monotone. Some leading, some following, and some, perhaps Derrick, getting out of the way, Randa thought.

After several minutes the wooden cellar door was jerked open and Derrick reached his hand down to Randa.

"Y'all come on up from there, and get in here by the stove," he said.

Randa was up the steps for what she hoped was her last time, ever. "We are all freezing," she said.

Mattie was up and offering her hands to help the children climb up in a steady single file, each of them looking carefully from side to side to see whatever was the matter.

Randa led the children to her classroom, urging them to put on their coats and gather around the stove. She was curious to know what was going on. She walked over to the doorway and peeped toward Mattie's office door where Danny, Jake, and Derrick were moving aside the wooden chest of drawers.

Suddenly she felt a hand press into the hollow of her back. She gasped and spun around as he said "Hello, darlin'" in a Conway Twitty voice.

"ROYCE!"

She sprang into his arms to hug him tightly, noticing he used his right arm as a protective shield over his incision.

"I . . ." she buried her head into his shirt collar as he caressed the back of her neck and gently kissed her.

"I . . ." she stammered.

"Hold that thought, while I see what we've got in here," he said, moving away from her hug toward the office door.

CHAPTER EIGHTY SEVEN

"Mr. Silcox, this is Sheriff Royce Hawkins! We're going to unlock this door now, and when we open it back I want to see you laying spread-eagled across the floor. I want you to shove your weapon over here to this door, now. I want to hear it bump the door. Do you understand?" Royce said feebly.

Derrick approached and handed Royce his 357 Magnum. "In case you need to take him out."

"Right." Royce gave a perplexed smile as he took the gun from this stranger.

"Silcox? I want to hear your gun hit the door, now," Royce tried to pull his voice up to a shout.

A shot rang out and the bullet hole appeared in the door, almost as if by some slight of hand magic. Silcox had indeed hit the door as Royce had directed.

"Take him," Royce commanded Danny and Jake.

Danny chucked the bottom of the door with his boot causing it to fly open. The wild-eyed Silcox dropped his gun out in front of him. Jake held his gun, and Danny his shotgun, toward the man's head. One look down the barrel of the shotgun that had killed his brother made Uncle Eugene weaken.

"Get your hands up behind your head," Royce said. "Turn around."

Danny jerked the weapon from Silcox, slinging it across Mattie's desk. Jake pulled the man's hands down to put handcuffs on.

"Take him on out to the car," Royce directed. "They need to get things back to normal in here."

Danny and Jake steered Silcox by the handcuffs through the hallway out to the front doors. Randa moved over to Royce. "Are you okay?" she asked.

"Yeah," he reached for her hand. "This is it . . . it's over now. I'm sure."

"Sometimes I don't think it will ever be over," Randa said. "How did you get out of the hospital?"

"Danny came down . . . he gave me a ride."

She put her hand up to his face, "Does Brodie know?"

"Yeah. I put him in a head lock and forced him to sign me out."

"I'll bet."

"On our way up the road, we heard this call come in," he explained.

"And you just couldn't go home with all of this excitement coming down?" she teased.

"Course not . . . not with my best girl in the middle of it. You know I really thought I could be your Knight in Shining Armor, but it looks like someone beat me to it," Royce said giving a nod to Derrick, who seemed lost now that things were over.

"Royce, that is my brother Derrick," Randa said.

"Really . . . and he carries a side arm?" Royce held up the 357.

"He sells drugs. Oh God . . . no. I mean, he sells pharmaceutical drugs to hospitals. He travels a regional sales territory, and apparently feels a need to carry a gun in the car," Randa explained.

"Thank goodness he does. He stalled that guy off for us," Royce said.

Derrick entered the hallway.

"I've heard a lot about you, Sheriff Hawkins," he reached out to meet Royce's hand shake.

"Thank you for your help here today."

"I thought you might think I had taken the law into my own hands," Derrick worried.

"They were in need of some serious help, and you were the man that God sent here on that mission," Royce commended.

"Actually, I just stopped by to see what kind of bath tub Randa wants in her new trailer. The insurance agent said the mobile home people are waiting on that decision," Derrick laughed.

"Miss Randa?" Donna-Dean called from the classroom door.

"Kin I come see Sheriff Royce?"

"You sure can," Randa said.

Royce turned to reach his hand out to her. She ran to him, dragging her coat on the floor behind her.

"He come to git me. Didn't he? I don't want to go with him!"

"You won't have to go with him," Royce promised.

"You know whut?" she looked up his long body and giggled.

"What?"

"Peggy Beasley saw you kissin' Miss Randa!"

"She did?"

"Yep. She says you're sweet on her."

"Well, what do we do about that?" he laughed as she leaned her head back to look into his eyes.

"I dunno. Maybe you wuz just warmin' her up."

"That's right. You can tell Peggy Beasley that Miss Randa was so cold that her lips were turnin' blue!" He glanced at Randa, who had clasped her hands over her blue lips to hide her laughter.

Donna-Dean ran back to carry the kissing information to her friend.

"Warmin' you up . . . wuz I," he drew her close.

"I'll say!" Randa quipped.

Jake approached them. "Chief, you need to come see somethin' out here."

Royce kissed Randa's forehead. "See you later. Stay warm!" he said to her as she walked into the classroom. She looked over her shoulder to see him moving his eyebrows up and down in a Grouch Marx-ish leer.

She pointed an admonishing finger at him, and warned him to "Behave!"

CHAPTER EIGHTY EIGHT

The phone rang from somewhere under Royce's leg. He jumped up from the top of his desk and jerked the receiver.

"Yeah . . . Wyn? This is Royce Hawkins, were you able to trace that post office box number? Really. That's what I thought. I knew Marietta was real close to Atlanta. I've got this guy sittin' his big ole tattooed ass here in my jail. Yeah. Sure will. Okay, thanks, Wyn. You boys do good work."

Royce hung up the phone and circled the desk to ease himself into the high-backed desk chair.

"Damn."

He smacked a pencil across a note pad, smiling confidently to himself. A knock brought Francine's beauty-shop hair cautiously around the door frame.

"Sheriff? Dr. Caldwell's huntin' you. He's on the phone, again. You want to talk to him this time?"

"Just tell him all hell's broke loose over here, and I'm tryin' to get it settled so I can go home. Tell him I'm fine. I'll call him later. Oh, Francine, have Danny bring Silcox in here . . . please."

"Okay . . . but you don't need to be doing any of this. You'll wear yourself out," she said, noticing him wave his hand to brush her warning out of his mind.

Moments later, Danny led a hand-cuffed Silcox, accompanied by a court-appointed attorney, into Royce's office, where he dragged wooden chairs from various places in the room and positioned them in front of the desk.

"Okay, according to this Georgia driver's license you were carrying, you are Norvel Eugene Silcox and you live at 483 County Line Road in Marietta, Georgia. Is that correct?" Royce asked.

"Maybe . . . maybe not," Silcox quipped.

"Are you Norvel Eugene Silcox?"

"Maybe . . . maybe not."

"Well, what should we call you?"

"You can call me Jack Shit for all I care," Silcox blurted.

"Alright, Jack, you have asked for an attorney to be provided for you, and Mr. Tucker has agreed to serve you as a Defense Attorney. I'll be explaining the charges brought against you. Mr. Tucker will sit here and listen to the questions I have for you, and he will advise you on the points of law that will be in your best interest. Again, as you were told earlier, anything you say can, and will, be used against you in a court of law. Do you understand?"

"Yeah."

"You have the right to discuss anything I ask you with Mr. Tucker before you give an answer. You'll also have the opportunity to talk privately with him when you go back to your cell," Royce explained.

"Okay," Royce drew a deep breath, stretching himself up from the incision on his right side which had, like Brodie and Francine, begun to nag him to go home.

"I want to start by giving you an opportunity to explain why you came up here from Georgia to get this little girl?"

"You do not have to answer that question, Mr. Silcox," Tucker warned.

"Cause, he woulda wanted me to have her," Silcox said.

"He?"

"My brother . . . Robert."

"And why would he want you to have her?"

Silcox looked perplexed. He snickered nervously, while twisting in the wooden chair, "Cause . . . I'm her uncle."

"Look," Royce began, "we know what y'all were into out there. The boy told us, in his writings. He kept a journal. Told us everything, named names . . . referred to you several times. We've found the money that was buried on the place, plus Robert had received several envelopes of this stuff from you, the day before he was shot. You might as well come straight."

Royce noticed Tucker's hand clasp onto Silcox's arm.

"I ain't sayin' nothin' lessin' it's to a judge."

"Well, I've got one right down the hall," Royce threatened.

"I never really did nothin' to them kids. Just poked around on em' whilst he took the pitchers. It wuz all his idear from the git go."

"Mr. Silcox," Tucker shouted, "you cannot say things like that. You should not let these questions lead you into any admission of guilt. I strongly advise that you do not . . . ."

"Y'all made some good money," Royce lured.

Silcox was silent.

"You came back up here huntin' his money, didn't you?"

Tucker's hand, again, griped Silcox's arm.

"Didn't either one of you Bozo's know this was against the law?"

Silence.

"Not to mention how you were harmin' these children. You did some awful bad stuff to the boy," Royce charged.

"Me? I didn't do nuthin'. Robert wanted David-Jack to do what he sed, when he sed do it, and the kid would always argue back. Made Robert get mad and he ended up doin' worser stuff then he'd ever planned to do."

"It's easy to blame this all on a dead man. Fact is, Robert has left you holding the bag."

Royce got up from his chair and walked around to sit on the front corner of his desk.

"Why did you want this little girl?"

"Cause."

Royce moved himself toward Silcox's face.

"Cause you wanted to continue your little business with her?"

"That's for me to know, and you to find out," Silcox smirked.

"Sheriff?" Tucker objected.

"You guys are all alike," Royce said, "having some cock-eyed 'idear' on how you can make some quick cash. Turn some big money. The sad thing is, you can always find somebody who will fund your little plan. With this pornography shit you can always find a market. If nothin' else works, you can sell it overseas. So . . . now there are two people . . . well, three, if you want to count your brother, who are dead; and a little girl who's left alone in this world, with a head full of nastiness that will be with her the rest of her life."

"Can't blame none of that on me," Silcox gloated.

"How do I know you are Robert Silcox's brother? You got any proof of that?" Royce continued. "You got any proof that you were . . . shall I say . . . his business partner?"

"That's a criminal charge. I don't think you want to answer that, Mr. Silcox," Tucker warned.

Silcox grinned like a Cheshire cat.

"Well, speaking of charges, I think I can come up with a few off the top of my head. There's assault with a deadly weapon on these school children, negligent discharge of a firearm within the school building, suspicion of dealing in child pornography through the federal mail service. Mr. Tucker, I assume you will explain the word 'federal' to him, and how it relates to his case."

Tucker glanced at Silcox, who appeared skeptical.

"Now," Royce continued, "when you were booked here today, a strip search was conducted. Incidentally, we do that on everybody who is jailed. And, we discovered that you have a very unusual tattoo . . . in a very unusual place. Is that right, sir?" Royce asked.

"Don't say anything, Mr. Silcox. Remember, what you say can be held against you," Tucker advised.

"Bet that hurt like hell, having that put down there!" Royce taunted.

"No . . . as a matter-of-fact, it tickled!"

Tucker squirmed. "Again, Mr. Silcox, I strongly urge you to . . . shut up!"

"It's odd that your unusual tattoo just happens to match the tattoo on the gentlemen in these photographs found in your truck," Royce said.

"Mr. Silcox, I warn you, do not say a word." Tucker pointed a stern finger at Royce. "Sheriff, I think we need to conclude this meeting. Apparently my client is going to ignore my words of caution, and you are letting your questions get way out of hand."

"Sorry." Royce said as he dumped the shoe box full of pictures out across the desk.

"Do you have children, Mr. Tucker?" Royce brushed his hand over the photographs, scattering them before the attorney. "If you do, sir, you might want to warn them about such as this."

Tucker glanced up from the photos to meet Royce's eyes, slowly shaking his head from side to side.

"Danny . . . would you take Mr. Jack Shit back to his cell."

Tucker grabbed his briefcase from the floor. "Let's get on with this preliminary hearing, if the judge is available this afternoon," he said.

"I'm all for that," Royce said. "I need to get the hell home."

When the door closed, Royce picked up the phone to call the T.B.I. Crime Lab voice-mail.

"This is Sheriff Royce Hawkins, I need to call a meeting here in my office at 7 a.m. tomorrow morning. My deputy tells me that your blood people are on their way here now. They can reach me at my home phone, and I'll come back to the office. Got a major turn around in this case, and we've got a suspect in custody at this time. Sorry this meeting takes up another Saturday morning, but I've got to move quickly. Thanks."

CHAPTER EIGHTY NINE

Becca opened the front door, balancing a large white box on one arm. "Hi, come on in. I hear you two have had an exciting day."

Donna-Dean ran into the living room to search for Gabriel.

"Royce isn't here, yet. He's still at the office. I hope he's alright. Brodie's frantic," Becca said.

"He's doing too much," Randa said. "He's going to crash sooner, or later."

"Everybody in town has been sending things. Lots of food. The Hi Ho Restaurant has sent a whole country ham with biscuits. The Toot-N-Tell has sent what must be twenty pounds of his favorite barbecue ribs. And there are cheesecakes, and fruit baskets."

Becca pointed across the room to a huge cardboard box. "And . . . Benson's Furniture Emporium has sent him a recliner. Can you imagine . . . a recliner . . . for getting shot!"

"That's really nice. He'll enjoy that, if we can get him to sit down, ever again," Randa laughed.

"Oh, Royce would like for Derrick to stay here tonight. No need him staying in a motel. And we've got plenty of food to eat," Becca invited.

"Derrick should be calling soon. I'll ask him. That's very nice. Thank you."

Becca dropped the white box from her arms onto the coffee table, and flipped open the top.

"I've spent all afternoon getting some things out of the attic. I figure it's about time to take my wedding dress home. It's been six years."

271

She fumbled through the folds of her bridal gown to find a white, leather photograph album.

"This is the wedding album I had made for my dad. Donna-Dean, you might enjoy looking at these. There might be someone you know in there."

Donna-Dean took the album and perched herself cross-legged on the couch. She carefully picked through each page, oohing and ahhing at Becca, the beautiful bride.

"Oh . . . lookee here, it's Sheriff Royce," she thrust the album over toward Randa. "He sure is handsome."

Randa looked past Donna-Dean's fingers to the smiling groomsmen surrounding Becca as she sat on the steps of the church. Royce was extremely handsome in the black tuxedo, with a criss-cross tie tucked under his chin.

Becca sat down beside Donna-Dean. "You've got to see the garter picture." Donna-Dean looked at her, quizzically.

"The groom takes the bride's garter off of her leg and tosses it over his back to the groomsmen. The one who catches it will be the next one to get married," Becca explained to Donna-Dean.

Randa glanced at the photograph of Royce with the bride's garter landing smack across his chest. His hands were at his side, and he seemed to be leaning backward out of the garter's path. "Did Royce catch it?" Randa asked.

"No. He was afraid of it. He let it fall to the ground. Everybody kept chasing him with it all afternoon, but he never claimed it."

Becca turned the page to another photo. "Funny how all of these other guys are married now."

"I got pitchers, too," Donna-Dean scrambled down from the couch to run to the Barbie house where she had hidden the Polaroids Randa had made of Royce, Donna-Dean, and their snowman.

"See." Donna-Dean handed the photos to Becca. "He sure is handsome."

"Now which of these men are you calling handsome?" Becca teased. "This big fat one made out of snow, or this big old country boy who's holding on to you."

Donna-Dean flung herself onto the couch cushions in a fit of laughter.

CHAPTER NINETY

As Royce started to leave the office, he grabbed the ringing phone from Francine's desk, hoping it was the T.B.I.

"Royce . . . get yourself home . . . now!" Brodie ordered.

"I'm on my way out the door, Bro. Honest. I've finally got this Silcox mess wrapped up. Danny said he told you what happened over at the school."

"Yeah. I'm not sure you were up to all of that."

"I lived through it."

"Well, the main reason I needed to talk with you is the funeral home has David-Jack ready. They want to know if you plan to come by to . . . uh . . . see him?"

"Oh. I don't think I could handle that."

"They want to bury him at eleven o'clock tomorrow morning at City Cemetery. They wanted me to make sure you knew that."

"Would you tell them I'll be there. I think Randa might want to go with me," Royce said.

"Okay . . . you are going to go on home now, aren't you?"

"Yeah. I'm going. Oh, Brodie . . . thank you for everything you've done for me and for David-Jack. Tell all the Rotary people I'm grateful."

"Don't mention it, Royce. I just want you to put this all out of your mind for tonight, and get some rest."

"Sure will," Royce said wondering if it was a sin to flat out lie through your teeth to such a good friend.

CHAPTER NINETY ONE

Randa passed a cup of hot chocolate to Royce. "You know something? Last night, when we came here with Becca, everything felt so strange."

"Strange?" he asked.

"Yeah. Things were just all wrong without you. Something was missing . . . the house, even Gabriel, reminded me that you weren't here. It made me realize just how much you mean to me."

He leaned over to give her a kiss. "And I was lyin' up in that hospital, countin' all the little holes in the ceiling tiles, wishing I was here with you."

"I sure have become attached to you, and so has Donna-Dean. Which reminds me, what in the world are we going to do about her?" Randa asked.

"Actually, I've been planning to have a big discussion with you about Donna-Dean."

"How's about you becoming a daddy?" Randa decided to go straight to his heart.

"Oh no, you've had a big conclave with Becca," he fussed.

"No. Why?"

"I had tossed out the idea of adoption to Becca at the hospital yesterday. She thinks I'm crazy. I also told her that I'm very much in love with you."

"And she thinks you're crazy?"

"No. I can tell she's delighted."

"That's sweet."

"I thought I should tell her some of these things while she's here, rather than having to tell her on the phone after she's gone back home."

"That's good. She will feel like you have included her in your decision making."

"She suggests that I give you full priority. And, I want you to know that I fully intend to do that. Becca thinks I shouldn't cloud the issue with the idea of adoption."

"Maybe we should think of Donna-Dean as our joint project," Randa said.

"Interesting."

"All I know is, I have had a wonderful man land in my lap, from out of the blue, and under very odd circumstances. I need to follow my heart. If I fall behind your love for Donna-Dean, or Becca, or for your love of being a sheriff, then I will gladly be in that line," she said to his smiling, blue eyes.

"I think Becca's point was that you must immediately go to the head of that line . . . and you will," he said taking her in his arms. "I just don't want you to think that my love for you came about because I wanted a mother for . . ."

"And . . . I want you to realize something," Randa interrupted, as she reached up to grab his cheeks with a teacher's grip.

"When you enter a room with the two of us, you always look for me first, then for Donna-Dean. You always draw me to you first, and Donna-Dean second. What you do to show your love, you do in some sort of subconscious order. Coming from the kind of horrible family life she has had, I don't think she would be aware that you do this, but a lonely old-maid school marm like me, has very much noticed."

"Thank God my subconscious is doing something right," he said. "Derrick and Becca are grounded in reality, they're not out here in the love galaxy like we are. They are probably astounded that we seem to know we are in love with each other, so quickly."

"Would things have been any different if, say, Brodie had set us up on a blind date?" Randa asked.

"Nah. We would still have talked and laughed, and looked into each other's eyes," he said.

"I could have fallen in love with you when you had the roses delivered to our table at the restaurant," Randa said.

"I could have fallen in love with you when you jerked me around by the coat collar to give me a goodnight kiss there under your trailer window. For me that was the match that torched the flame," he said.

"See. It's not the time factor. Not how many dates we've had, or how many steps we've gone through to build a relationship. Sometimes, I guess, it's right there on the surface," Randa said.

"I think my parents had that kind of love," Royce said.

"Mine didn't, and I always wished that for them. I wanted them to have a heart felt love that everyone could see, especially me and Derrick. Maybe that's the best thing you and I have to offer Donna-Dean . . . is that we are two people who care deeply for each other, and we want to draw her into that love."

"God, you are wise," Royce hugged her tightly. "But, I don't want you to ever think . . ."

"Let's don't think," she kissed him over his words. "You are sweet to let me know that you are troubled over some second-fiddle situation, but don't worry. We should just sit back and enjoy all that love can bring," she coached.

"Sometimes I think what I know about love, I learned from rock and roll music. Lots of first loves, and true loves, and burnin' loves," Royce laughed. "Lots of prayin' to the stars above."

"Those early years were good teachings, but in the late 60s everything got entirely too groovy," Randa teased.

"Seriously, we need to look at what's at hand for Donna-Dean. I think I've organized my thoughts, but I want to know what you are thinking," Royce said.

"You mean about adopting her?" Randa asked.

"Yeah."

"I've been watching you two bless each other's hearts with a joy that's almost holy. I'm sure she would not find that in any other person," Randa said.

"I was wondering if you might have an interest in adopting her?" he asked.

"Is that what you would like for me to do?"

"If you want her . . . sure," he said.

"Wait a minute. The next thing we'll be doing is tossing a coin, or counting potatoes, or doing eenie-meenie-miney-mo!"

They laughed.

"Royce, be honest with yourself. You want this child, and I'd say you would be willing to walk across the hot coals of the court system to get her."

He ducked his head. "Do you think I'm crazy?"

"No. I happen to think you two are meant for each other."

"I just want to make doubly sure that she, or any of the problems she might bring with her, won't jeopardize our relationship," he said.

"I know. You are a man who likes to have all of his ducks in a row, that's your way. Maybe we should just realize that there are no guarantees in life. This will be a great undertaking for all of us.

"I think we both understand that she will have a lifetime of questions about her parents. Why they did what they did. The burnings. The killings. She may need the kind of special counseling anyone would need who had lived through such an ordeal. Even as an adult, these things that were done to her may haunt her and affect her for the rest of her life. But we can help her work through things each step along the way. That's all we can promise the court, and it's all we can promise each other," Randa said.

"And we'll do it. You know why? Because we have the desire to. But, the only drawback in my mind is that somehow her being here, all of the time, wanting my attention, might cause me to lose you," he said softly.

"You've said that you love me. And because I accept that love, I know that you will love me and need me in a whole other way from the kind of love, and self-gratification, you will get from raising a child," she took both his hands in hers. "And, you forget, I love her too. I want a good life for her. A child needs to have something to look forward to every day, and for Donna-Dean that would be coming home to you . . . perhaps us."

"Judge Ferrell is stopping by here this evening. It's time to lay things out on the table for him. He'll probably have a multitude of reasons why this can't be done," he said.

"And, you will have to prepare yourself for that," Randa said hugging him tightly.

CHAPTER NINETY TWO

"Royce, are you sure you're up to this? We can meet some other time," Judge Ferrell said.

"No. I'm fine. Come on in." Royce stepped back from his front door. "Let's go upstairs to my office."

"Beautiful place you've got here," the judge said as they walked up the steps. "I remember when your daddy built it. He'd be proud of the way you've kept it. Fact is, he'd be mighty proud of you all the way around. You've done right well for yourself. Everybody's awful proud of you as sheriff . . . it seems to suit you."

"Well, thank you. I enjoy it. Sort of exciting every now and then. Even gettin' shot wasn't as bad as I imagined it to be." Royce led him to twin winged-backed chairs, by the windows.

"Judge, I've got a proposition to make to you. As I told you, in the hospital, this little Silcox girl means a lot to me. I've done a lot of thinking about what's going to become of her, and I've decided that I want to petition the courts to adopt her."

"I had a feelin' that might be the direction you were headin'. What makes you think you want to take that on yourself, Royce?"

"I want a good home for her."

"Well, now . . ."

"But, more than that, I want her to have a good loving daddy while she's still got some childhood years left," Royce continued.

"I think that's what we all want for her."

"I've got a good home here. I've got money. I can provide for her. Get her anything she wants. I can pay for counseling, put her through college . . ."

"Hold on, son. Don't you have the cart before the horse?"

"What?" Royce asked.

"You don't have the one thing she needs . . . possibly the most important thing . . . a mother."

"I know that. And that is certainly a point in your favor."

"Something tells me you're working on that too, aren't you?"

"Not per se. I've met someone who's an absolute angel . . . and that seems to have fascinated a lot of folks . . . but, I don't want to recruit her as a mother, not yet."

"We talkin' 'bout Miss Randa?"

"Yessir. She knows all about this hair-brained idea, and she's the only one who doesn't think I'm crazy. So . . . what do you think, can we work a deal?"

"Maybe. But, I'll tell you this, if I didn't know you . . . know what a fine fella you are . . . I'd laugh at your notion. I'd probably be advisin' you to not get into nothing you can't get out of," the judge laughed.

The phone rang on the desk across the room. In the middle of the second ring, someone downstairs picked up.

"We might have some legal maneuvers to make," the judge added.

"And what might those be?" Royce asked.

A small tap at the door. Royce stepped over to open it. Randa, accompanied by Donna-Dean, said "You have an emergency call from Danny . . . sorry."

"Y'all come on in, I'll take the call. Judge Ferrell, you remember Randa . . . and this is Donna-Dean." Royce turned to his desk to take the call.

Randa led Donna-Dean to the chair where Royce had been sitting.

"Danny?" Royce said, as he moved the telephone across to the front of the desk. "What's the matter!"

"Hello, pretty girl. How are you?" Judge Ferrell reached over to take Donna-Dean's hand.

"Fine," Donna-Dean said shyly.

"We've been having an indoor picnic with all of the food everyone has sent for Royce," Randa said.

"You have got to be kidding me," Royce shouted into the phone. "What in this world?" He paced the floor in front of the desk and chuckled a loud "God!"

"I like that cheese pie." Donna-Dean said to Randa.

"Cheesecake," Randa explained.

"It had Velvetta cheese in it?"

"No. Not Velvetta . . . a different kind of cheese . . . cream cheese."

"Well, take Jake with you and go. I can't leave now," Royce directed. "Get back with me after you bring it in . . . for God's sake wear those rubber gloves and use one of those big plastic bags."

Randa smiled nervously, meeting Judge Ferrell's skeptical eyes over Donna-Dean's head.

As Royce hung up the phone, Randa held out her hand to Donna-Dean and moved her quickly toward the door.

"We'll head back downstairs. Maybe start thinking about going to bed. We've had an exciting day," Randa said.

"Goodnight, sweet girl," Judge Ferrell said shaking the tips of Donna-Dean's fingers.

"Night," she said.

As they passed Royce he reached a hand out to step Donna-Dean up onto his desk chair to meet her eye-to-eye.

"I'll see you later. Leave me some of that cheesecake." She leaned out to hug him around the neck. With one hand holding Donna-Dean, he reached his other hand out to Randa.

"Goodnight, Judge Ferrell," Randa said over her shoulder.

"Goodnight."

As the door closed Judge Ferrell said. "If I didn't know any better, I'd say y'all were a ready-made family."

"Yeah. And 'daddy' has just been called back to work tonight. Some trucker has reported a leg in a boot standing upright on the side of the interstate."

"Jesus," Judge Ferrell said, almost smiling at the thought.

"Yeah. Donna-Dean would be subject to my being a sheriff. That's another point in your favor."

"But your natural born children would be too, unless you gave up sheriff'n."

"I could do that."

"The whole county would suffer."

"So, maybe I've given them enough of my life already," Royce said.

"Well, son, in all of your plannin', try to do what will make you happy."

"I want to be sheriff. I want to adopt Donna-Dean, I want to get married and have about six more children to fill up my daddy's big ole house, and die with forty notches in my gun belt and y'all can bury me in City Cemetery. Which reminds me, we are burying Donna-Dean's brother over there tomorrow morning."

"Brodie told me. I'm proud of you for seeing that the boy gets a proper burial."

"Does Donna-Dean understand any of this?"

"She's been very non-reactive. I don't think any of what we we have told her has sunk in," Royce said.

"Well, I'll get things under way for you to get some sort of custody. Now, what might be the better thing to do is to make you, and Randa if she wants, foster parents for awhile. That would give you some time to work on your relationship. That would stop any intervention from other authorities. Donna-Dean would be 'placed' for all intents and purposes."

"Then, if I was to marry, I could formally adopt at that time."

"If and when. And, I'll plant the idea that I want you to let me perform the ceremony," he said patting Royce on the back.

"Could you believe . . . . me, married." Royce laughed.

Chapter Ninety Three

Royce and Donna-Dean sat upright in the new recliner, each of them too restless to go to bed.

"Let's go back, again," Donna-Dean begged as she squirmed herself deeper into the plush cushion.

Royce pushed backward, feeling a pinch of pain across his incision, as the chair raised up his legs and eased the two of them onto their backs.

"It's fun," she said.

"Yes, it is," Royce replied.

They lay there quietly, looking up to the rafters crossing the ceiling. Donna-Dean snuggled herself to his side.

"Donna-Dean, can you tell me about this man who came to school today?" Royce asked.

"I don't want to go with him," she said, playing with Royce's fingers.

"Well, I don't want you to go with him," Royce said. "I don't like him."

"He's mean," she said. "He wuz gonna make my momma go off with him."

"Why?"

"He loved on her."

"He did?"

"Yeah. He loved on her a lot and they wuz always fussin' with my daddy. Made me sad. Daddy'd always tell momma to go on and git out and go be with him."

"Did she want to go?"

"Yeah. David-Jack said momma was gonna do somethin' bad to my daddy. And David-Jack was sorta glad 'bout that. Sed my daddy would git what was comin' to him."

They sat in silence. Royce hoped she was getting sleepy.

"I don't want to go," she said.

"I know that. I don't want you to go anywhere. So let's don't worry about that now," he said.

Silence.

"Do you know whut a lullaby is?"

"Yeah."

"Whut is it?"

"It's a song you sing to a baby . . . or to anybody, I guess. It helps them to go to sleep."

"How does it do that?"

"Well, it's sung all soft and low, and it makes them relax. Why do you want to know about lullabies?"

"It wuz in a story we read at school."

Silence.

"Kin you sing one to me? I never had a lullaby before."

"I'm not much of a singer. Maybe Miss Randa could . . ."

Donna-Dean quickly put a sticky little palm up across his lips. "No . . . it's gotta be you."

"Hmmm," Royce stalled. "I don't know any real lullabies. But maybe this will do . . ." He put his arm around her and drew her close. "You are my sunshine, my only sunshine. You make me happy when skies are gray. You'll never know dear, how much I love you. Please don't take my sunshine away."

She looked up at him and whispered, "I don't want to go."

"The only place you have to go is off to bed," he whispered back to her as he brushed strings of hair away from her sleepy eyes.

Randa and Becca had watched the scene unfold before their eyes, as they stood in the kitchen doorway. They looked at each other and shook their heads. Randa blotted tears from her eyes with a dish towel, and drew a deep breath before walking over to coax Donna-Dean toward the bedroom.

CHAPTER NINETY FOUR

"I really appreciate you all coming up here so bright and early this morning to eat Krispy Kreme doughnuts with me," Royce teased the four agents seated around the office, each of them sniffling, or coughing, their lack of enthusiasm at working on a weekend.

"I've got some hot stuff on this case. And I've got Robert Silcox's brother sitting here in jail on some piddly-assed charges he can probably walk away from. I want this bird to go to prison . . . big time. So, it's my goal here this morning, to piece all of this evidence together and wrap this case up in one solid package. What I'm driving at is, I don't want his attorney to be able to plea him out of anything. I've got a personal interest in this case now," Royce said.

"Personal interest? What are you up to, sheriff?" Agent Jackson spoke around the wads of doughnut stuffed into each cheek.

"Oh, it'll all come out in the wash," Royce said. "Just believe me, I'm truly after a conviction here."

"What have you got for us?" someone said from the back of the room.

Royce related the entire school incident. "This idiot just drove a truck full of evidence right up here from Georgia, and dumped it in our laps. And no, I don't think he's mentally incompetent. He's just a damn fool!"

Royce noticed he had them awake and attentive. No longer were they concentrating on doughnuts and Danny's coffee.

"We've matched his prints to the prints on the axe that killed David-Jack," Royce announced.

"Holy Jesus," someone muttered.

"Thanks to your blood people, who've been working through the night, we've matched a bloody footprint in his truck, and a bloody rag that was stuffed up under the front seat. It's David-Jack's blood," Royce tried to hide his excitement.

"He probably wiped his hands off to drive," Jackson said.

"His prints match those found on the axe. So he's pretty much our boy on the killing of David-Jack," Royce alleged.

"At any rate, we want to go over everything here this morning. Let's fit every piece into this puzzle. We want to be very careful with the physical evidence. Do this by the book, so nothing will be contaminated. I don't want any loopholes. I don't want any kind of legal technicality," Royce preached.

"Did this guy kill the mother?" Jackson asked.

"No. I think Robert did that," Royce said. "The blood guys are working with those two bodies over at the morgue. They wanted to re-evaluate some of their prints. So far, they tell me Robert's prints were all over her body parts. Good stuff."

"Why did she call Robert to come home from work," another agent asked.

"Well, late last night I read the last of David-Jack's Red Chief tablets. He says in there, that his mother was layin' plans with ole Eugene, here, to have Robert dig up all of his money. Then they were going to kill Robert and run off together. That's why David-Jack had been digging up some of the money as soon as Robert had planted it under the fence. He was going to use that money to get himself and Donna-Dean out of there," Royce said.

"So she calls Robert at work, to come home and dig up his money?" Jackson quizzed.

"Well, God only knows what she told him to get him to come home. In the meantime, David-Jack has not gone to school, because he knows this is the day something is coming down. So, he hides and watches things unfold when Robert gets there. The last entry in his little tablet journal is that he has watched Robert axe his mother almost in half, as she was trying to run out of the kitchen door. Robert then dragged her on out in the yard to that old mattress. David-Jack says he tried to set fire to the mattress, but it wouldn't burn fast. So he took the axe and chopped her up."

"Can you imagine the boy watching . . . and this was his mother?" one agent said.

"But . . . this was a violent mother who had stuck a pin through his tongue, and done God only knows what else to him," Royce said. "He says in the tablet that the only thought he had, was to get to Donna-Dean and get them away."

"So, can we assume that the mother told Donna-Dean not to come home from school because she knew they were going to kill Robert?" Jackson asked.

"Who knows? I've got a hunch that David-Jack had some sort of confrontation with Robert and Eugene when he arrived, perhaps over the pornography, or the money, or that he had seen Robert murder his mother. And, while Robert buried Ma in the cellar, Eugene stalked David-Jack," Royce surmised.

"So, you think Eugene switched allegiances once he learned that Rowena was dead; how come the two brothers didn't get into it over her," Jackson asked.

"Well, I believe they had, shall we say, shared her over the years. Rowena's mother, who is a bit off of her rocker, told me that there was 'fornicatin' going on among this bunch," Royce said.

"I am currently working on the thought that these children are not Robert's. I believe they are Eugene's. On Donna-Dean's birth certificate there is an X on the line for father of the child. Both of these Silcox's do not write. They sign everything with an X. The Marietta, Georgia post office says they write out addresses and money orders for ole Eugene to do his little business by mail.

"At any rate, I have a DNA thing underway. and if I'm right, it means this ass-hole axed his own son to death. And that's the brass ring. If the DNA matches, we can send him up the river."

Silence around the room.

"I look at all of this, and I try to convince myself that it doesn't matter who did what, and to whom. But somehow it does matter . . . to me. Maybe because the boy died in my arms.

"Later on this morning, when we're putting this boy in the ground, I want to have some sort of 'why', even a 'why' that we've all conjured up, but one that seems to be the most logical reason for this boy to have lost his life," Royce said as he sat down at his desk, and rested his case.

CHAPTER NINETY FIVE

11 A.M. Saturday morning. This dead-of-winter rainy day, when most fourteen-year-old boys would be sleeping late, or watching cartoons on television; Royce and Randa were waiting on the gravel cemetery road. The hearse from McCaskey's Funeral Parlor was on its way with David-Jack.

The grave, on the sloping hillside before them, had been dug earlier and was banked with a fake green grass, roll-out rug. The grave diggers, standing nearby propped on their waiting shovels, were morbid sentinels in the fog rising up from the hollow beyond.

Randa took her gloved hand and turned his face from the sight before them. "Tell me what you're thinking."

He took her hand and clutched it across his chest.

"Is this the way you thought you would fall in love?" he asked.

"I think so . . . minus all of the high drama. I know that you are what I had almost given up hope of finding. You are an endangered species."

"Oh, sure," he laughed.

"I wanted someone who was sweet, and loving, and sensitive. Somebody I could be silly with," she explained.

He smiled at the flattery.

"I've always wanted to find someone just like you. You've touched my heart. Simple as that," Royce said. "I'm constantly thinking about you . . . what would make you happy, what would make you laugh."

He raised his left hand to adjust the rear view mirror, anxious now for the hearse to arrive. Randa noticed he had words written in ball point pen across his palm.

"What's this?" She took his hand and began to move his splinted fingers.

"Something I have to remember," he said pulling his hand away. "I think I see them coming. Over there." He pointed down the narrow roadway that circled its way around to the wrought iron archway at the cemetery entrance.

The clouds seemed to grow darker, closing in over the trees and in around the hearse as it moved slowly toward them.

Royce opened the truck door and stepped out, stretching the pain away from his incision. Randa slid across the seat and stepped out behind him, pulling up the hood of her jacket.

Royce positioned his Smokey-the-Bear hat down low over his eyes. The misty rain made glistening sprinkles across the brown felt brim.

The hearse pulled past them. The three funeral directors stepped out and began their work.

"Sheriff?" one of them approached, extending his hand. "Dr. Caldwell said I should give these papers to you."

"Thank you. Very much. I appreciate what you've done here," Royce said.

"Thing like this is hard."

"We'll walk over there with you," Royce said.

The men opened the rear doors of the hearse. Royce noticed the pall of red roses blanketing the top of the casket.

"It's from me and Donna-Dean," Randa said.

Royce drew her close and hugged her tightly.

The men eased the coffin out, and gripped its handles to walk across the cemetery lawn.

As Randa took a step to follow behind them, Royce drew her back. "You know . . . his death . . . and not his life . . . drew us together."

"Maybe that is what he was destined to do," Randa said.

The rain stopped. As the men approached the grave, shards of sunlight broke through the dark clouds, forming a heavenly backdrop.

"I think the Lord is ready for us to do this," Royce said.

Randa noticed one of the funeral directors looking back to see if they were coming.

"Hey," Royce said, breaking the eerie silence. "I've got something I want to show you. It's sort of silly for me to be showing this to you . . . here . . . at this place. But, it's sort of burnin' a hole in my pocket."

"What?" Randa asked.

He dug into the shirt pocket buried inside his leather jacket.

"This is something that was my mother's." He pulled out a small, red velvet box and opened it to reveal a diamond ring.

"Royce!" she gasped.

"I want this to be yours. But . . . I'm not going to give it to you . . . I mean, I'm not going to propose to you . . . not now, not here," he laughed. "I don't want this to be your memory . . . that I asked you to marry me in a cemetery!"

She kissed him in mid-sentence.

"I'll ask you soon . . . at some really romantic place. I'll get down on one knee."

She kissed him again over his words.

Royce snapped the little box closed, and put it back into his pocket. He took her hand and they walked through the headstones toward David-Jack's grave site.

"Sheriff?" the funeral director said, "We generally read somethin' from the Bible. Everybody deserves some words read over them . . . especially a chile. And, Frank, he sings in the choir at First Baptist, so he can sing somethin'. Then we'll give y'all all the time you want."

He stepped away to stand at the head of the casket, opened the Bible and sent the age-old words wafting out across the misty fog, "Yea, though I walk through the valley of the shadow of death . . ." and "Jesus said, suffer the little children come unto me . . ." "He taught us to pray . . . Our Father, who art in heaven . . . for thine is the kingdom and the power and the glory."

Frank began to sing. Randa buried her hand inside Royce's coat to hold him around the waist. She felt his body tremble against the powerful song and emotional words, "Precious Lord, lead me on . . ."

At the end of the song, that seemed to go on forever, the funeral director continued, "As Jesus once held the little children on His knee, loving them and teaching them about Heaven, may He therefore hold this one close to His Heart and comfort him as he was left un-comforted on this earth."

Royce moved away from Randa's hug. She was surprised to see him move in close, and reach out to touch the coffin with his right hand. He raised his left hand to read the words written in ball point pen.

*"He will raise you up on eagles' wings, bear you into the brightness of the dawn, and hold you in the palm of His right hand through eternity."

*Adapted from lyrics "On Eagles' Wings," © 1979, Jan Michael Joncas. Published by OCP. 5536 NE Hassalo, Portland, OR 97213 All rights reserved. Used with permission.

Made in the USA
Las Vegas, NV
03 August 2021